Playing with Water

Playing with Water

Kate Llewellyn

FOURTH ESTATE • *London, New York, Sydney* and *Auckland*

Fourth Estate

An imprint of HarperCollins*Publishers*

First published in Australia in 2005
by HarperCollins*Publishers* Australia Pty Limited
ABN 36 009 913 517
A member of the HarperCollins*Publishers* (Australia) Pty Limited Group
www.harpercollins.com.au

Copyright © Kate Llewellyn 2005

The right of Kate Llewellyn to be identified as the moral rights
author of this work has been asserted by her in accordance with
the *Copyright Amendment (Moral Rights) Act 2000* (Cth).

This book is copyright.
Apart from any fair dealing for the purposes of private study, research,
criticism or review, as permitted under the Copyright Act, no part may
be reproduced by any process without written permission.
Inquiries should be addressed to the publishers.

HarperCollins*Publishers*
25 Ryde Road, Pymble, Sydney, NSW 2073, Australia
31 View Road, Glenfield, Auckland 10, New Zealand
77–85 Fulham Palace Road, London W6 8JB, United Kingdom
2 Bloor Street East, 20th floor, Toronto, Ontario, M4W 1A8, Canada
10 East 53rd Street, New York NY 10022, USA

Llewellyn, Kate.
  Playing with water.
  ISBN 0 7322 8131 8.
  1. Llewellyn, Kate, 1940– . 2. Women poets, Australian –
  Diaries. 3. Authors, Australian - Diaries. 4. Gardening –
  New South Wales – South Coast. 5. Lifestyles –
  New South Wales – South Coast. I. Title.
A821.3

Cover concept Jenny Grigg
Cover and internal design by Kate Mitchell Design
Illustrations by Julia Pedde, www.lotsoflove.net
Typeset in 13/16 Perpetua by Helen Beard, ECJ Australia Pty Ltd
Printed and bound in Australia by Griffin Press

70gsm Bulky Book Ivory used by HarperCollins*Publishers* is a natural,
recyclable product made from wood grown in sustainable forests. The
manufacturing processes conform to the environmental regulations in
the country of origin, Finland.

*To Avis Parry
and to the memory of Lucy Halligan*

Contents

Finding Grace	1
The Fall of a Leaf is a Message to the Living	11
Growing Easily	35
Rain, Rainbows and Indian Summer	65
At Dusk an Owl Flew Down	111
A New Garden	149
Butterflies and Bombs	173
Bees and Bonfires	203
Stitches in the Earth	245
Champion of Camellias	267
A Different Geometry	297
Flash Point	311
A Barefoot Good Samaritan	329
Counting the Trees	359
Glorious Days	393
Bibliography	422
Acknowledgments	424

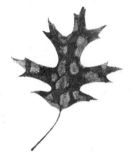

Finding Grace

THE DAY

Under its grey hat
of sky
a scarf of clouds
the day departs the dawn
and firmly shuts the door.

Busily it passes
with white egret stalking.
The day has purpose
it does not stop to stare.

It has a lot to get through:
lunch, dinner, rose-planting
and other priorities.
A million factories to start
and stop
schools, offices, road works
and other mighty operations.

Oh busy happy
beautiful day.
How many are there
of you left?

*H*ouses are like marriages, it is not always the first you wanted that you get. Yet, later, it can seem that what you had your heart set on would not have worn so well, nor made you as happy as what you finally got. And so it was with me. I had loved an old stationmaster's house at Bulli, further up the track. But the agent had not told the owners of my offer for a week. Because I needed somewhere to put my furniture, as my own house was sold, I turned away and looked elsewhere.

When I bought this house I knew I would make a garden.

At first I slept in the yard under a big nameless tree. The furniture stood around in the moonlight. It looked like a theatre set. All night, trains drew coal down to ships and their horns made me turn endlessly in the green canvas swag's cocoon. The carved oval mahogany mirror standing on the chest of drawers reflected the stars. The moon shone down like a caretaker's torch. Spiders wove webs above me while I coughed through the night, recovering from pneumonia. After some days the floors were sanded and ready so the furniture and I went in.

The day I walked outside from the bath wearing only a towel I saw there was no privacy. I turned back indoors and knew that the first thing to do was to plant creepers as shields. Geoffrey, the man who used to help me in my Leura mountain garden, came and built five panels from wooden lattice and the wire-screen doors from the house. I bought ten creepers — white, blue, pink and yellow.

Around each creeper I tipped a bucket of blood and bone, and it was this, I think, combined with the semi-tropical climate and the rich soil washed down from the rainforest in the mountains that the house faces, which made the plants grow so fast. That, and my terrible need. Within nine months there was privacy. The green screens made the garden feel like a Persian king's walled garden. Which is what the word 'Paradise' means.

When I first looked at the place, there were aviaries cemented along the back fence. I asked the couple who had sold me the house if they would take them and they did. I hailed a boy on a bike one day and asked him if he would like to dig up the cement where the aviaries had stood. He came in, nodded, went away, came back with an enormous crowbar and dug up the cement. He took out the Hills hoist too. The boy asked: 'Are you going to put in another clothes line?' I answered: 'No, I am going to plant a tree.' And I did. I put a *Magnolia stellata* in the hole.

Along some of the galvanised iron or wooden fences there were hibiscus; purple, scarlet or pink. These gave me hope. Otherwise the whole aspect was gloomy. An above-ground swimming pool had been in the centre of the back lawn. It had left a great dent. The side driveway leading to the back garden was cement with gates halfway down and a place where a caravan had been set.

A yellow egg-shaped pine tree grew at the front bedroom window and this tree hid a big pink oleander and a frangipani that hung in a crushed, yet valiant way over the wire fence. Behind the pine, a *Murraya*, or mock orange bush, had been planted flat up against the bedroom window. There was another *Murraya* at the front fence in a corner of the drive. These were in full bloom and their orange-blossom scent wafted around. Every life, every house and every garden needs grace notes. These two bushes gave them and I took heart. What was good could be multiplied, and what was not good could be removed. Sometimes I used to clench my teeth and mutter when I thought of that: 'But not necessarily in my lifetime.'

The soil here is rich. Even after the pine was taken away with all the draining, poisoning effects that they have, white cosmos two-and-a-half-metres high waved over the new cream wooden fence. In one of those Sunday afternoon television interviews with politicians at their homes, which are done, I think, for want of any better news, I had seen a man standing before his front fence which was covered in ivory and white rose bushes in full bloom. It was somewhere in Adelaide. As soon as I saw it, I knew it was what I would try to do in the new garden. So ten roses went in behind the new fence.

It was the *Yellow Pages* and hailing men in utes in the street that brought good workmen. For instance, one day riding my bike past the oval I saw a man digging a hole. I dismounted and asked if he dug holes freelance. He seemed puzzled but, after I had explained I was making a garden around the corner, he agreed to come and look. This was Dave. An artist of the hole. 'Most people dig holes like ice-cream cones,' he said, halfway through one of many. 'I dig them square. That is the only way a hole ought to be.' Dave toiled for me many afternoons. He'd knock off work and arrive with his tools on the back of his black motorbike. His sweat sprayed around as he dug. For the work of the men who helped make this garden I am grateful. There is something deeply human in the toil and modesty of the hard work these men did. They asked for nothing except their wages, they took coffee with pleasure, smoked their cigarettes sitting under the big tree in the backyard and returned to the work. I was always glad to see them. Their faces were soon red, yet they never seemed to mind the work. It may be an accident that toil rhymes with soil, but perhaps it's not just coincidence. A wooden sundeck was built out from the back door and along it a hyacinth blue trumpet-flowered creeper, with cat's claw thorns, now grows. Claudio, Dave, Ben, Peter, Robbie, Dieter, Jason, Brett, Mal, Geoffrey, Bill — I remember you all with gratitude.

Day after day, I lugged water from the slow-running back tap to the new trees. Sometimes I felt I had gone back to childhood. Playing with water around a sandcastle, waiting for the next wave to fill the moat. It seemed much the same as this pouring of water onto the garden, which is a form of green moat around the house. Ladling out fertiliser dissolved in water from the watering-can, stirring with a wooden spoon the bucket of water and fish emulsion, these too seemed little different from what we children of the desert did — playing with water.

To sit here and see the sea through the leaves of the big tree waving in a breeze is a return to childhood. The gulls swoop down when I throw out bread, the sparrows flutter in the birdbath, spinning water out in circles. As I ride my bike on the bike path south, a blue crane struts through a small creek that flows from the mountain. A white egret stands as if turned to stone, waiting for a fish. Wild duck and seabirds float in creeks, rills, small lakes, a lagoon and also in puddles. Above, the wide blue sky, the breakers on one side, my grandson, Jack, in a yellow raincoat riding ahead, to whom I call something he does not hear entirely and he shouts back to me and neither do I hear, but the wind hears all.

The Fall of a Leaf is a Message to the Living

GHAZAL 5

On this windy day, run out
gather quick, lemons from the tree.
Indoors, while we laugh and kiss
rain can lick lemons from the tree.

The fence is falling. Frugally
every week we prop it up.
The neighbour's boy, left at home
all day, bored, tempted, taking all
comes to nick lemons from the tree.
When I go to town to teach in suit and
heels,
the garden looks weirdly snug
blanketed in hay. And on this
lie sick lemons from the tree.

'This is very hard, Gwen,' I say
looking for a rhyme remembering
how she clapped her hands as we found
when coming round
a wall of brick, lemons from the tree.

All those old recipes
for posset, flummery, syllabub and
marmalade.
The luxury of saying, 'I can give you,
if you'll wait a tick, lemons from the tree.'

Kate, the word integrity should be
your shield. If you fear your past mistakes
and their effect sometimes
you can assuage sorrow and regret
by going out to pick lemons from the tree.

Sunday, 2nd January

The front door of this house faces due west, where the diminishing tail of the Blue Mountains runs south down the coast like a dinosaur sprawled along the continent. The back door faces east to the sea but it can't be seen from there as houses interrupt the view. From the dining-room table though, through the big tree, there are small glimpses of bits of blue from time to time when the wind shifts the leaves. Sometimes the blue is the sea and sometimes the horizon mixing sea and sky.

The railway station is nine doors north and has a big bauhinia tree and a coastal banksia by the steps leading up to the platform and the ticket office. I wanted to live near a station, so I could zip up to Sydney easily and not drag luggage very far. Especially at night coming home from teaching I love to have the house so close to the station; it almost feels like cheating.

Along this street, running parallel to the train line, the small houses have trim lawns, some have azaleas blazing beside the house and cement drives leading to a garage. There are few trees and coming from the mountains it all seemed hot and bare.

One day, walking back from the beach, I looked and, in that way that sometimes comes, saw clearly what a contrast all this was to where I'd lived before. I felt appalled and thought, What have I done? Now I think that was useful because I became galvanised like a mad woman. The energy this gave me was marvellous. I couldn't bear to live in so barren a place. The sun blazed down with hardly any shreds of shade.

My friend Peri came to stay yesterday from Mosman with cuttings and plants. When I said, 'I don't know how to describe this street,' she countered with, 'You're introducing a different aesthetic.'

I have thought and thought about why some people are opposed to having trees in their garden or along their street. I think it could be they are afraid of branches falling, roots in pipes and leaves in gutters. If you worked all day down a coal mine, as many people did who owned these cottages, I don't suppose you'd like to come home to dig out roots or clean gutters. A lawn's a lovely thing when you want complete control and have very little in other parts of your life.

Along the railway line a row of casuarinas runs and these baffle the noise of the trains and screen the line. I bless the person who planted them and long for more of the seedlings to grow.

Peri said when I sat at her kitchen table a few weeks ago admiring a futon tree, looking out at the skyline of trees she's planted outside her back gate: 'Futon trees aren't good street trees, they drop branches. Cape chestnuts are better. They make a pink umbrella when they bloom and they only drop their leaves for about six weeks, which lets the light through onto the clivia growing under them. The rest of the time they're green and shady.' I leaned over and took an old envelope and began to write down what she said.

Peri has an organic rare tropical fruit orchard near Currumbin in Queensland, really a sort of holiday house that has some acres with it, and she's let me stay there in the wintertime for years. She called it 'Bend of the River'. On one side of the orchard she's had a wooden sign erected with 'Don Quixote's Last Stand' burnt into it with a stick. (The sign is there because on the surrounding hills houses are spilling over like milk from a jug. The whole area is filling with houses, even the caravan park, which was next door to the farm, has been taken over by houses. Pink-roofed suburbia spreads like sunburn over the green paddocks.) I helped Peri plant this orchard with our skirts tucked up. Japanese golfers watched as they hit off on the course nearby. I remarked that those men might go home and tell their wives that Australian women worked in paddocks planting.

Peri has taught me a lot about gardens. When we first met I lived in an old rented house with a pink verandah at Balmoral Beach. She walked down the path one day and spoke to me as I stood in the garden. 'You've got a tremendous lot of weeds here,' she said, gesturing to the sea of sword ferns and other nameless plants. 'Oh,' I replied, 'I love all this greenery. I didn't know they were weeds.' Then, inspired by what she said, I ignorantly cut down the big wisteria that grew all over the balcony. It grew back and bloomed again.

I am a person who takes advice in a lot of matters. Most especially in things that I don't know anything about. People are surprised when they see what has come to pass from an idle word or two.

Peri had 'Plant more trees' printed on the back of her envelopes. Once when I was staying at 'Bend of the River' I saw a sale of native trees for a dollar each. I decided that, as I owed seventy dollars for the phone bill in her house, I would plant seventy trees instead. Julie and Anton, the caretakers, and I planted a double avenue as a windbreak down the side of the orchard. When Julie told Peri she swore. She thought I'd blocked her view to the river. The trees are almost fully grown now and small birds flit in and out in a way they don't do nearly as much in the orchard.

A hare lives there among the tall grass, which isn't mowed as the orchard is. From time to time we see it leaping with its long ears alert. Everybody loves that hare.

Here, underneath the big tree, Peri told me to plant bird's-nest ferns and clivia. I had always thought that shade in a garden was something to be ignored and it should be left to grow whatever it would. Now I love the shady part on the northern side of my garden which runs down towards an old gum and a plane tree.

Coming from Tumby Bay, on the Eyre Peninsula, the gardens we had there were made from washing-up water, seaweed mulch and liquid manure which men made in old bathtubs from seaweed left soaking for weeks. I can't remember much shade except on the verandahs, which often ran right round the houses. In the sun our parents grew tomatoes, zinnias, daisies, Geraldton wax and spinach. Come to think of it, nobody planted trees then either. Maybe trees are a modern idea? Our trees were mainly *Tamarix*, which loves the sea, and quandong. When the *Moonta*, the weekly supply ship, was due in and we had run out of fruit, women made quandong pies and stewed quandong topped with sponge, which now would be called *clafoutis* I suppose. Nobody thought anything of quandongs then except that they provided our only fruit and meagre shade and they gave us their stones to use as sheep and cattle in our endless games of farming. I've been back to Tumby Bay many times and there are quandong orchards now. The beautiful glossy scarlet fruit sits among dark green leaves and I wonder why we didn't think it lovely then. Too common, I suppose. What we would have thought beautiful would have been a magnolia or peaches or apricots. I didn't see a magnolia until I was over twenty and then I didn't know what it was.

What is it that makes a person long for a garden so that days and nights are full of work or plans? The idea takes over and conducts every day and fills it, seething almost like a love affair. Is it something like oxytocin, the hormone that floods the mother when she holds the baby? The same chemical that releases during love-making and stealthily bonds us to the other regardless of who or what they are? I wish I had known about oxytocin earlier. I might not have been able to combat its tremendous addictive force, but I'd have been able to think about it and know what it was that made me such a fool. But nobody ever regretted making a garden. (Unless they beggared themselves and lost the lot perhaps.) This is a clean pure love, wise at last. A noble obsession, released from the ignominious by age, grace and experience. I intend to relish this. This is my rejoicing and my last stand for something truly worthy. A small suburban garden, but to me a form of salvation.

To explain exactly how this place lies, think of a clock. The front door faces twelve. The side path runs down to six and a lattice screen with white potato vine stands at two. At three the big deciduous unnamed tree. The gum and a small camphor laurel are at four. The plane tree grows at five. A jacaranda staggers in too close beside the plane tree at six, with purple bougainvillea twining through its branches.

Coming up the southern side now, at seven what I call the meadow garden, a small sunny plot with white cosmos and opium poppies, leads to the lemon tree at nine. The little shed's at ten with blue potato vine beside it and a screen next to that with more vines. Then the house begins and leads up to the pink oleander and the frangipani joining up to almost twelve. Outside the gate, at eleven and two, the olive trees grow with pink geraniums below.

That's the layout and now all I need is time to get it to perfection, to have realms of shade and luxury, privacy and peace. A glory that is mine to share with whom I wish.

It is the finest form of freedom to be able to say that all the mistakes are my own and the successes, the things that grew to fullness and to bloom, grew from advice, fertiliser and a passion that gripped me like a bridle.

Saturday, 8th January

Sowed basil seed beside the shed. The seed was gathered by Terry, my neighbour, from his basil last summer.

Terry lives with Daphne, his wife, on the southern side of this house. A retired mechanic in his seventies, he stoops over his big oblong vegetable patch in a straw hat looking like Mr McGregor with Peter Rabbit watching. He has taught me to soak many kinds of seed in warm water for half an hour. Those that sink first are the most viable and so, if there is little space for sowing, it is best to use the seeds that sank first. I use all the seeds, just in case, as there is plenty of space.

Every Thursday, Philippa comes south from Thirroul to spend the day working in this garden. When we both lived at Leura, in the Blue Mountains, Philippa taught me a lot about gardening as I watched her make two gardens one after the other when she moved house. She just digs holes and plants. No clearing or digging out weeds, no cutting out big beds. Nothing but a knife and a plant and in it goes. It is an extremely cheerful way to begin and it works. Philippa used to be a fibre artist while she reared her children but she seems to have abandoned this. I nag her to begin again. She prefers gardening and it too, I suppose, is a form of fibre art. Thin, with blonde curly hair, she is immensely strong, body and soul. I watched her walk up to the church alone and upright at the funeral of her son, Alexis. Nobody else I know could have done that with dignity and silence.

At dusk, we sit on the deck facing the sea, looking down into the garden. Sitting with a drink, talking about the day, making plans and looking at the garden has been useful. Often just passing through or working in the garden, I don't look closely at the whole. Each plant or tree takes the eye one by one, but sitting a while, looking, does show gaps and mistakes. We see what is thriving and where things have been planted mistakenly. We look and look and point.

The sea is at the bottom of the garden. The sea that goes right round the world. This world which is the garden of the universe.

Sunday, 16th January

An electrical storm with heavy rain is beating down on the garden. After weeks of no rain, it is a relief. The Meyer lemon in a big pot at my bedroom door has caterpillars eating the new leaves that sprouted after a disease turned it to a skeleton. I got rid of the caterpillars and fed the lemon with Thrive fertiliser and tea leaves. It is a strange thing that two plants in almost the same position will grow so differently. For instance, the cumquat *Fortunella japonica* in a pot has been heavy with orange fruits and is now in bright green leaf. Perhaps it is simply that the lemon is just where the butterfly laid the eggs, nothing more to it than that. Around the edges of these pots lobelias' deep blue flowers are spilling over. But not as many as I would wish, because, curiously again, the pot holding the tormented lemon has healthy lobelia and many of those planted around the cumquat died and more must be planted there.

Last week, after waiting more than a month for a Sacred Lily of the Incas (*Ismene festalis*) to come up, I thought it must be dead and almost dug down to see. Then it came up with dark green strappy leaves. It is best to be patient, even when in doubt. If I had dug down, not being certain where the bulb was, I could have ruined it. This white spider lily has a most delicious scent. There are about forty species of these *Hymenocallis* lilies. I bought the bulb in Woolworths in Corrimal because of the story in Sophocles' play, *Antigone*. Ismene was the one who would not help her sister, Antigone, bury their brother, Polynices, when he was killed and, at King Creon's behest, left for the birds.

And still down comes the rain. The wheelbarrow is my rain gauge. At a glance it shows how much rain there's been.

The two olive trees I planted on the front nature strip beside the road have been ravaged by vandals. Two days ago I dug up an olive tree which I had planted in the back garden rather too closely to the new blood orange tree. I took this one out to the road where the other olive had been torn out and hung upside down in the branches of its sister tree. I had replanted the torn-up tree after soaking it in a bucket of water, but it died nonetheless.

So now a third tree is in the hole. The first was stolen, never to be seen again. Terry kindly searched the district for me, looking over fences and in the school yard that adjoins our back fences, but he found nothing.

People had told me I would not be able to grow trees in the street and it began to look as though they were right. Rage rose in me and I rode off to a hardware shop. Phil, my neighbour on the other side, had told me that only star pickets and cement would save the trees. Not sure what star pickets were, I asked Terry and he said that I would only be giving the vandals a weapon if I used them. They are simply a long star-shaped iron picket used for fences and staking. I bought star pickets, instant cement and a roll of barbed wire and one of chicken wire. With the energy that comes from pitting your will against another's, I dug holes and filled them with cement and stuck the pickets in. Then I wrapped the wires around the pickets that surrounded the trees. In a few hours the trees were wrapped as if in a war zone. They looked strange but beautiful; the emblem of peace in barbed wire. I put a bath towel over the newly planted tree to shade it on a hot day. The towel was taken while Philippa and I had morning tea. Now Terry has given me old shorts which were dusters to shade the tree. It has gone into shock, but is well watered. People shake their heads and tell me it is hopeless, but I am not giving up yet. Paragon, Verdale and Manzanillo are the best olives for this area, I read in the newspaper, so they are what I planted. 'You'll never grow trees in this street, Kate,' Phil said. Well, we'll see about that.

Speaking of olives, here is a recipe that uses quite a lot of olive oil.

Caponata

1 small bunch of celery or half a big one, chopped

4 or 5 large glossy eggplants, chopped

4 onions, peeled and cut into chunks

1 cup of vinegar (not balsamic)

½ cup of capers

2 tablespoons of brown sugar

½ cup of tomato paste

olive oil

salt and pepper

1 cup of olives

Method:

Fry the chopped eggplant in batches until soft and slightly browned. Place in a big serving bowl.

Add more olive oil to the pan and cook the celery. Don't let it get soft. Place this into the bowl with the eggplant. Add a little more oil to the pan and fry the onion until clear but not browned or unformed. Put in the tomato paste and about a cup of water and cook for 3 minutes or so, gently boiling. Add the vinegar, sugar, olives and capers. Bring to the boil and then taste. It may need more sugar or salt.

Mix all the ingredients in the big bowl. Grind pepper over it.

Serve at room temperature or warm.

It is good with bread and fish or chicken.

Thursday, 20th January

Old white cosmos plants were piled into the wheelbarrow. A stack of weeds too, from the bed at the curve of the path down the outside of the house which leads to the back steps. This bed was like a meadow with old roses and a few pink and scarlet zinnias. All these annuals had been planted in one day from a heady mix. In a hurry, I had soaked five packets of seed and sowed the lot, thinking, 'Now we shall see what likes it here.' It became one of the most beautiful beds I have ever grown. I took some plants from this bigger bed and put them down the side path too. The white cosmos wafted its starry flowers above the bright blue cornflowers. Towards the back of the bed, a few zinnias stood and among them some surprising greenish-white ones, stalwartly claiming their space and making the whole beautiful and strange.

The cornflowers went in later than the packet advised, as they ought to be sown in winter. But still they thrived in the heat and lasted four months. Some are still flowering among the last of the cosmos, which are not quite done yet either. Behind them, four pink climbing roses have almost covered the side fence since they were planted in June. A Lorraine Lee rose I bought among twenty others from Heynes' Nursery in Norwood, Adelaide, is two metres tall. There is an Albertine I brought here from Leura in a pot at Easter and two old Rugosa roses my son Hugh dug out from under the big tree, where they languished for years in the summer shade. We call this tree the Mother-in-law tree, as when I first saw it I asked the owners of this house the name. The man told me his wife's mother had given them it as a seedling so they'd named it after her as they knew no other name. The Eureka lemon tree and the pink crepe myrtle (an advanced tree I got from the Leura Nursery) are also along this side fence. The myrtle has just bloomed and is three metres high. It has doubled in size, as has the Eureka lemon, since they were planted here. It is the good soil and the climate, as well as the blood and bone fertiliser, that set them roaring. When I move house, the first thing I plant is a lemon.

Not a single basil plant has come up from the seeds I sowed for winter. Terry says that one hot day can kill the lot in the early stages. I thought I had taken care not to let them dry out. They were sown under a sprinkling of old lawn clippings with no soil at all on top, as he taught me.

My friend Jennifer came two days ago to begin taking photographs of the garden to show whatever happens this coming year. We are full of hope. Anthony, Jennifer's husband, walked around as I picked the first tomatoes for them to take home, smelling the plants while saying: 'Tomatoes smell so wonderful; they have an old-fashioned smell.' There was a plate of Rouge de Marmande tomatoes ripening in the sun on the back table. These were handed over the fence by Terry, who grew them from a self-sown plant that sprang up having fallen from a bush onto the path and been trodden in. If you hold your palm up and turn your fingers in slightly, that is the outline of the shape of this beautiful prawn-pink fruit. Rouge de Marmande tomatoes are good planted earlier than Grosse Lisse and others I am told.

The genus name *Lycopersicon* is from the Greek meaning 'wild peach', but the Swedish scientist Carolus Linnaeus named the tomato *Solanum lycopersicon* although the original applied to an unrelated Egyptian plant and so the name has remained, a little incongruously, with the tomato. The tomato was looked on with suspicion by Europeans when it arrived from Central and South America and was not widely accepted until the early nineteenth century. Had people known how to dry it in the sun, as we do now, it could have saved lives in times of famine. No doubt people dried food in suitable climates, but it seems that they did not use the method for tomatoes.

Grown commercially, tomatoes are not always staked but simply harvested, plant and all, from the field. As I had no stakes, mine are not tied up, but sag and crawl like green lions around the garden.

Panzanella

Take some good ripe tomatoes and cut them up. Sprinkle with salt and pepper.

Take some good bread, preferably but not essentially sourdough, and tear it up into bite-sized pieces.

About half a loaf will make enough for four people. But a whole loaf will be suitable for six or more.

You will need about the same volume of tomatoes to bread.

Place the bread in a bowl of cold water. Squeeze this with your hands. Discarding the water, mix the bread with the tomatoes.

Tear up a cup or two of fresh basil and stir this through. Pour over a cup or two of olive oil depending on the amount of salad you have made. Sometimes chopped peeled cucumbers are added to this dish.

Serve at room temperature. This is good with lightly grilled tuna or canned tuna on a hot day.

Thursday, 27th January

This morning, tossing a bucket of bathwater onto the white cleomes which were drying out under the shelter of the eaves by the side path, I found the Geraldton wax hidden in their shade. This delicate-looking yet hardy native is one of the earliest memories I have of any plant. It was practically the only flower my mother had when we lived on the edge of a desert by the sea on the Eyre Peninsula. I put this one in beside the wall on the northern side of the house and then forgot it. It grows to three metres with large airy sprays of waxy pink, lilac and white flowers. It is prone to rootrot so possibly its dry position will be good for it. In Western Australia where it comes from, as the name implies (Geraldton is a port on the western coast of WA), there are great avenues of it waving beside the roads. They are used as oleanders are in Crete; a highway from Heraklion has thousands of pink oleanders which grow for many, many kilometres. It would not be hard to plant like this in dry areas with short wet winters. The effect is beautiful and they need no maintenance.

GERALDTON WAX

As we drove into Yanchep
the foam of the bushes

reared up like the sea
around the boat.

White or pink or pale-grey,
others of magenta,
the utter lavishness of it
hit me
like a sudden knock
on my front door.

My mother had one precious bush
of this
in her desert garden.
No rain fell for nine months
of the year
and then only ten inches,
rarely more.

The wax bush bloomed
outside the kitchen window.

She poured the water on it
from the grey tin basin
of the washing-up.
Occasionally
women from the church
would come
and pick it for a wedding
but one day

one such came
and cut so deeply
she turned the bush
into a basin.

It was never the same again,
something had gone
from its heart.

My mother grieved.

And there at Yanchep's garden
I saw that in certain times and places,
waves of flowers bloom
with nothing put on them
by a person's hand.

But something makes them grow
like unexpected uninvited love
blessed with clement weather.

Friday, 28th January

Kate Grenville got me going on compost. 'Oh, I always have a compost heap. I am a believer in compost,' she said when she was pregnant with her son Tom, staying with me at Leura.

Last night I spread two barrowloads of compost on the garden. It was dusk and birds came out of the trees to peck the earth. Compost makes good mulch and even though the soil here is rich and black, as I've said, nonetheless it improves the growth of everything. The compost heap is only a three-metre-square patch that was once a fowl yard. There is a lot of daunting mysterious talk given out on composting. It is better to pile up leaves, cuttings and vegetable scraps and let it all rot than throw it into a rubbish bin — and that's mainly all that's needed. Lime or dolomite sprinkled on the pile from time to time helps keep the compost sweet and hastens the breakdown into soil. Last month's salad is this month's soil. It gives me pleasure, appealing as it does to a frugal streak; something good that costs nothing at all.

Peri bought a book in the Kangaroo Valley second-hand bookshop and cafe, which she read out over her tea and cake. It was Mary Pickford's autobiography, *Sunshine and Shadow*. She read it out because we had been discussing roses and what are good roses and what are poor or ugly. There are some mighty ugly roses.

This is what she read, holding up the old blue cloth-covered book:

> Whenever I got a penny, at the age of five or six, I would go to the florist and buy myself a rosebud, which I took home and carefully tended. One day, after making my purchase, I pointed to a full-blown rose that

seemed to be falling, and asked the florist: 'May I have that rose, if you don't want it anymore?' The florist gave it to me for nothing and that became quite a ritual: my rosebud for a penny, and a fading rose for the asking. After repeating this performance three or four times, the florist asked me one day what I did with the rose that he no longer wanted. 'I eat it,' I told him.

And that was the simple truth. It had tasted very bitter at first, but I thought that if I were to eat it, the beauty and the colour and perfume would somehow get inside me.

When we drove home we saw arum lilies growing wild in a bog at the side of the road. I had been looking for them as I'd seen them before, so we stopped. I dug up some and piled them into the back on top of the mulch we'd bought and the pair of *Robinia* trees. By the time we got home it was dark, but I dug holes in the shade of the Mother-in-law tree and filled them with water. In the glow of the outside light, which the previous owners had put in for parties, I dug and the lily flowers glowed like lustrous pale fish in a dark sea.

Growing Easily

WINDOW

There is always a woman
at a window
arms folded
or resting on the sill
waiting, waiting, waiting
for the plants to grow
bulbs to thrust
leaves to turn
or the friend to come.
Gaping at the world
and death only a beat away
trying always to remember
while drinking from this chalice.

A nun of memory
she reads the Bible of the day.
The weather, birds and plants
seem the same
yet the text changes daily.
The Just Joey rose has faded
now to ivory.
Somehow the nameless tree
seems bigger.

I woke in tears
because Apollinaire is dead
or that he died so young —
flu and shrapnel killed him.
I understand nothing
attempting to notice everything.

My chair scrapes on the floor
and so my neighbours know
that I am home.
Signs are all we have
and half of those aren't understood.
I mourn no one but Apollinaire.
In the halls of my unconscious
spiders spin nothing but
wild silver webs
catching only blood
and crystals.
Lately dreams have laughter in them.

The window in the morning
opens on the green kimono
of the garden
naked I shrug it on
and step outside

roses, cornflowers
and white stars of cosmos
embroidered on my back.

I want to be buried face down
so that I can wear the earth
this garden
blooming on my back
the light gleaming
on the silk birds flying over
and the sash, the wide blue sea.

Tuesday, 1st February

In her book, *You are Now Entering the Human Heart*, Janet Frame wrote about shading and shadows: 'All things, even kettles and fire shovels, stood under the sun, complete and unique with their shadows, fighting to preserve them.'

It is the shadows on the lawn in the early morning that are beautiful. The Mother-in-law tree's shadow shakes like a green fan on the grass. Imagine a world without shadows. All things standing forever lit from above with no shadow falling, even around a tree trunk, as if everything were permeable by light and so without substance, like things made by dreams. The Surrealist painters dispensed with shadows and it's partly that which makes their art so dreamlike.

The blue potato vine (*Solanum seaforthianum*) is climbing onto the roof of the shed. In full bloom now, the mauve-blue star-shaped clusters of flowers hang near its bunches of bright orange berries. There are fourteen hundred species in the genus including trees, shrubs, perennials, annuals and climbers from around the world. Potatoes and eggplant belong to this genus, yet many other types are poisonous. Told that this divine blue-flowering creeper is slow to grow, I became defiant and planted it to hide the ugly little shed anyway. I did not want the whole place covered in the white version of this vine, even though it is lovely and extremely fast growing. The white one, *Solanum jasminoides* or Alba, now covers some of the flywire doors from the house, slung up above the fences to make screens. I longed for blue. I'd pull the sky down if I could. Fed and watered, the blue vine grew quickly and reached the roof in eight months.

The Australian rainforest vine *Pandorea jasminoides*, Bower of Beauty, has pink trumpet flowers with dark crimson inner throats. I don't know why it is that a label on a plant can depict a pink flower yet on the back it's described as cream. There is, though, a variety called Lady Di with white flowers and cream throats. This creeper needs a warm temperate climate with rich well-drained soil and plenty of water.

There was a time when every outdoor lavatory was covered with some kind of flowering vine. Indoor lavatories were rare then. You could sit with the door open, dreamily looking at the flowers of a vine like the purple ones I saw last week from a train; a sort of pea-flower. Or you could stare out at the pretty orange-coloured blossom of lantana (shrub verbena). This was about the time lantana escaped into the bush and became a pest.

The scent of lantana flowers takes me back to dreamy summer days reading the Deaths column of *The Advertiser*. Since I knew nobody who had died, except my Grandfather, I do not know why I was so drawn to those sad columns. I read them in the cool dark cave of the lantana-covered lavatory.

Near my house there is a garden with a lantana cultivar called Radiation twined and topiaried. I got off my bike to look. It felt a bit like seeing a wedding bouquet made of weeds. But what, after all, is a weed? Nothing more than a plant you decide to call a weed. For instance, at Leura, in my old garden, Philippa dug out a driveway of blue *Agapanthus* because we had decided that they were weeds. Crowding out other plants, they took all the space and could not share. Yet those Februarys full of blue were wonderful. I used to love walking down the drive through an avenue of blue. Maybe we shouldn't have done it.

When I came to live here by the sea, I longed for flowering trees. I wanted them so that if things were not to my liking on earth, I could lift my eyes to the sky and see something beautiful. Hibiscus were hard to grow in Leura, though some people did manage. But after years of struggle, I have come to a simple conclusion. And that is that it is almost always better to grow what will flourish easily. It has taken me years to learn this. It will probably take me a bit longer to administer it.

Hibiscus thrive here so I planted a great wanton *Hibiscus rosa-sinensis* called Surfrider by the shed. Philippa was horrified. She hates these great colourful hybrids and likes older simple kinds. To cover a bare patch of fence on the northern side next to the path I planted *Hibiscus arnottianus* which is a cultivar called Wilder's White. Five petals around a scarlet pistil. The label says it will grow to two metres, but the *Encyclopaedia Botanica* says it grows up to five metres. I stare at that ugly space and watch the hibiscus sprout with the ardour of a gambler watching a roulette wheel slow.

I've decided to lift the Surfrider before next spring and plant it outside the bathroom window on the southern side of the house. I will be the one to see it most and it will give more privacy. It is a pleasant thing to look out at a tree or shrub from the bath, or even cleaning your teeth. There is something primitive about it.

The Rose of Sharon, *Hibiscus syriacus*, grows easily here. There are two big shrubs, one each against the northern and southern fences. (The house faces due west.) The cultivar Bluebird grows like a weed in this garden, but the only trouble with it as a covering for fences is that it is deciduous. All winter, after I had

French windows put in my bedroom, I lay staring out at those bare branches waiting for spring to mask the fence with a thousand leaves and mauve flowers. And now it has. But it will go again.

At night, the horns of the trains bleat 'Help!' like a drowning man. Sometimes a horn sounds like laughter in a corner. Another, the cackle of a hen; sometimes like bandages being torn and at other times a trumpet. From the bathroom the noise of the carriages full of coal sounds like gorillas mating. During the day I rarely hear the trains. It only took three months not to hear them in the daytime. My son said, 'Aeroplanes are an assault, but the sound of trains is romantic.' I clutched at that during the first weeks, thinking I had made a terrible mistake coming here.

SUMMER

> There we are six at tea
> at the black oval table
> I later sold for a lot.
> The man at one end,
> the woman at the other.
> The boys are fighting over
> the custard skin
> and we are putting cream
> on the ice cream on the custard.

No wonder the man died young.
An austere abundance fills the house.
All things are polished —
our shoes, our hair,
our noses too,
which are peeling.
Outside on the mallee roots
in the wheelbarrow
the dishpan is warm from the sun
and beyond that
tomatoes are hanging red and green.
We don't know anyone
who doesn't speak English
except Eraldo the prisoner of war.
We have never seen our mother cry
and we don't know men can.
After the meal,
one at a time,
not changing the water,
we were bathed,
the woman, then the man used it.
I always felt sorry for him
as the water was cooler by then,
but he said he didn't mind.
Last to bath,
first to die.
Who will be next?

Wednesday, 22nd March

Summer's over. Yet still the great tree that blocks the sea from this window where I sit is green and in full leaf. In Adelaide, where I went for the Festival of Arts, my friend Jane showed me her garden and there, behind the shed where she makes tiles, was a tree about a metre high and then she told me its name. When I said I'd tried for so long to discover more about this tree, she took me around the block and pointed to a big tree sheltering a verandah. It was the same as my own. The *Ailanthus*, also called the Tree of Heaven, and in Adelaide sometimes it is called the Marryatville Tree. It seeds in any newly dug land and in the suburb Marryatville it became a weed, flourishing everywhere. And so it is here. For weeks I have been pulling up thriving seedlings hidden among other plants. *Ailanthus altissima* is a native of China. In some places it is valued for its ability to endure pollution. A great green dome of a tree, it has insignificant flowers, but salmon-coloured bracts in summer among the deep-green pinnate leaves. So the mystery is solved. The Mother-in-law tree becomes the Tree of Heaven, becomes *Ailanthus*. Now I remember that Don DeLillo has it growing in New York in his book *Underworld*.

There is a white horizontally growing *Datura* lily in Jane's garden. In the moonlight, when we walked outside, it shone there, white, almost silvery glowing trumpets, whiter than swans at dusk on a lake. Jane is saving its green seed pods for me.

When I came to this coast I was full of an ardour to have semi-tropical trees. I knew I'd miss the great trees of the Blue Mountains if there wasn't something sensational to replace them. I wanted *Datura* lilies outside my bedroom window, either apricot or ivory, and also oleanders, orange trees, bauhinias, Dutch tulip trees, all the flowering trees that brush the sky. I soon forgot this plan. There are no *Datura* lilies yet. But this week I will get one if I can. *Brugmansia suaveolens*, called Angel's Trumpet or *Datura*, has orange-red flowers. I have never seen this tree, but found a photograph of it in *Botanica*. True *Daturas* are short-lived plants with capsular green fruits. All parts of both true *Daturas* and *Brugmansias* are narcotic and extremely dangerous. I once knew a boy who smoked some *Brugmansia* leaves and went blind, completely and utterly blind, for several days. Then his sight gradually returned. But that was during the seventies and some of us felt invincible then. There was no AIDS that we knew of, people tried anything in nature, smoked strange leaves, made love to strangers without exchanging names, and thought they could fly. Some jumped from buildings, arms out like wings.

The way the lily trumpets of the *Brugmansia* hang down and its night scent makes it a wonderful plant. Cecil

Beaton photographed women against this tree, and he knew what he was doing. I feel like riding down to Shirley and Jim's Nursery at Corrimal and buying the pale apricot Charles Grimaldi immediately, and also the Candida which is ivory.

The David Austin Claire rose I bought in Adelaide with my friend Clare Guthleben, which was with all the other roses planted last August, is now four metres high and swathes this window. Three green arms reaching for the stars. The yellow Charles Austin rose back in the garden among the white cosmos has arched over almost to the fence and is growing through the lemon tree. Soon there will be yellow roses among the lemons.

This whole long empty street, with only the two young olives wrapped in barbed wire, would be fabulous with about two hundred *Gordonia axillaris* trees. They used to confuse me because, even though they are so huge, I thought they were camellias, to which they are, in fact, related. With their glossy leaves and big flat white flowers with golden stamens they are one of the most beautiful trees for a warm climate. Perhaps they grow in a cold climate too, as all these camellia types are natives of South China. I would give anything to get the Council to agree to *Gordonias*.

Because it is autumn I will give you a recipe I love, to go with the season.

Patricia Harry's Dried Fruit Autumn Dessert

15 grams of sugar

1 litre of water

100 millilitres of brandy or rum

zest and juice of an orange

cinnamon stick

600 grams of dried fruit (prunes, figs and dried apricots is a good mixture but any can be used)

Sponge Topping:

4 eggs, separated

110 grams of caster sugar

85 grams of plain flour

1 teaspoon of ground cinnamon

Method:

The night before, mix together everything in the first list of ingredients. Boil for 3 minutes and leave to cool. Drain and keep the fluid. Place the fruit without the cinnamon stick in a casserole dish. Cover with the fluid.

Sponge:

Heat oven to 190°C. Beat egg yolks with half the sugar until thick and creamy. Beat the egg whites until stiff and add the remaining sugar.

Fold a cup of the egg white mixture into the yolk

mixture. Add the spice and flour and gently fold in the last of the whites. Pour this immediately and gently onto the fruit and place in 190°C oven for 10 to 15 minutes. Remove when light brown and set. Dust with icing sugar and serve warm with cream.

Saturday, 25th March

I have been picking flowers. Visitors from Bathurst are coming for the weekend. Helen and Len gave a hundred trees they had grown from seed to my friends Barbara and Ruth, who had bought a small farm near Peel called 'Girra Girra'. When I stayed with Barbara and Ruth we dug the hard earth among rocks and shale and planted trees. We watered them with buckets lugged up from the dams. So I am keen to hear, when Helen and Len come, if they have been over to see the trees at Peel.

When asked, Helen, sitting beside me, explains that she and Len learnt about tree-growing through trial and error and through getting to know the land they were planting on. That, she says, and understanding the seasons, helped them to grow seeds into trees. They went to a workshop on propagation of native species.

'It is not always the case,' she continues, 'that eucalypts need fire to open their outer skins. The capsule will open in a paper bag. In some types, it will open when the flower dies, without any interference at all. You see, the seed capsule forms, the twig dies, then it falls to the ground and can, in the right circumstances, without any fire or help from people, sprout and grow. After I collect my seed, I usually fill a tray with a mixture of river sand and potting mix. I just sprinkle the seeds on the top and cover it with more sand and water. When the seedlings get their first true leaves I prick them out into tubes that we get from Yates. Sometimes we use milk cartons, which are good, but there is a problem with storing them, because they take up more room than the tubes and also they get eaten by mice and silverfish. It takes up to a year, depending on the season, before the seedlings are ready to plant out onto road edges and paddocks. At least that is about the time it takes. I mean, if I sow in spring, sometimes they can go out in autumn, but it depends on the season. It may well be that it isn't until the following spring that they are ready.

'With the larger seeds such as *Acacias* and *Hardenbergias*, I pour boiling water over them and leave them for twenty-four hours. Then they go straight into the tubes or milk cartons with a mixture of half potting soil and half river sand. Wattles in trays grow too fast, and so the roots spread out and are a bugger to prick out. But some trees can be grown at first in seed trays.

'We get about two-thirds' survival rate, when we plant the seedlings out into the paddocks. That is, as long as it is a reasonable season. Len and I have propagated about five thousand native trees in the last three years.'

When my friends have left I stand and watch the stars glitter above the garden like sequins on night's bow tie. It is said that it is wise to grow seeds on the waning, not the waxing, moon, which right now pours down its silver light. Night's milk spills over the silent garden. All is still except the sea which roars on endlessly.

Perfume is to a garden as music is to religion. I long for some night-scented flowers. Then I turn, sigh and go to bed — a woman on her own, happy as a nun.

Wednesday, 29th March

Two days ago I sowed sweet peas (*Lathyrus odoratus*). It was one of the plants used by Austrian biologist Gregor Mendel (1822–1884) when he experimented in hybridising and so began the foundations of the science of genetics. I have never had any luck or success with sweet peas before, but that was because Leura is so cold. Also, I never mastered getting the wire erected in time for the plants to climb. They would end up sprawled among other low plants, tangled and rumpled with only a few blooms. Sweet peas are demanding. They must, except the dwarf prostrate kind, have wire to climb. Unless you are prepared to have a wall of wire netting or wires strung between posts, which looks ugly (until it is clothed and covered like a pastel patchwork quilt on a washing line full of scent), the peas won't thrive.

When I walked into Terry's garden, while the peas soaked in a bowl of water, he told me that they are one of the few seeds that are best not soaked. They are treated with a chemical before packaging and the soaking removes this. I had gone to ask his advice on any last-minute things he might be able to tell me — too late!

One packet I had soaked is called Old Fashioned and is the highly scented frilly kind, and the other is from an old packet called Bijou and marked 'Best used before August 1995'. This type is used for borders and window boxes and needs no training wires. So I shall see if they are still viable out-of-date and after soaking. Many seeds outlast their recommended planting dates. In nature, when there are droughts, seeds come up after years of waiting for rain. But perhaps the wild are specially adapted for that purpose.

The traditional date to plant sweet peas is St Patrick's Day. Since my friend Barbara married Patrick Pak Poy on that day, her birthday, it isn't hard for me to remember. In today's newspaper Cheryl Maddocks, who was my neighbour in Leura, writes that dolomite or lime are good for sweet peas as they like an alkaline soil. Since I tossed lime around the outer side of the front fence for the hedge of lavenders I had hoped to grow there, and of which three big bushes now survive, it should be good for the peas. Cheryl also says that for the past seven years the Sweet Memories series of sweet peas has won the Chelsea Flower Show Premier Award in London. Mr Brackley, a fourth-generation sweet pea breeder, sells these seeds through Tesselaar mail-order catalogue. The telephone number for a free copy is (03) 9737 9811 or you can look at their website at www.tesselaar.net.au.

Arriving in Britain in 1699 from Sicily, the sweet pea became the symbol of Edwardian England. The scent of sweet peas, and that of stocks, takes me not to Edwardian England but to an old tin town hall on the Eyre Peninsula on the day of the Agricultural Show. The flowers were put, one bloom each, into a bottle for judging. They were also put into vases with other spring flowers for the flower arrangers' contest. The flowers stood on trestle tables covered with white sheets with new wire netting around to protect them before the judging. After the judging, the netting was taken away.

The competitors and others streamed into the hall when the judging was done and we rushed to see how we had fared. My mother had a firm idea that one should praise all others and ignore one's own victories. But it was acceptable to point out one's failures. It was a good lesson, painful and hard at first, especially when about ten years old. Yet I understood the ideals behind the attitude. After one show, my mother said consolingly to me, 'Oh, Mrs Young gave you such awful flowers to arrange. I don't know how she could have given you those terrible purple larkspurs with those orange wallflowers.'

I planted the sweet pea seeds along the outside of the front fence and along the cast-iron edging on the front verandah. Some were sown around the wire that wraps the olive trees and then they were all dosed with some buckets of bathwater laced with fish emulsion.

This garden by the sea has been made with mainly seeds and cuttings. There are some trees I bought, it is true, but on the whole the first packets of seeds have gone on to become flowers whose seeds I gathered and planted, or else they sowed themselves. Now I am keen to discover if cosmos will go on through the mild winter and if the rocket will do the same. I imagine the impatiens will go on forever as will the geraniums and roses. The basil might self-seed and the nasturtiums have gone two rounds already and could last through winter, perhaps. The idea of these cycles of planting and gathering is satisfying. Bog sage comes on again,

Philippa tells me, after it dies down in winter. Here on the coast, blue salvia doesn't have to be treated as an annual as it is in other places, but continues for two or three years at least. I know this because the seedlings I brought from the mountain garden are in bloom here after a full year.

Friday, 7th April

Beside me, on the table I am writing at, are bulbs. They are from the international Melbourne Garden and Flower Show, where I went last weekend.

I am lucky to have them. I was robbed at Spencer Street Railway Station, but the fellow didn't get the bulbs and for that I was grateful. I had been looking for some tulips that my friend Mrs Judd, who has one of the great gardens of the Blue Mountains, plants as her favourites. They are Angelique, a double pink and white, and Upstart, which is taller and a deeper shade that she puts behind Angelique.

There's nothing like bags of bulbs piled up to give a feeling of hope that whatever the winter is to be, spring will come and with it waving flowers from these brown onions. And here there is not so much to dread at all, compared to the winter of the mountains which I used to find harrowing. In fact, I used to flee north and once, when hanging around in Queensland for two months, afraid to go home to the cold, I decided it wasn't the way to live. So I made up my mind to find a place by the sea. And now here I am, with white *Lilium longiflorum* (Christmas lilies); white Erlicheer daffodils; white Monet tulips; mixed daffodils; pink and white hyacinths; the semi-double tulips, Upstart, a delicate soft pink; and white St Brigid anemones. Also, Dutch irises and other things that have lost their labels.

On the matter of tulips, Mrs Judd is peerless, 'Now with tulips I plant them the second week in May. They are fed with blood and bone and dolomite. The whole area is dug up, fertilised and then that is turned down. Tulips have to be planted a spade's depth. You mustn't burn the bulb with the fertiliser. We never put them in the fridge — it makes them a month early. Growers tell you that it makes them deteriorate. I get my tulips from Tasmania from Vogelvry and Van Diemen's and also from The Lakes in Dandenong. They must be fed again after they flower before they are lifted.'

I remember she said they are fed a week or two before flowering. I will ring her and find out what she uses then. She has over one thousand tulips and keeps the bulbs in orange netting bags in her cellar. Tulips won't last long if left in the earth all year round. I found that out the hard way because I didn't believe it.

Tuesday, 18th April

Quinces. I have been gathering quinces with Ruth and Barbara from wild trees on the banks of a creek at Peel. We drove out looking at the golden globes hanging by the hundred. A wrecked wattle-and-daub house stood in a corner of a paddock.

Cydonia oblonga (common quince) grows to almost four metres but those old trees were probably taller than that. They hung tantalisingly over the empty creek and were swathed in blackberries that were also in fruit. Ruth went home and got a ladder. I remember my father slinging a ladder into a great tangle of blackberries at Yallunda Flat where they grew on the edges of the roads and in the ditches. It had seemed to me, at the time, a stroke of genius to think of the ladder. It was probably a common thing that he had seen others do, but to me it showed how clever he was.

So with me standing on the base of the ladder to anchor it, Ruth climbed up and flung the quinces back under her arm to the ground, where Barbara gathered them. Full-size quince fruit are about the size of a woman's fist. A furry skin and bone-hard interior. Ruth said, 'If gathering apples from trees is called scrumping, what's the name for getting quinces?' Barbara said at once, as if she'd been thinking about it, 'Mincing.'

Now I am home, there is a big bag of small hard quinces here to cook. My friend Sheridan Rogers' recipe for baked quinces with black rice pudding is one of the best autumn desserts I know. Black rice is sold in Chinese grocery shops. White or brown rice are not suitable.

Quinces do not withstand summer humidity so it is not clear to me that one would survive here. But there must be room down the back for a quince tree. When it stops raining I will ride down to Shirley and Jim's Nursery and buy one. They are hardy and grew like weeds at Angaston in the Barossa Valley where my mother grew up. She and her sisters used to pelt each other with quinces. 'One day you girls will want for fruit!' screamed Granny from the verandah. And she was right. My mother went to live where the only fruit that grew freely and without cosseting was the native quandong. Many a day she'd have liked quinces to cook.

AUTUMN

> Waltzes on the radio
> birds singing.
> One breast heavier
> than the other.
>
> The sad young smell
> of autumn.

The mutabilis rose
droops on the dressing table.
The celestial blue
forget-me-not is stalwart.

Wind swings sweetly
through the Ailanthus tree.

Daily I visit the pond
waiting for frogs.
Silver circles appear
but never the song
of the frog.
A small ramp of log
leads to the water
they only need to take it.

Here is the feast frog
insects galore
and deep water.

Here is the day, woman
everything ordinary
peaceful and blessed.

Thursday, 20th April

I'd like a rain gauge. The barrow I use just gets full and falls over. All night it rained and most of yesterday too.

The El Niño drought may be broken. A meteorologist speaking on the television said the waters around Chile are cooling and this could mean the droughts will break. The sea is a darker grey than the silver-grey sky. More and more of the sea is visible from this chair as the Tree of Heaven sheds its leaves.

I sowed coriander and more sweet peas yesterday in the rain. I forgot to tell Graham, the man who mows the lawn, that the sweet peas were planted around the olives, so they were lost. The slips of box hedging I took from my friend John Miller's garden in Newcastle are dark green. They take about a year to grow to a few centimetres. Jane told me she is using a Greek myrtle (*Myrtus communis*) in her garden: 'It's got a white starry flower with a faint eucalyptus scent. Beloved by Zeus.' Hearing that I went and got one and now this myrtle is thriving in the back garden's problem area. It can be used in parterres and is faster than box. Jane is making a parterre herb garden with her myrtle hedging. Parterres are a whopping lot of trouble in my opinion.

Monday, 24th April

A sunny day. The unnamed blue vine on the back deck has big clusters of flowers waving and sparrows are flicking about gathering insects from the leaves. Philippa is making a new bed from lawn inside the front gate. Big winds yesterday brought down the *Thunbergia grandiflora* vine on the front verandah. And the Claire rose fell from this window where it now lapses and droops. The white *Alyssum* seeds I sowed last week are up. They will go into the yet to be dug bed where a car can be parked inside the gate. I am tired of looking at that bare ugly patch, so we are going to sow it with groundcovers. The other sweet peas are up. Two days ago, having a heavy heart and nothing better to do, I sowed stocks in a newly dug bed.

Yellow chrysanthemums are starting to bloom in the back among red, apricot and yellow nasturtiums. I had dug them up from the row at the front fence six months ago. Some remain and are flowering among the cream Edelweiss rose. Philippa doesn't like yellow in a garden but she looked up while sitting on the lawn digging with a trowel and remarked that they look alright among the roses.

When you take on somebody else's garden, in a climate you haven't lived in before, things reveal themselves slowly. The old yellow chrysanthemums are a pleasant surprise.

Saturday, 29th April

A green orange. I found this globe swinging from the Valencia orange tree at the back step this morning.

Quickly I went around the other seven citrus trees to see what they held. The mandarin, too, has small green fruit and the blood orange has a single minuscule fruit hanging on the top branch. Both the lemons also have some tiny fruit.

Very reluctantly I sprayed all the citrus yesterday with white oil. The leaves were falling after curling up with an insect infestation. Shirley, at the nursery, told me that there is only one cure and it is to spray with the oil as the insects can't lay their eggs on the slippery surface.

I see now it is important to put out snail killer at the end of March or early in April. Something had made a lacework of vines and many plants. It bewildered me, but Philippa, who has a fine eye for infestation, began stamping on snails last week and said there was a plague here. She bends and looks under plants and shrieks the name of any bug she spies.

Today I sowed blue lobelia and Pacific Giant pansies. The coriander and the stocks have sprouted green on the grey soil. With what ardour I go out each morning peering through my reading glasses. Yet I miss so much. For instance, why didn't I see the new fruit coming when I sprayed the leaves? I was looking at the leaves, that's why. Sometimes I see people pass by as I stand at the front window. Many do not look to the right or left. They seem blind. But I tell myself this is not a test of intelligence, the person looking at the cement path may be thinking of how to end the play he is writing, how to pay a bill, or a thousand other things. Virginia Woolf walked down The Strand seeing almost nothing while thinking of her novel *To the Lighthouse*. But some people do look at trees and plants.

A blind man came towards me as I stood at the gate yesterday. I had just moved the white magnolia from the back step, where Peri had told me that it would overshadow the garden. I planted it between the olives in the lawn outside the fence. Then, having only one spare star picket available, I used a roll of barbed wire to wrap it; every bud was draped. I stepped out and engaged the man with a white cane in conversation. We discussed the beautiful three days' weather we have had. Then I told him of the magnolia. He asked what kind, saying that if it was the gigantic one, it was not suitable for that place. But it was a smaller tree. Then, because somebody had parked their car on the path and broken a cement block covering a pipeline, I showed the man this hole. He knelt down and put his hand in the hole, feeling the depth of the cement blocks that had given way. This man seemed more interested and aware than some of the sighted. One day, as he is passing, the scent of the magnolia (full of buds now) will tell him that it is the tree we spoke of. It will be a few notes of Bach for him, perhaps.

Birds galore. I stand and watch the sparrows dart and flit across the back lawn with the mynah birds, starlings, magpies and, in the last three days, seven black currawongs. As Philippa and I sat on the deck at dusk, a very young rosella flew onto the guttering. Its head still too big for its neck, with its scraggly feathers, it watched us. Philippa ran and got cake to crumble onto the railing. She held some in her hand but it wouldn't come. Next day it returned. The sparrows are helping the plants. I see them dart about picking insects and then suddenly a group of sparrows fly off like the sweep of a brown brush against the blue.

Rain, Rainbows and Indian Summer

GHAZAL 10

Certain days I know contain
elements of the sublime.
For instance, the impulse today
to dance beside the sea. Over and over
was the refrain,
elements of the sublime.

After rain the sun came out,
white lilies became chalices above the mud
sheets and towels dried on the railing.
Always in the domestic domain,
elements of the sublime.

Day after day I wonder
how I ought to live. Spreading mulch
and compost, watering, then dusk falls.
This holds, I can't complain,
elements of the sublime.

Mozart played by two Oistrakh
accompany passing clouds. Rosellas
drink from the white grevillea.
Nothing in nature will disdain
elements of the sublime.

As I ran on the sand today,
the sea was white, the bathing sheds
have been graffitied, bins are overflowing.
Yet I hold within my suzerain
elements of the sublime.

Kate, if you can only learn to long
for little, and by looking close
you will find much that will pertain
to elements of the sublime.

Monday, 1st May

A damp day. I lugged buckets of bathwater mixed with a cup of fish emulsion down the back to three camellias having a dry time. Many gardens have tough, neglected areas. The only two gardeners I know who see these and deal with them are Nan Evatt, my neighbour at Leura, and Peri, who is coming to stay today. For years I did not see sad corners, ugly bits, my eyes glided over these places, called and beguiled by some plant or tree in flower or great leaf. Not unlike my life. It is in a dry place near the compost heap that these camellias struggle, neglected and thin. Yet two are in good full bud and, since the big rain last week, look better.

On Peri's tropical fruit farm in Queensland there is a front patch she called the Badlands. For years she and her caretakers, Julie and Anton, struggled to get anything much to grow. Yet, after about five years of half failing, spreading manure, watching some trees die, some live, it suddenly responded. A micro climate developed there. The trees made a windbreak on the slope going up to the house on stilts; warmth and moisture did the rest. But many people would just give up on places like this. So Philippa and I are going to sustain interest in this curved bed where plants struggle. It looks like a bad housing area, a slum where nothing much of grace exists and every inhabitant struggles to simply stay alive. Hopelessness and weeds invade. By heaven, this area is going to have some care and bloom in spring in mighty abundance.

Birds, the fish of the air. They catch those insects, the garden's krill, and turn it into song. Singing fish. Yes, there are such things. I heard a woman saying to another on the bike path by the sea that, as the schools of fish travel, she has heard them sing.

'You can hear them coming,' she said. 'They are singing in the water.'

The white *Luculia grandifolia* is giving out scent in the damp air this morning. I bent down to smell it as it drew me like a thread. Later as I stomped around, fork in hand, planting bulbs, Terry brought a sunflower head to the fence and handed it over. 'Would you like to plant this? It's how we knew we'd have bees for our vegetables in the country when I was a boy. They bring the bees.' Then he added, 'You can give them to the birds if you like. They are full of oil. Or you can eat them yourself.' I planted some around the compost heap and left the rest by the birdbath. As I bent, planting ten white liliums near the gate, the post came. In it were photographs of my friend Margaret Sharpen, three weeks before her death. I kept on planting the liliums and said, these are for you, Margaret. Forty years a midwife and never able to have a child of her own. A sort of gardener of babies. Plant or person, we all return to the earth.

There are now snowflake bulbs in the drive, which has been dug up. These were my mother's favourite flowers. The first garden she had as a child had these bulbs under a tree. Cream freesias went in here too, and some mixed Dutch irises into the new bed, edged with white primulas. Yesterday I planted blue cornflowers. I'd sown these into a box months ago and almost forgot them. Double white hyacinths were put in also.

Into three big pots I put pink and white tulips, thinking all the while of Mrs Judd and her advice to bury them a spade's depth. And for a scent at the back step, I put half-a-dozen pink hyacinths. These are not as chic as blue or white hyacinths, but they went in anyway as they were cheaper.

I see now that it is important to give the tough areas some of the best plants. It is easy to veer away from the ugly parts of the garden, just as it is with people, ignoring what is too difficult to confront.

Terry was right when he said, 'Don't let anyone tell you that you can't grow potatoes here all the year round.' My second crop is doing well, and when the trees above them shed all their leaves, they'll be in full sun.

Newly dug potatoes are delicious. I thought I knew what fresh potatoes tasted like because I had eaten white new potatoes from shops. But it is not at all the same. A bit like the difference between freshly caught fish and two-day-old fish.

But where, with all this talk of seeds sprouting, are the *Datura* seeds I planted? I stare at the ground and it stares back. Perhaps I soaked them too long. Perhaps they take longer to germinate than the seeds of annuals. Jane sent them, calling them Floral Moonlight. And that is what those flowers are like. The silver moon on the sea.

Small honeyeaters and sparrows flew around where I had been digging potatoes. Silver eyes, perhaps, I do not know their name, like a thumb with wings. So small, one hung upside down, drinking nectar from a yellow chrysanthemum, its throat exposed like a woman making love. Suddenly, as if to a drum, they flew off into a hibiscus and began to drink from the scarlet pools of flowers.

Wednesday, 3rd May

Rain. It has rained for two days. Within hours of the bulbs being buried it began. I rode to Wollongong in my

Driza-Bone coat. This trip showed how right my late sister-in-law Jan had been when she told me. 'Your coat needs a fresh coat of linseed oil.' We were in her stable, rolling our swags before setting out to cross the Simpson Desert. If ever you wish to abandon gardening, cross the desert when it is full of wildflowers. For hundreds of kilometres, great sweeps of flowers of every colour cover the red sand, like the floor of heaven. People stand speechless. Some have tears in their eyes. It is a calamity of beauty. Gardening seems like the act of a fool in the face of such enormous loveliness.

One recovers. But it stays in the mind. Such a grand scale — a colossal untended garden. It certainly puts digging with a trowel in perspective. Or opening a packet and soaking seeds in a bowl. Yet there is something that makes some of us long for greenery and beauty around our houses. It is enough for many to have merely the greenery of a lawn and cement paths. But that does not satisfy everyone. And by now, I don't think anybody who does not love gardens will be reading this.

All along the train tracks a version of the liliums I planted have been blooming in their thousands. It is like the white Madonna lily called *Lilium candidum*. This is *Lilium formosanum*, a native of Taiwan. It is easily grown from seed and has naturalised all along the east coast of Australia. It may have naturalised elsewhere too, but I have not seen it. When I first came to Sydney, I was astounded one Anzac Day to see these fabulous lilies growing wild along the roadside. I got the driver to stop and leapt out and ran back with a big bunch. I couldn't believe they could grow in such abandon.

Thursday, 4th May

Aquilegia. The word woke me. '*Aquilegia*! Go back to sleep. *Aquilegia*.' After a few moments I gave up and began wondering if it was time to plant them. Their common name is Columbine, which comes from the Latin name for dove. The flowers, when looked at closely, seem to be birds drinking from a bowl. Nan Evatt rang from Leura and I asked her about *Aquilegias*.

'Yes, you plant the seed in autumn. Do you remember I gave you a barrow of the plants and you put them down the drive?

'Some,' she said, 'are perennials, but some of the new hybrids may need to be treated as annuals.'

I love flowers that move and wave in the wind. A little above other plants, they seem like hands waving to the birds darting above. But it may be that they are this way to wave at bees, and so be fertilised, in a form of dance.

The rain has stopped so I am off to buy the seeds.

There is a blue nasturtium that had been thought to be extinct. It was found in an Oxford garden.

Tropaeolum azureum is a rare perennial climber that has lance-shaped leaves and grows to about a metre. It has creamy-yellow centres with blue petals. Nan and I shared a packet of eight seeds bought by mail order, but neither of us were successful. I want to try again, but they are hard to find.

Tropaeolum is the botanical name, and if you look up nasturtium in the encyclopaedia you will find only watercress. In the nineteenth century a white nasturtium was bred, only to be lost.

The wild gardens along railway lines often have great swatches of nasturtiums. They grow, too, on the banks of creeks and rivers. In Adelaide, whole stretches of the banks of the River Torrens are covered by these lovely flowers. Monet's garden makes good use of them too, where they are allowed to spread like green water over a wide path.

Later. *Aquilegias* are in. Shirley at Corrimal sold them to me and at the same time I ordered a *Magnolia soulangiana* called Scheherezade. It is watermelon pink, like a great tulip. Don Burke had three new magnolias on his television show and it was there that I saw this fabulous flower. Jim, Shirley's husband, was out among the trays of seedlings with a punnet of strawberry-pink foxgloves in his hand. I bought them to plant among the rocket which has self-seeded for the third time around the side path. This is the most successful part in the whole garden. It may be that the house and fence shelter it, or that the soil is not worn out, as it was concreted as part of the ugly drive and the edges left to weeds. It could be that it gets more sun and, being narrower than the two back beds, is easier to weed. Whatever the reason, the plants there thrived. The roses bloom, the *Alyssum* and rocket are profuse, the lavenders have grown fast and the cleomes and cosmos waved above until last month. This place is a boost to see. Everything went right.

I got more pink tulips too, and when the rain stops will plant them among the foxgloves in between the corners of the slabs of stone that make the path. Then it will need a lot of that celestial blue bog sage and something white to cool it down. Sometimes I think I ought to be planting trees. I ask myself, why am I fooling around with annuals? Yet a small garden can't be full of trees. Though I suppose it could.

I saw a program on the Prince of Wales' garden at Highgrove on television yesterday with Sir Roy Strong, Rosemary Verey and Marjorie Olein Wyndham-Quin, the Marchioness of Salisbury. Each, one at a time, walked with the prince around the parts of his garden they had helped design. Rosemary Verey was wearing a dress the colour of the blue gate at her own famous garden. The Marchioness was wearing the same hat, shoes and long soft skirt and jacket she wore in a photograph in *Gardens Illustrated* magazine. As I watched, a wisp of wind blew and she clutched the jacket modestly around her chest. She is in her seventies and has made two famous gardens. The present one is at Hatfield House in Hertfordshire. She planted mop-headed *Ilex* trees in pairs down either side of her East Garden. First she had considered pleached limes. Then she thought of the Boboli Gardens in Florence. The *Ilexes* were sent from a nursery near Pistoia, Italy (in case you are looking for them). But I imagine some are sold here — somewhere or other. Not surprisingly, this is a mighty aristocratic attitude towards gardening.

The Marchioness said plants had always been important to her because she spent much of her childhood with her Irish grandparents in County Limerick where her grandfather had an arboretum. 'He used to take me for walks and talk to me about the trees,' she reminisced.

I feel certain that talking to children about plants and helping them make a garden of their own, or even just to plant things and to sow, begins what can be a lifetime of pleasure. Gardening is sometimes a little like bird-watching. It gives great pleasure and doesn't, as a rule, make a noise, pollute or damage anything. There are a few mistakes that cause damage, it is true, in every gardener's life. A tree pruned too hard, or something not watered. But mainly those are silent things, the plants simply respond with leaves and flowers. Plants don't yell.

Even princes make mistakes in the garden. Walking around with Rosemary Verey, Prince Charles pointed to an area saying it was a disaster and he would have to try it again. He was beginning to learn disaster and, as a result, parts of the garden did not work. This man likes to dig and to plant. 'When Adam delved and Eve span, who was then the gentleman?'

For ages I have wondered what pleached limes could be. Somewhere, I can't think where, I saw this method illustrated. Bamboo stakes are used to help weave the branches of the trees into a tall wall, beneath which people can walk (if the lower branches are cut and the higher ones encouraged). Or the pleaching can begin quite low with the bamboo stakes holding the branches. The tree, of course, is not a citrus lime, nor the kaffir lime used mainly for its leaves in cookery, but it is *Tilia europaea*, the European Linden or common lime tree. This tree can grow up to forty-five metres tall, has heart-shaped leaves and pale yellow flowers that are sometimes used for making tea.

The pleaching of limes is a form of haute couture in gardening. Mainly, I think, because it is so much work and because it needs a large area of land. However, it can be done to one or two trees in a smaller garden. But then it needs a practical purpose, such as sheltering flowers or vegetables, or simply covering a wall, rather than making an avenue.

In the same program Dr Miriam Rothschild appeared briefly, talking about the meadow she had taught people to make. She has a particular mixture of seeds she calls 'The Farmer's Nightmare' which comprises red poppies, daisies, grasses and other wildflowers. Her own garden and house, she says, cause some to say that it is so wild nobody could possibly be living there. It is naturalness and wilderness that she is attempting. Now in her nineties, like my other hero Mrs Judd, Dr Miriam gardens with great originality and passion in a way that others copy.

For Australasian conditions there is a fabulous Wildflower Carpet Mix of seeds, containing white *Alyssum*, blue love-in-the-mist, blue Chinese forget-me-not and red Californian poppy, which Digger's Seed Sower's catalogue offers. They also sell another mixture called Wildflower Meadow Mix, which flowers from spring into summer and contains red Flanders and orange Californian poppy, blue cornflowers, rosy Silene and alfalfa.

Today, while I was mulling all this over, Jane rang from Adelaide and said, 'I have the Digger's catalogue here and I am going to order their cosmos called Yellow Garden and their green and white zinnia seeds.'

In one of those coincidences that some friendships mysteriously breed and flourish on, I said, 'Well, I've got it too and I'm going all out for their Wildflower

Meadow Mix.' I privately thought, 'I'll have some of what she's having.' Because Jane's been gardening a lot longer than I, she knows more so I often copy her. And the yellow cosmos sounds unusual.

It is hard to find cleomes and there's a pink cleome seed offered in the catalogue and I'll order that too. The address of Digger's Seeds Club is PO Box 300, Dromana, Victoria, 3936. Their Garden of St Erth is open to the public and has a nursery attached as well. The garden is on Simmons Reef Road in Blackwood, Victoria. You can phone them on (03) 5368 6514 for opening times.

I thought of building a wall of old bricks right across this back garden, splitting it in two with a beautiful mysterious doorway leading through its centre. Gardens need private, secret areas and the wall, on both sides, could bear roses. It would be a radical thing to do and could be wonderful. It would certainly be original. From Sydney to Nowra there is almost a continuous line of Hills hoists running as a steel avenue along the sea. Washing on the steel trees is like a flower flapping and billowing in the wind and can be beautiful. At least it is quick to dry, but I will never have one.

Saturday, 6th May

It's been raining since Thursday night. Suddenly this morning it stopped. A high wind is blowing the leaves from the Tree of Heaven. More and more sea is coming into view.

Today I realised I can't just keep shouting the names of annuals into the storm like Lear, and then race out to sow the seeds while the rain pelts down. I must lay out compost and feed my flock.

Yesterday I went to Sydney to see my grandson, Jack, for his birthday. I took a report on the garden he planted full of roses named for the American presidents. We put a mottled pink rose of not much virtue among them called Princess Grace of Monaco. Philippa snorted when she saw this rose. I admit it is strange with its cream frilled lolly-pink petals. But at the time I was desperate, and bought it in a bundle from a supermarket.

In the city, almost a gale was blowing, umbrellas blew inside out. Great cream camellias were in full bloom in Edgecliff. I saw how immense jacarandas can grow. Some, in a row going down to the sea, were as big as two-storey houses. Morton Bay fig trees alongside did not dwarf them. The jacaranda in the back garden has doubled in size since I came here. Glorious purple bougainvillea is beginning to climb more thickly through it, and beyond this a glimpse of sea.

Perhaps birds just open their mouths and drink when it rains. Each drop, like a grape falling into their open beaks. I think this, because I have not seen any at the birdbath since Friday. In the rain, the birds neither sing nor bathe nor eat, they merely sit and seem to dream, swaying on a branch in the wind.

This is the cake Jack always likes for his birthday.

Jack's Lime Coconut Syrup Cake

1¼ cups of self-raising flour

1 cup of coconut

125 grams of butter

1 tablespoon of lime rind (or lemon rind)

1 cup of caster sugar

3 eggs

½ cup of yoghurt or cream

½ cup of milk

Method:

Beat together the lime rind, butter and sugar until pale and creamy. Add the beaten eggs. Fold in the rest of the ingredients in two batches.

Bake in a moderate oven (180°C) for 45 minutes in a spring-form pan which is greased and floured.

Syrup:

⅓ cup of lime or lemon juice

¾ cup of sugar

¼ cup of water

Method:

Boil this mixture for 3 minutes. Allow to cool slightly.

Stand the cake on a tray or plate, to catch the syrup, and gently pour the mixture over the cake, pricking with a fork as you go.

Thursday, 11th May

It's hot and the wind has dropped. Philippa is pulling snails from daisies and removing leaves with rust on them from geraniums. Today she is digging up the last of the buffalo grass from the drive. She sits, wearing her floppy blue hat, digging with a garden fork she's just mended, tearing out the deep roots and flipping them into the overloaded wheelbarrow. 'None of this can go into the compost,' she says, 'it must all go to the tip or it will grow again.' I hate the waste of the good dirt on the roots, but I know she is right, and I'm grateful.

The sea is bright blue, the blue of the tiles on the back table. Red geraniums are blooming in pots leading down to the jacaranda which is almost bare now. Sometimes I wish for a bright garden. These wan vistas of green, grey and white, which I have been so keen on, seem a bit insipid. In a magazine somewhere I read of a professional woman gardener who said she grew all the bright colours — red, orange, yellow — at home because all her clients wanted white gardens. Her own garden in the photographs looked beautiful.

Nasturtiums, red geraniums and the masses of lemon chrysanthemums with blue salvias are in full bloom now and give a lot of pleasure and some of the brightness I want. The real trick is, I think, to have these colours when the weather isn't boiling hot.

Learning about gardening without doing a course is hit and miss. Yet some of the greatest gardeners, Rosemary Verey for instance, like some of the great cooks, did not have formal training. They learnt from their mothers and then they taught themselves. Maggie Beer, Gay Bilson, Stephanie Alexander — none was formally trained. Peri, is bringing me some *Hortus* magazines from London. My son and daughter-in-law are giving me a subscription to *Gardens Illustrated*. I ordered a whole year of the 1997 *Gardens Illustrated* as well. I want to learn quickly.

Rosemary Verey said something about beginning to learn by making her own famous garden which still amuses me every time I think of it: 'I knew that there was no hurry.' (Oh, here is a knock and here is the year's copies of *Gardens Illustrated* magazine held out in a man's palm.)

I simply cannot imagine being given a huge piece of land with a house on it where a garden was needed and not feeling hysterical with the wish to plant. Rosemary

Verey sat and thought, consulted gardeners, went to the Chelsea Garden Show, and began very slowly. In that time an olive grove could have been planted and already be three metres tall.

Monday, 15th May

Mothers' Day has been and gone. A million chrysanthemums decorate headstones and dining-room tables. Mine are on this dining-room table that I am writing at, three white blooms, each as big as a fist.

This morning I pulled out all the spent annuals. Terry said, 'It's the shortest day next month.' This surprised me because it is still warm. No bulbs are up yet. The garden feels like a loaded gun. Lying bare and forsaken-looking. Yet at any minute it could explode.

'Well, I'm off to buy some Lady's Mantle.' Jane said on the telephone this morning. I asked what it is. 'Its real name is *Alchemilla mollis*,' she said, spelling it for me as I scrawled the letters down. I'll have some of what she's having, I thought again.

Botanica says this plant is a herbaceous perennial, low growing and ideal for ground cover. Jane said it is often found on the edges of perennial borders in English gardens. Raindrops are caught in the wavy, slightly cupped and frilled leaves which make a sparkling look. The flowers are like *Gypsophila* and are greenish-yellow.

Still no sign of shooting from the seeds of that Floral Moonlight white *Datura* Jane sent me. I posted three lots off to friends in Bathurst. Helen, the tree grower, might have success. I sent some to the two girls on the farm at Peel where we planted all the trees. Big rains there, as here, so the trees are looking good, Ruth said on the telephone.

Lord, I long for the day I walk up their curving drive and see the swerve of trees leading to the house, all waving in the wind and higher than our heads. If trees will grow in that arid rocky soil, they will grow anywhere. It is strange that it seemed to make utterly no difference whether we planted a tree with compost, or with sheep manure, or with just a few rocks around as compost, they fared much the same. At first, shocked by the look of the soil, we ardently packed rich homemade compost around each sapling. Then, after a day or so, I remembered native trees do not always flourish with compost. So we desisted and simply scraped rabbit droppings around the base and dropped a few rocks on. Some in the end got nothing but the soil dug from the hole. Others got a spadeful of sheep manure, aged and matured, brought in from under Len's and Helen's shearing shed. So there it is: the trees are, as far as we can tell, flourishing and of equal size, or dead. It may be that the effects of shock and the amount of water are the only important factors. I enjoy a good conjecture, as you see.

It takes ten years, I heard today, for an orange tree to reach its full potential. On the River Murray, the orchards are being ploughed up because the Valencia oranges which had been planted for juice are not selling because of cheap imports. Fresh oranges now sell best, so navel orange trees are being planted instead.

To dig up a fully grown orange or lemon tree is horrible. Once, when we built something in our back garden in Adelaide, a great sprawling lemon tree had to be taken out. It was like killing an animal. My baby had lain in the pram beneath that tree, gurgling, looking up into the branches. The smell of the blossom was beautiful. And then we tore it up. I cried, but it had to go. A garden should have lemons so one day, years later, I rode home on my bike from university with a Lisbon lemon tree in the basket behind the seat. Its leaves were in my ears. It seemed to be singing to me. Its branches were around my waist. It felt like a lover. I put it behind the front gate and it grew about two metres a year. Great oval lemons came from that tree, yet you couldn't exactly park a pram beneath it, as it stood between the side fence and the drive.

But we got lemons alright. Ever since, I have made it a habit to plant a tree when a lover leaves me. (And no, I don't have a forest.) The lemon tree had been for that reason, and later I couldn't remember his name. But he had big feet.

LEMON

Bitter breast
of the earth
I've picked this one
from a dark green laden tree
this is a cold hard
obdurate fruit
yet one swift act
releases the juice
enhancing oysters
fish and almost everything else
the acerbic aunt
of the orchard
beautiful in youth
yet growing thorny
in old age
irritating
irritable
when I move house
the first tree I plant
is a lemon
biblical
dour and versatile
I much prefer it
to those cloying salesgirls
the soft stone fruits.

Lemon Soufflé

This is an old recipe so it uses imperial measurements. I've not changed them to metric in case it spoils the soufflé.

4 eggs, separated

4 ounces of caster sugar

½ ounce of gelatine

2 lemons (when doubling the recipe, which is sensible to do, use only 3 not 4 lemons)

½ pint of cream

½ pint of warm water

Method:

Whip the egg yolks with sugar and lemon juice. Place over a pan of hot, not boiling water and make sure the water does not touch the bowl. Beat the mixture until thick, which takes about 10 minutes. Remove from heat and beat until cool.

Beat the egg whites until stiff. Whip the cream. Gently fold both these into the cooled yolk mixture.

Dissolve the gelatine in the warm water. Gently add this to the lemon mixture. Chill, covered with a plate or film of plastic.

Serve with whipped cream and strawberries spread on the top.

Wednesday, 17th May

Bulbuls. A pair of bulbuls have come to the water bowls. There are blue wrens too. They were here last year, went, and now have come again. Whether the grey Persian cat, Carmel, who visits the garden ate the wrens, or whether they come and go regularly, I do not know. One day I did find grey feathers on the lawn. Terry said, 'If you feed birds in grass, they can get caught.' So now I throw the bread and scraps into the centre of the lawn, so the cat can't easily creep up.

The sea is grey today and I can't tell where the sky begins and the sea ends. 'Oh, what a beautiful day!' a friend of mine, Franz Kempf, once said, flinging open a window on a grey day in London. 'A silver florin of a day!' I wasn't there, but this artist's friend told me, laughing, as it was such a shock to him, a dentist.

I have been out treading among the mint and nasturtiums, winding roses up above the side back fence onto the shed's roof.

My fingers smell of nasturtiums. There's a glass vase of them beside me, burning orange, lemon gold and rich brown. I used to think nasturtium seeds were capers. But although they were used for pickling during the World Wars and, even now, sometimes still are, it is the caper bush *Capparis spinosa* that gives the true caper. Caper bushes grow wild not only around the shores of the Mediterranean, but in Australia and the Pacific region. The flower buds are gathered before they show any colour and are preserved in salt. Maggie Beer says in her book, *Maggie's Orchard*, that after the flowers die, berries form, and these too can be used in an antipasto or with pork. An old recipe for pickled nasturtium seeds comes from *The Experienced English Housekeeper* by Mrs Elizabeth Raffald, who was cook and housekeeper to Lady Elizabeth Warburton at Arley Hall in Cheshire. In 1759 Mrs Raffald 'wrote down everything she knew' and this book is the result. I do not believe it was everything that she knew, but that is what the authors of *The Perfect Pickle Book*, David Mabey and David Collison, say when they quote her recipes. Here is Mrs Raffald's way of pickling nasturtium seeds:

Mrs Raffald's Pickles

Gather the nasturtium berries soon after the blossoms are gone off, put them in cold salt and water, change the water once a day for three days, make your pickle of white wine vinegar, mace, nutmeg sliced, peppercorns, salt, shallots and horse-radish; it requires being made pretty strong, as your pickle is not to be boiled; when you have drained them, put them into a jar, and pour the pickle over them.

Thank you Mrs Raffald.

Monday, 22nd May

Chrysanthemums need dark nights to bloom. A streetlight shining on the chrysanthemums will be regretted. I gleaned that from a book Peri lent me when I stayed with her this weekend. It was called *Green Thoughts* by Eleanor Perenyi.

Star of Bethlehem (*Ornithogalum umbellatum*): a plant mentioned in the Bible, very pretty too, but a terrific weed once established. It invades all parts of the garden, and the slippery foliage breaks off when tugged and leaves the bulbs safely behind.

A friend who lives on a hill above Blackbutt Park brought home from Paris packets of seeds. Among them one of wild grasses. I think that could be the same as plague. But he swears he won't plant them.

There are many kinds of ivy, but the dark green climbing one is a devil of a weed unless contained by cement walls and even then, when birds eat the berries, it is transported. Given time, ivy can kill a giant tree. I see trees being strangled in gardens where the owners, perhaps thinking it beautiful, let the ivy run. A great blue spruce in the garden next to me in Leura went that way. It remained, in the end, a dark thin finger pointing accusingly at the sky as the ivy abandoned it and crawled, with the fervour of a hunter, to a couple of fifty-year-old Japanese maples. I am glad there is no ivy in this garden, and while I am here there never will be.

Heavy rain for two days and wind too. A leaf floats down as I stare out this window and the Claire rose waves and tosses in a green arch as if searching for an anchor in that sea, the air.

Bulbs are up. As I walked through the gate, holding an umbrella like a puppet being dragged along, I saw the first daffodils and irises are up. No sign of the liliums. I read, after they'd gone in, that these bulbs ought not to be planted deeply. Just under the earth, almost poking up, the book said. Too late. They'd been in for a fortnight, so it seemed best to leave them.

Tuesday, 23rd May

This is the land of rainbows, I thought and looked up and saw one. When I came to live here, there were rainbows almost every day. Jack and I, riding south, would see one sometimes with one foot on this house and the other in the sea. I leave it to you to imagine how we interpreted such rainbows.

I've been out in the back garden tangling great green rainbows, the climbing roses at the side fence, to each other to keep them from being blown to the ground.

The white dahlia is bowed down to the wet earth. Anders Dahl, a Swedish botanist whom the dahlia is named after, procured dahlia tubers and, by his death, in 1789, had produced some hybrids. A celebration to honour the dahlia plant was held by the Spanish king at the Madrid Botanical Garden in that same year. Dahlias were discovered by Europeans in Mexico. The superintendent of the Botanic Gardens in Mexico City, Vincente Cervantes, sent dahlia seeds to Abbe Cavanilles, the director of the Royal Gardens of Madrid, and it was this man who named the dahlia.

Until recently I did not know dahlias could be grown from seed. Daphne, Terry's wife, showed me a small plot with some green shoots in it months ago. She said they were from dahlia seeds she'd gathered. The flowers are now in bloom and I will walk next door and see how they are.

Later. The dahlias are finished. Cut back to stalks and their seeds gathered. Terry was out staring at his sugar-loaf cabbages, watering-can in hand. There was some kind of liquid fertiliser in the can. He began to tell me that he had lost many parsnips in the heat.

'I sowed row after row of carrots and parsnips; I even kept them under planks. But the ground was too hot. Boy, when I did get some, you saw hundreds of baby carrots. And I mean baby carrots. The ground was too hot and they just stopped growing. You remember the stunted parsnips I gave you?'

Yet now there are two rows of parsnips thriving, their green tops waving in the strong wind.

'You thought seeds needed heat to germinate, didn't you?' Terry continued. 'Well, they do, but the heat can kill them too. Even in the shade under the verandah in pots they died. I lost all my beans and all the lettuces.' He gestured to the peas growing up a trellis and to where the rows of beans once were.

PARSNIP

Earth's long ivory tooth
in a buried smile
which becomes
winter's snarl
tugging at the hem
of my skirt as I walk by
looking for a cabbage
bending to see
into the heart of the
green thornless rose
that is not yet ready
but this parsnip is
spilling earth
as it comes out.

> A life spent in a grave
> beneath a green fern
> it lies on the path
> like a fish
> dying in the air.
> Walking indoors
> shaking off the soil
> that gave me this parsnip
> to boil
> all it needs now
> is pepper and a bit of butter
> but the hole most surprised
> born in that wrenching moment
> lies there gasping in the sun
> dark and thoughtful.

Terry returned then to the topic of olive trees and the magnolia in the street. While I was away the magnolia was pulled up and left lying. Terry waited until a break in the rain to replant it. When he went out, council workers driving past saw him and stopped. They replanted the tree for him, and for me. Terry went inside and did not see them take the barbed wire away from all the trees. I suppose it is illegal. But that was fifty dollars worth of wire.

It is a mistake to think that the ripping up of trees means hatred of trees. It is just something to do when idle, perhaps, just something to do when irritable with drink. I keep thinking that it is important not to take this personally, either as a form of hatred of gardens or trees or of myself. We are all connected, but while I may have provoked those who have pulled up the trees, it's better for me not to blame them, or myself, but put it down to an act of nature. I am struggling to deal with another grief, and seeing the trees, so seemingly unprovoking and benign, being attacked makes me think it's best to just plug on. Some kind of hope, some faith, is necessary and, above all, no bitterness. Give me a gracious acceptance of my lot.

One day, I hope I will harvest olives from my three trees. One day, I hope my olive oil can be used as a form of stock for soup. I mean by this, that if you don't have any stock, vegetables and olive oil make good soup. For instance, Peri wrote out the recipe for the soup she made for our dinner; more a list of ingredients to boil than a recipe. Here is the list: tomato paste, soaked chickpeas, a tin of tomatoes, garlic, onions, water, plenty of oregano and good olive oil. Boil until chickpeas are soft.

There are several other very good soup recipes in a book using olive oil as the essential ingredient. Here is the best lentil soup I've had:

Faki Soupa

150 grams of brown lentils

1 large onion, sliced

2 cloves of garlic, crushed

1 small tin of tomato purée

200 grams of fresh peeled tomatoes or 1 x can of tomatoes

3 tablespoons of olive oil

900 millilitres of cold water

salt and pepper to taste

Method:

Soak the lentils for an hour or two, rinse and cover with cold water. Boil until tender, with all the other ingredients. Then blend or just mash the mixture. Either way, don't make it too smooth. Season and serve with good bread and more oil.

This recipe is best doubled or trebled, as I can't see the point of making just enough. This is for four people at one meal.

Thursday, 25th May

Moss. In the cracks on the footpath beside the highway in Corrimal emerald-green moss is growing. I stepped up from the gutter and saw it. Moss can't grow in pollution. It can be used in gardens, playgrounds and other places, like canaries were used in mining, as a warning of danger. Roses are used in this way in vineyards, to warn against disease threatening the vines. Here and in France there are vineyards with a rose planted at the end of every row.

That the bright moss could grow there beside the road, with cars drawing up beside it at the lights, snorting out fumes, is amazing. David Bellamy, the botanist, reviewing a book called *Moss Gardening: Including Lichens, Liverworts and Other Miniatures* begs people never to collect living mosses, lichens or any other plants from the wilderness. And never to use peat under any circumstances, because peatlands are some of the most endangered living systems on earth. He says to use peat substitutes, which are easy to buy.

There is a lot of peat for sale at almost every nursery I visit and I wonder if the sellers know it's endangered.

This little spill of moss, so bright, innocently growing there beside the cars and trucks, put a spring in my step all day. It was so valiant, such an emerald splash, squandered there by the gutter. What this moss also means is that there are spores wafting through the air by the million, waiting to fall on a suitable spot to grow. Many of these plants, lacking common names, are known only by their Latin names. So this drizzle of emerald that I saw probably has a Latin name. People were hurrying past with their shopping, or walking into the optometrist nearby. It gripped me and it still does. I cannot get over it. It seemed so emblazoned, so unexpected, and such a gift, as if a tree had bled there.

Friday, 26th May

The liliums are up. Knowing that they were planted too deep, I have been out there looking daily. Yesterday I planted pink foxgloves and tulips. Said I'd do it weeks ago. But saying a thing is about to be done is not necessarily doing it.

Only a couple of the pansy seeds have come up. And a few of the *Aquilegias* too. This sowing of seeds is addictive. Something in it is atavistic. For so long humans have worked in agriculture that it may be something deep being fed in me when I sow. It is also the thrill of a gamble. A bit like throwing dice. Whatever the reason for it, I am devoted to sowing. I turn first to the seed racks when I enter a nursery.

In Tanzania, I saw women sitting sorting seeds in the shade of an open iron shed, piles of seeds alongside them. Their babies lay beside them, or strapped to their backs. From time to time the women fed the babies and returned to their sorting. Some had a leather bottle with them which held a mixture of mashed banana and something else, I am not sure what. A woman would take a swig of this and give some to the baby.

Each time I tear open a packet, I remember those women laughing, working, feeding their children beside the piles of seeds.

Gerberas, impatiens, nasturtiums, stocks, these were some of the flowers my friend was growing for seeds on his farm beside Mt Kilimanjaro. The price per kilo of impatiens seed on the international market is fifty thousand US dollars, and when you look at the seed you can see why.

SEEDS

> The pomegranate seeds have worked.
> You fed her those at dinner
> in that old pink hotel by the lake
> like a farmer feeding Ratsack
> mixed with liver to a crow.
> But you have reckoned without me.
> You've announced in numerous legends
> you'll not be leaving your wife
> I hope to God you don't —
> ruin three lives, not four.
> I know you're smitten,
> you only use seeds
> when you've spotted something
> you want and know you can't
> otherwise have — and is half the age

that you are. Yes, I admit
she's enjoying the darkness
down there in your lair of secrets,
dead birds and bones.
But she's a creature of light,
of the sun, beaches.
Your cold gloomy pool lit with forty-watt globes
won't satisfy her in the long run.
She'll want to come up to the light.
I know you don't care
how much you've cost
and what you have ruined and smashed.
But read Birthday Letters and think.
Do us all a favour, go hunting,
let her go
shoot a crow
kill a stag
be a man
give her the antidote —
it's not too late
although there's a chill in the air.

A honeyeater has just landed in the Tree of Heaven. Now another has landed. They flitted off together before I finished the sentence.

A bright windy day. I am off to town to gather my grandson to stay here for the weekend.

Hallelujah.

Saturday, 27th May

I have been out sniffing the white *Luculia* flower. A warm white perfume, it smells like powder spilt on a dressing-table. I can still smell it, as though my nose has caught it. Perhaps that is what it is, simply pollen up the nose. Warm days, cold nights. Perfect weather. Although the pipes have burst, I am glad I am here. Last week the Water Board came after sending a great bill four times the normal. I think they must have lost some clients to suicide, because they came with such alacrity and without being asked. The man prowled around, a kind of water diviner without the stick. He found a leak behind the shed, the only place I never tread or see. Jack and I are bailing buckets from the bath, this time to do the laundry because the washing machine is in the shed and the water there is turned off. The plumber comes on Tuesday to put in copper pipes. One plumber said, 'The place is jinxed,' because we had so many leaks. But I don't think so.

The Tree of Heaven is full of tiny birds. Round and through it they are flitting like planes at a frantic airport. Jack put birdseed in the feeder hanging from the branches. The first food there for months.

Here is my mother's scone recipe, which is very good. In fact, she fed a family of six for almost a year with the big bag of flour (donated by the local flour mill) she won annually at the Gawler Show for these scones.

Muttee's Scones

3 heaped cups of self-raising flour

½ teaspoon cream of tartar (many of these ancient recipes use cream of tartar, which is available on the baking shelf of supermarkets)

2 eggs

2 tablespoons cream or melted butter

1 cup plus 1 tablespoon of milk

pinch of salt

Method:

Sift flour and cream of tartar. Beat eggs with cream or melted butter and add milk and salt and whisk together. Fold the fluids into the sifted flour with a knife and knead gently with your fingers. It is essential that the mixture is handled as little and as lightly as possible. Roll the dough out and then fold it over once. Roll out again. (This makes the split in the side of the scone.) Cut out using a cutter or a drinking glass. Dip your fingers in milk and dab onto the scones. Bake in a very hot oven for about five minutes. In four minutes take a look and see if they have lightly browned and risen. Remove as soon as they look ready. Wrap in a tea towel immediately and allow to cool a little. Serve with jam and cream or with smoked salmon, fresh dill and sour cream.

Sunday, 28th May

A pair of rainbow lorikeets are standing in the food bowl. How they discover food is here, I do not know. Never seen for months, they appear within hours of food being put out. Their acid-green backs are moving up and down and their bright blue heads pounce on the seed. Perhaps they watch the flight paths of smaller birds. But where they sit to do this is a mystery. Word gets out, but how?

When Jack and I came from the train, the stars were out. Some were green, sprinkled on the deepest blue, in a pattern we could not fathom. God's tongue, the sea, spoke its language to the stars. We came inside and banged the door.

A pair of small dark birds have landed on the railing. Brown-breasted with a clerical collar, on the throat a tan spot. I wish I knew their name.

Yesterday we rode to Corrimal. White egrets were fishing and several kinds of duck were swimming in Bellambi lagoon which runs behind the sea. A pelican took off in a stately fashion. A young cormorant stood beside some reeds while ducks kept it from the water. It looked frustrated, cawing softly in the sun.

At times, this lagoon is full of bright-green weed. Fishermen go there and drag it from the water. They use it for their bait. The weed has gone at present, swept out by the wind, perhaps. Or possibly the rain or tides took it out to sea. The only thing I know is the train timetable and that is because it is printed. A month ago I put out onto the front nature strip benches that were rotting where the shade house used to be. A woman came with her brother and took them. She asked to see the garden and I showed her. Her name was Beryl and she told me she has old roses and gave me her address. Last week, at Corrimal, I called in. She's got a sheep and a goat and a garden packed with shrubs and roses. The neighbours built a second storey and took away sun from half her garden. So she pulled up the roses and planted camellias down the side.

The usual dreamer of garden dreams, Beryl invited me inside and showed me gardening books. Pictures of gardens that she loves. We sat there at the kitchen table as she pointed to photographs saying, 'Oh, look at this one. Isn't that beautiful? How would you like to have that?' A week later, a flowering ginger plant, some Green Goddess lilies and a pot of snail vine were left on my front step.

The lorikeets are back. They look like two orange seals facing me, peering out together.

Friday, 2nd June

An Indian summer's day. Philippa is cutting back hibiscus, May bush and a big native fig. These are shading the side path and need pruning. It is not until Philippa gets working in a bed that we see how the weeds — *Tradescantia* and onion weed — have been thriving. Snails have made daisy bushes into lace. Once snails get up into a plant, the bait on the ground is useless. I learnt that today. The snails must be pulled off one by one.

I have been to Balmain, staying with friends, Philip Martin and Jenny Gribble, for a few days. Their garden is a balcony and the harbour. Yachts and ferries are their flowers. What's the Opera House then? A great frangipani blossom floating on the water, as they do in gutters around the city. Few things are lovelier than a flowing gutter full of frangipani blossoms with a few peaches floating by, dropped from overhanging trees.

I'm making an old recipe for visitors. My Godmother Isabella told me that when my mother made this cake, my three brothers kept asking for more and each time they did she said, 'You can't have any,' even while she was cutting more.

Aunty Beck's Chocolate Cake

1 cup of self-raising flour
1 cup of sugar
½ cup of milk
2 eggs
2 tablespoons of cocoa
3 tablespoons of melted butter

Method:

Beat all the ingredients in a bowl for 3 minutes. Put in a greased ring tin. Bake for 35 minutes at 180°C.

This morning, on the phone from Adelaide, Jane said, 'I've put two myrtles in huge pots and I'm staining the pots with umber. Then I saw Zeffirelli's *Romeo and Juliet*. Do you remember at their wedding the walls were that wonderful old pink? So I thought that was what these pots need. So I'm putting pink onto them today to give them a bit of a vague blush.'

Can't say I did remember.

Philippa has been planting Oriental poppies in her garden. She said, looking at a picture in *Gardens Illustrated* after lunch, 'Oh, look. Look at these poppies. I must get some more.' And she lifted up a page to show me a meadow of weeds, daisies and poppies.

At one time it was illegal to grow opium poppies in your garden. I was told at Leura that I was breaking the law. But those great grey plants, with buds from which salmon-pink petals like crushed moth wings burst out, turning then to pods like those of Egyptian waterlilies, always grew in my garden. There may be a way to make opium from the seeds, but I don't know it. Opium was not always a forbidden drug, as shown by Elizabeth Barrett's letter to her friend Miss Metford in 1839:

> Can anything grow anywhere or any way with this terrible wind? The temperature of my bedroom is kept up day and night to 65 degrees and I am not suffered to be moved from bed even for its making — and yet the noxious character of the air makes me very uncomfortable and sleepless. I took two draughts of opium last night — but even the second failed to bring sleep. It is a blessing this — that sleep — one of my worst sufferings being the want of it. Opium, opium, night after night — and some nights, during east winds, even opium won't do, you see!

'Never try to move a poppy,' writes Eleanor Perenyi. She goes on to say that the annuals should be sown where they are meant to grow, but that the perennial, the *Papaver orientale*, which grows about a metre tall, has only one drawback and that is that it disappears for months after flowering. She says the hole can be disguised by a nearby plant of baby's breath. This poppy has a very long taproot and, if bought in a pot, should be planted out with care. Perenyi also advises that the less attention paid to Oriental poppies the better, except for a metal hoop to keep them from falling.

My mother was fond of Iceland poppies and used to send me to the grocer's shop saying, 'Now ask for a packet of Iceland poppies in sunset colours. Don't forget, sunset colours. I don't want those other colours. And get a yard and a half of saxe-blue ribbon. You need new ribbon to go with this dress I'll finish tonight.' She'd give me one shilling and sixpence, and I'd walk up the wide empty street to the shop with the wide verandah, enter on the bare splintery floorboards and do as I was told. For this reason, poppies have always reminded me of saxe-blue taffeta ribbons. Speaking of blue, at other times my mother would say, 'Go and buy me a reel of blue thread. Take this piece of material and match it.'

'I don't need the material,' I'd say. 'I can remember the colour.'

'No, you can't, blue is the hardest colour to remember to match. You have to take the material with you or it won't be right.'

Biting off a thread from the smocking, she'd push the piece of material towards me across the table. 'Take this piece.'

Off I'd go. And that was how I learnt about blue.

The blue sea outside the window would need a scrap of cloth to match it, and then it would need scrutiny to say just what blue it was. Celestial, saxe, the blue of Madame Bovary's eyes, hyacinth, I really can't say. A mixture of all these and something of this perfect sunny day, with the pale grey-blue sky on the horizon.

Now I have got off poppies and onto blue which I did not mean to do. But you can see the reason. What I meant to do was quote Virgil on poppies to you. Here he is, and I see now how wrong it was to think that crop rotation was an Oriental invention:

> *A field where before you raised the bean with its rattling pods*
> *Or the small-seeded vetch.*
> *Or the brittle stalk and rustling haulm of the bitter lupin.*
> *For a crop of flax burns up a field, and so does an oat-crop,*
> *And poppies drenched in oblivion burn up its energy.*
> *Still, by rotation of crops you lighten your labour, only*
> *Scruple not to enrich the dried up soil with dung*
> *And scatter filthy ashes on fields that are exhausted.*
> *So too are the fields rested by a rotation of crops,*
> *And unploughed land in the meanwhile promises to repay you.*

At Dusk an Owl Flew Down

OWL

The owl flew from the tree
slitting the air like silk.
We were sitting drinking
in the dusk.
Owl! It's an owl!

Foolishly I ran to get meat
or any gift
to make the owl welcome.
But I was too late.
Again it flew from the tree
and we watched the pale scissors
of its wings
slice the blue dusk
into two dresses
for my granddaughters.

I walked back inside
with my arms full of silk
and began threading a needle.
Now we have dresses
and no owl.

Thursday, 8th June

𝒜 fat grey pigeon is walking through the violets. It is looking for the grain fallen from the birdfeeder hanging above. Yesterday, as I walked down the side path (my pride and joy), I saw the first violets blooming. These plants were left for me at the back step when I was away, by a woman whom I met one day when she was about to put a note in my letterbox saying that she wanted to buy a house around here. Penelope Ferguson said she had a big garden at Coledale, north of here, and had sold it, but was still living there. She said she would bring me cuttings from her garden.

At Leura, my neighbour Phyllis had hundreds of pink violets lining paths. Behind these were clumps of lily of the valley. Growing wild and filling some paths were dozens of hellebores (also called Christmas roses). Phyllis, almost beaten by the beautiful wilderness, this abundance of what others try so hard to achieve, said, 'Come in any time and help yourself, Kate.' So I took the wheelbarrow and filled it, clearing a bit of the path of hellebores. I wish I could go back. The hellebores would do well in the shade of the big tree, although Philippa says they need cold. She's probably right. But I believe in having a go.

Right now, Philippa is outside, pulling leaves from geraniums afflicted with rust. I cannot properly describe the anguish that rises in me as I see her sit at this slow task which seems so entirely useless to me. Philippa says that taking off the rusted leaves stops rust spreading. But I believe in letting it run its course. No doubt she's right, but as I see the weeds thriving in both back beds, and the soil soft and damp ready to give up the weeds, my urgency reaches hellish proportions. Why don't I go out and do the job myself? Several answers to that. One, I am inside trying to make a living. Two, I am baking a fruitcake, making caponata, boiling potatoes for lunch and mopping the floor with kerosene in hot water. Another reason is that Philippa doesn't really enjoy my working beside her. I get in the way. My best job is to bring the wheelbarrow round to where she is working, she'll tolerate that. But, ideally, she prefers to be left alone. Undemanding, energetic, knowledgeable and diligent, with a passion for plants, her taste and style are wonderful. I ought just to keep out of it. And largely I do. Philippa is going to plant *Alyssum* seedlings, which are ready now beside the shed where they were sown. The stocks I sowed a while back are ready to plant out too. I want big scented stocks stinking their sacred scent.

Last week I had Sophia, my two-year-old granddaughter, to stay because she had a cold. She weeded beside Philippa one day, bucket in hand, fork in the other. I heard a conversation that later made me howl in bed with laughter until I thought I'd wake her. It went like this: 'Don't be ridiculous, Sophia, *that* is a cornflower!' Since there is no sign of a flower on any of the plants and they are only a year younger than Sophia herself, I don't see how she could be expected to know the difference between a weed and a cornflower. But, and she may be right, Philippa said as we sat eating chicken noodle soup at the back table, 'It is best to sort things out and then treat children as if they are twenty.'

There's been a lot of rain. When I went on the train at dawn to collect Sophia, the line had a slippage on it. We limped into Thirroul. The phone queue curled round the building. From time to time, announcements through loudspeakers were made, which, in essence, seemed to say, 'We do not know what is happening. We think there may be some buses available. Some may come from Kiama. Some are full. There has been a landslide at Waterfall. All trains in both directions have stopped. We hope to move you soon.' Variations on this theme came for an hour or so as the rain poured down.

Horses in paddocks, looking forlorn and ravished, stood up to their hocks in water, sadly trying to tear at a bit of green on a bank. I have never understood the stoicism of animals. They do not write letters to their owners or politicians, but stand stolidly enduring the torrent in silence. I often wonder if they are making a plan, or if there is hope or faith in their hearts, that the sun will come and the earth dry up and they will be warm again. Or do they just exist in the awful moment?

During this great rain, Sophia and I spent a couple of days indoors, dashing out only for a quick slippery dip. On the first day, seeing a great high slippery dip as we got off the train, Sophia ran to climb it. I stood there, umbrella and luggage hanging on me, and saw her little boot slip on the wet top rung and she fell, clunking down with a thud. Luckily, her boot had caught in a rung or two as she fell and it slowed her. The thickness of her nappies cushioned the fall. We staggered home to lick wounds and to talk it over and over.

While we were stuck indoors, I wrote to the Department of Parks and Gardens, councillors, the mayor, our MP, six in all, asking for trees to be planted around the 1950s' playground for shade in summer. I've asked, too, for trees to be planted in the street and a few other things as well. 'A creaking wheel gets the oil,' an old man said on the radio yesterday and it struck me.

Friday, 9th June

An owl! An owl in the big tree. At dusk the owl flew down. Philippa and I were sitting drinking claret at the blue table. It was like a feathery ghost in the bare tree, its white face, barely glimpsed with a pale brown body. It swooped to the lawn and back to the tree. A holy visitor. Philippa stood at the railing to watch while I went to get more wine for us and meat for the bird. The owl flew off.

It is dusk again and I have put the big outside light on, as it was last night, but cannot see the owl. It might have come for old soup bones that I have thrown out from time to time, or fish heads or scraps of meat the smaller birds leave uneaten. 'Only connect,' said E.M. Forster. He put that as an epigraph at the beginning of *Howard's End*. And while he didn't mean if you throw out bones you'll get owls, it strikes me that the smallest act has significant consequences. Of course, it could be that the owl lives in the tree and because it's bare we saw it, that's all. Nothing to do with me. What does this owl presage?

Saturday, 10th June

I am soaking seeds with a use-by-1990 date. I found them on a shelf. No name on either of the two packets, but it seems a pity to throw them out.

I keep thinking about that enduring horse in the rain. Did the horse think, my parents suffered more than this? Or, my mother is dead and one day I will be dead. All this will pass away. I am simply a horse in a long chain of horses. Or, my mother is dead and I wonder where all the things she knew have gone? Do they pass away, just fade out, or do they float about waiting to be known or learnt by some other horse? And what of the paddock my mother grew in, where she learnt to tug at grass standing beside her mother, then suckling and sleeping beside her, sheltered by her body from the wind? Where has that wind gone? Is that hanging around somewhere too? The way my mother knew how to jump hurdles — what happened to that when she died?

Was there any thought that horse might have that would keep it enduring with hope? Or would it just stand there without anything to support it until it dropped or the water soaked away?

Tuesday, 20th June

'Storms and strong winds have damaged houses.' That's the radio at lunch time. It is snowing at Leura. When I spoke to Kathy at Megalong Books she said snow was falling onto car bonnets. It is the first really cold day I have had since I came here. Suddenly I saw, looking out this window at the metal-grey sea tossing with white horses, how much we need change. Kept indoors all day, I snooped around with the gas heater on, somehow relishing the extremity of it all. 'Another perfect bloody day,' said Sarah Miles in that film set in Kenya in the forties — *White Mischief* I think it was called. I can't remember the name of her character but she was the one who wore the snake around her neck to the races. While I wasn't actually sick of weather that never got really cold, this snap has made me happy.

Wind: nature's pruner. The trees are bent, tossing like those modern ballet dancers who wear torn frocks and dash their long hair on the floor. I am always slightly embarrassed watching this kind of ballet. It seems excessive. Yesterday I rode home from Wollongong in the dark. It was raining. I stayed too long at a film. My bike has no lights so I rode on the footpath until I got to the bike path by the sea. I was frightened because riding beside lagoons and creeks, edged with bush, seemed dangerous. I hadn't known the film was so long. It was *The Horse Whisperer*. Wonderful scenery and very good clothes.

My friend Nancy Phelan asked today, 'How is the garden?' I said, 'What can I say? The geraniums are in bloom and so are the nasturtiums. There's a million plans with not a lot yet to show.'

Wednesday, 21st June

The sea has faded to the sky, both are almost white. I lifted up a page against it and there was hardly any difference. Still the wind howls on.

Thursday, 22nd June

The howling wind goes on. People have given up umbrellas, they just blow inside out. The big screen of white potato vine has blown down. It was, I see now, a sail that had grown heavy with the vine. It fell on the potato patch and one camellia that was already dead. The camellia died suddenly and I think it must have been poisoned by the gum tree near it. Pigeons have settled on the lawn, puffed up, catching a bit of sun on their breasts. Three crimson rosellas flew down to the feeder hanging in the tree this afternoon. Three birds of the one breed may mean a pair have bred.

The big bed of pink, orange and white impatiens is bent in the wind, tormented like the trees. Some trees have fallen in the park by the highway. I see now that trees growing alone are vulnerable in the way they aren't in the bush, sheltered by each other. Still the wind blows. On what day did God make the wind?

Friday, 23rd June

Peace. The wind has stopped. Birds get very thirsty in winter. I see them drinking and splashing in the bowls every time I fill them. The impatiens have been burnt by the cold, not much, just some blackened tips. The blue vine on the back deck, which shed almost all its leaves when it had Cabot's wood paint spilt on it as I painted the railing, has sprouted. I thought perhaps I'd killed it. Peri gave it to me as a cutting she struck in a pot.

Today Philippa is coming to work. We are going to dig up the hyacinth bulbs that have not yet come through and see what is wrong. I planted them very deep as the woman at a garden festival had advised. At the time it seemed odd, but she might be right.

Saturday, 24th June

'Grab the doona for me dog, will ya?' a boy called to another as they pulled up in an old blue van. Philippa cleaned out the shed yesterday. I piled things up on the grass outside the gate. Barely back inside, I turned as I heard him call. One boy leapt out, took two chairs and the moulting doona. 'And grab the blankets too!' It all went within five minutes of standing there. I had been planning on sending it to St Vincent de Paul and then thought that there were probably people around here who could do with it. All day that boy's, 'grab the doona for me dog' has been going through my head as I washed blankets and hung them in the sun. I'm over feathers. When I tipped the doona from its cover I saw why my room is full of dust.

As I watched two tiny wrens swinging on rose branches in the afternoon sun, more like monkeys than birds, I thought how strange it is that I have slept under feathers for a decade. Well, not any longer. It's back to wool. His dog can have my doona. 'Thanks very much,' the boy said as he turned to get back in the van. I thought of saying that I'd like it if, in return, the olives and the magnolia could be left alone each Friday night. Probably a futile corrupt bargain, so I didn't try it. I did think, though, that a bit of local goodwill might save a tree.

The mandarins are getting ripe. Which makes me think my friends who have an orange orchard may be harvesting. Jennifer and Anthony, who came here when she photographed the garden, have a place on the Colo River. Jennifer gave me the recipe for Peg and Dot's marmalade, which is used by several restaurants, Balmoral Beach Pavilion is one. Seville oranges come in a bit later than Washington navels, so it may be a little early yet.

Peg and Dot's
Seville Orange Marmalade

8 Seville oranges

2 lemons

4 litres of cold water

sugar

Method:

Cut up the lemons and oranges. Mix with the juice of the lemons, depending on juiciness, with 4 litres of cold water. Soak this overnight in a cool place. Then simmer all for two hours. Measure the quantity of cooked substance. For each cup of this, add one cup of sugar, one at a time. Bring this to the boil. Keep boiling until it jells. Test jelling on a saucer in the 'fridge. Bottle into sterile jars. Never let marmalade go off the boil as it won't set.

Friday, 30th June
'Girra Girra', Peel, via Bathurst

Frost. A white frost. I laughed when I touched Ruth's spinach, it was stiff as a hide of leather. Great dark-green leaves curled and solid. Lettuce and parsley were frozen too, but, being more frail, were softer and seemed doomed. Ruth said the vegetables have had many frosts and are not ruined by it as I'd expect. But if the sun hits the leaves before they have defrosted then they burn and spoil. So it is not the cold that they can't bear, it is the sun when they are cold. It is a bit like going on holiday and getting sick, just when you have time to get strong. The rest allows you in some ways to let up and permits the collapse your body longs for, so previously stretched and virulent with need and work. I said a white frost, because that is not the only kind. The black frost that killed my pink flowering gum tree at Leura was the first I had seen. I had not known there could be such a thing. God help some native plants when a black frost comes. That small tree died as if flashed by fire. It seemed instantaneous and irredeemable. Like a murder in the night.

I have come to stay at Girra Girra for a week. Later I will go out and look at the trees we planted. The tanks are overflowing and so are the four dams. Ruth and Barbara are not bailing out the bath for the washing machine as they did before the rain. We all bathed in the same water when I was last here. Because that was the way my family did it when I was a child in the desert, it seemed quite natural to do it here. When the explorers Len and Anne Beadell, with their baby daughter, Connie, went out to make the atomic bomb roads around Maralinga and Emu in the fifties, the baby had a bath in a bucket once a fortnight. There is a photograph of it in one of Len's books about his road building and exploration. Anybody who has lived with very little water, garnering every cup, can never really recover. I still feel like flinching sometimes when flushing a toilet.

Last night, while leafing through the book *English Food* by Jane Grigson, I asked Ruth what a bloater was. Neither she nor Barbara knew. I read out the description, which did not actually say what it was. Apparently they can be grilled and the best come from Yarmouth. In fact, if you want to eat the best bloaters, you still must go to Yarmouth. They should be eaten within thirty-six hours as the cure of salt and smoke is so light. They can be mashed with butter and turned into a paste to be eaten with hot toast, which was a favourite with the Victorians. And, like kippers, they can be raw in salads, with beetroot or apple, or, as the Poles do, eaten with cream and chives, topped with onion rings. But after reading all that we still didn't know what a bloater was.

We looked up several other books and then I thought, as a last resort, to see what a Frenchman had to say. In *Larousse Gastronomique* it says: 'Bloater. Craquelot — slightly salted, smoked herring served mainly in England for breakfast and for high tea. The bloater is grilled on a low fire and served with melted butter or Maître d'hôtel butter.'

All this connected with an idea I had had for days about gaps in knowledge and the importance of them. In the end, when you are trying to understand something, it comes down to context. I had suddenly seen, when thinking of my childhood, that the great unspoken space, a sort of gap above our heads that informed and caused everything, was the relationship of my parents. Their love for each other made the childhood my brothers and I shared the peaceful, graceful thing it was. Although we fought, all around and above us was the gap, the thing I never examined or saw. It was the relationship between the man and the woman and their love. On that hung all the law and the prophets. That got me thinking about other gaps I had not seen which are probably around a great many things that I take for granted. It had come as an illumination, but I was a bit embarrassed to tell anybody about this idea, as I thought it could be so simple and self-evident that it might be something others use daily when thinking about a subject. I tried it out at lunch yesterday with a Canadian anthropologist, Eva, who was visiting, Ruth and Barbara. On hearing my thoughts Eva said that it is the reason anthropologists don't usually study their own society, because it is just that gap in their vision that they can't see. They need to look at another society to be able to see, as an outsider, the gaps that everybody inside takes for granted.

On the matter of bloaters, it was plain that if I had looked further, I would have seen that Jane Grigson does say what a bloater is later in the book, when she states that, as a dish for breakfast and tea, bloaters have gained a Dickensian air of fog and domestic stuffiness which is not to their advantage. The name doesn't help: 'When Peggotty remarked in *David Copperfield*, that she was proud to call herself a Yarmouth bloater, she certainly didn't mean she was a fat, hearty creature, but that she was nicely rounded, and sweet, but well-spiced in character, and fit for a discriminating man.'

The name, Jane Grigson explains, is from the sixteenth century and, for people in the trade, it was a useful accuracy. It meant they were treated so lightly with salt and smoke that they were still plump, bloated, if you like, with moisture, unlike the dry, almost brittle red herrings.

We looked up bloaters in *The Book of Ingredients* by Philip Dowell and Adrian Bailey, with an introduction by Jane Grigson, where there was a photograph of a herring and a caption that said it can be baked, fried, broiled or grilled. Its extreme oiliness makes it ideal for curing, as in rollmops, soured and marinated herrings, buckling (what is buckling?), matjes, bloaters, red herrings and kippers. I don't think we have true herrings in Australia, but perhaps mullet are similar.

All this talk of fish meant Ruth got up and asked if we would like smoked salmon on scrambled eggs for breakfast, and is now making them. I can smell them — and the toast.

Thursday, 6th July

On Sunday, Helen and Len, who gave the tree seedlings for this farm, came to lunch. Helen and Ruth walked around in the deep cold, inspecting. There is a lot of erosion. Water just pours down the rocky face of the farm, taking whatever topsoil is not held down with grass or trees. So Helen is bringing out another lot of wattles to plant in a bad spot. She also said there is a machine that can dig a wide shallow drain that can be lined with straw or gravel and then planted with herbs. These drains help stop erosion, and the girls are thinking over whether they will try this. But what if the drain were to be half a kilometre long? What else would you plant in it? Hardy fruit trees perhaps? We don't know.

The Simon Johnson winter catalogue was delivered here yesterday. Ruth, who used to run the Sofala Cafe, read out a list of teas: 'Breakfast Earl Grey. This is a classic morning blend. A sumptuous and noble blend of full-bodied Ceylon tea, flavoured with the oil of bergamot — a small citrus fruit.' But there are two kinds of bergamot. The North American herb has pink, white and also mauve and crimson flowers that smell like Earl Grey tea, I think. The leaves were used by Oswego Indians for tea. The botanical name is *Monarda didyma*. And then there is the bergamot orange, or *Citrus bergamia*, used in perfumery and essential oils. We found that in *The Book of Ingredients*. The herb was also described in Rosemary and John Hemphill's *What Herb is That?*

Today I go home. I am getting a lift to Penrith with the girls, who are going there to be hypnotised to give up smoking. There's a herb farm at Capertee called Kadisha and we are going to try to buy bergamot to plant in our gardens. But where we'll get a bloater, I don't know.

Thursday, 3rd August

The sun was on my back last week when I weeded a front bed and planted out seedlings of stocks I'd sowed months ago. Then I saw big gardenias for sale in Woolworths for six dollars ninety cents. I bought three and put them in the back garden. One went into a hole left by the magnolia I'd dug up and planted outside the front gate. Exhilarated by this digging, and the way it is so satisfying to plant shrubs, I dug up three yellow daisies self-sown from a big bush against a side fence. These went outside the front fence near the olives. My theory is that the more the area by the public path is planted, the less tempted people will be to pull them up. If it finally looks like a garden, I think they'll leave it alone. It is the few sticks of trees that somehow offend them. As I've said, these trees, perhaps, seem an affront to people (drunk, wild or bored); the trees are too brazen, vulnerable and tempting.

Violets, violets everywhere and many a bunch to pick. They have spread out under the bare trees in the back garden and if you bend down you can sniff them or bring a bunch indoors.

At the back step, two daphne plants are blooming and daffodils are out too. I see now that the flowers a woman is given when she has a baby forever remind her of that time. Daphne, peonies and early daffodils came to me and it is these flowers every year that remind me of my son's birth. But I never did grow peonies. For all my talk and plans I have abandoned this idea, because I read that they like cold and finally I am practising what I preach and not trying to force something against its nature. It has taken sixty years to learn this but it's worth it. Yet every now and then I break the rule.

Outside the front gate geraniums in exotic colours, brought from cuttings gathered in Adelaide streets, are thriving. Bright pink, burning crimson, more red than red, and magenta, they are growing around the roses and the olive trees. The blue and white, pink and yellow schemes have been thrown out. Now gaiety is all.

Terry wearily points out that vandals have knocked one of the terracotta pots with pink geraniums in them and almost half the pot is shattered on the ground. But this was always a risk, and worth taking because the pots are bookends to the garden with the olive trees above them. I've just turned the pot around so it looks normal and what I'll do with it I'll think of later.

It all bears out Terry's worst fears and the warnings from Phil, the other neighbour, when the garden outside the gate went in. And yet there is a garden there, and people can pick the roses when they want to. I like them to do it. And a bit of lawn has grown trees. Begonias, which also grow easily from cuttings, are in these plots. They came from Peri's garden, and though it is sunny here they thrive and wave in the wind like small bamboo.

Saturday, 12th August
'Bend of the River', Elanora, Queensland

I am here on Peri's farm for a while. A peacock is honking that weird cry, like a cat fighting. Banana leaves are moving against a hill of bush. Between the banana and the bush, the river is slow and olive green with a silver snake of light floating on its surface. I am eating dried yellow stars made from slices of five-star fruit from the orchard. There goes the peacock again. It's like the trains at home. I suppose I soon won't hear it at all.

I have joined the Henry Doubleday Research Association. There is a pile of journals from this

Association here and I've begun to read them. The name comes from Henry Doubleday (1813–1902), a Quaker smallholder who brought Russian comfrey from Britain. He hoped comfrey might feed millions. This dream came from Doubleday's horror of the Irish potato famine. The Association's members range from:

> complete beginner gardeners to PhDs, and the interest of the work makes membership an absorbing hobby. It is not the kind of charity that gives away money, but information, on simple cheap methods that can be applied by any gardener, peasant or coolie.

The Australian Association is nationwide and is made up of organic gardeners and farmers who follow organic methods of gardening, growing crops and tending livestock. There is a monthly outing in Sydney and nearby country areas and a field day once a year. I am quoting from the hundredth issue — *Spring, 1994*.

When I get home I am going to start a worm farm. The instructions sound easy enough, as food scraps are simply wrapped in newspaper and put on top of a set of worms in their native soil (which I'm going to get from the compost heap). Once a week, a covering of fine lime powder is sprinkled on top of the parcels of newspaper. A polystyrene box from the greengrocer can be used, so long as it has some holes for drainage. I won't go on about how good the worm castings are for the soil, as most know this by now, I suppose. What I would like to know though is if the weeds can be used in compost heaps to make compost without spreading the seeds. As I said, Philippa puts all weeds into the rubbish bin and she may be right to do this. But when I lug out the heavy bin full of soil on the roots of weeds, I do not enjoy it. It seems a waste. For over a year now I have done it and I would like to stop.

The light is changing as the afternoon passes, a rooster is crowing. Peri said when I was coming here, 'Get Anton to sharpen the axe. There are too many roosters. But promise me you won't use the axe until it's sharpened.'

Daily I wind the clock ticking loudly on the wall. This dining room is darker now. Suddenly a shaft of light has made the leaves gleam and the fruit I picked this morning shines in a glass bowl; so does the butter in the black pan on the stove behind me, waiting to fry some onions for a tart I'm going to make for tomorrow's lunch. Two friends are coming down from Brisbane, so I've picked some limes to make Jack's citrus syrup cake. The chooks are laying about nine eggs a day. In the shed three goose eggs lie in straw in an old tea chest waiting for more. The geese are bold and irritable as it's mating time. A goose can break your arm with its wings if you annoy it, say by trying to take an egg while it's nesting. Or if you put your hand into the nest to see if any goslings are hatched.

A butterfly is flittering around the mango tree, making a wide circle like a big windmill flying. The sun also makes its wings glint. And speaking of glinting, there is no glint like that of a crow. Those black diamonds. One is calling now. Julie, the caretaker, says there is a plague of crows. But you can't shoot them, they are protected. A man at Burleigh Heads shot a crow and was fined five thousand dollars.

From time to time pink petals of the bauhinia float like birds onto the lawn. With a sudden gust, a flock, then two or three, then a dozen or so. They seem reluctant. On the dam there is a silver crucifixion of light, wide and bulky, like a Brancusi. Eggs are boiling in a pot and the clock ticks on.

Some days I ask myself, what have I learnt? What have I accomplished today? A letter to Philippa. Read the papers and was worse off than if I had not. Boiled eggs for tea. The list can get pathetic. Coolie or peasant? I ask myself. I read a book recently called *The Life of a Simple Man*, an autobiography of the life of a French peasant at the end of the nineteenth century. It was the kind of autobiography that Gertrude Stein wrote of Alice B. Toklas, as it was written by a man who had had the life told to him by the owner. When I go home I will quote some of it to show you why I liked it so much.

GHAZAL 6

> 'Look at Human things as
> smoke and as nothing at all.'
> Marcus Aurelius

Light steams through this still bright day
as insects rise like smoke.
Wattle birds come for more
than the pink camellias of May
as insects rise like smoke.

Small pleasures of the lonely,
running by the sea, polished furniture,
the garden mulched with hay
as insects rise like smoke.

Four deaths this month, three expected.
We know more will come
though who they'll be no one can say
as insects rise like smoke.

On Sunday roast that veal
when Claudia turns five.
Clean out the shed and make a cubby
where the girls can play
as insects rise like smoke.

Winter is the season of travelling north
or opera and balls — rug up, go out.
I'd rather stay at home,
I don't want to hear you say
as insects rise like smoke.

Kate, while you long for wisdom,
who do you think you're fooling?
You can't escape — a narcissist will pay
and pay
as insects rise like smoke.

Tuesday, 15th August

Yesterday I found a dead boy. I walked to the Pines Shopping Centre and saw an old yellow car parked on the side of the road by the golf course. I looked in to see if the person was alright and saw he was sleeping. I thought, how sensible to have drawn over to the side of the road and taken a nap. I took his number, just in case. Then, on my way back, two hours later — by this time it was noon — I thought how strange it was that the man could still be sleeping with the noise of the traffic so loud. I looked in again and there he was, a young lad, in the driver's seat, lying face down on the passenger's seat. I thought I had better look closer, just to check his colour. I saw, as I walked around to the passenger's seat, that he was very still and his face was suffused with colour. I looked for signs of breathing on the back of the fawn chequered shirt and could see none. The radio was playing softly, his wetsuit was in the back, tapes stacked by the radio. It was very peaceful. Suddenly I thought he could be dead.

I ran to the golf clubhouse, cursing myself, wondering if I ought to first have tried mouth-to-mouth resuscitation. But I felt too craven. God knows what I thought. Just a feeling of seriousness on a bright and gleaming day. There was a party of some kind in the clubhouse. Women in navy shorts and white tops were drawing out tickets, as if for a game, drinking brandy and Pimms and in full cry. I ran around asking for the manager or somebody else who worked there. Finally somebody said, 'Irene is here', and Irene came and gave me a phone and I dialled for the ambulance. I ran back to the car and another woman in navy shorts (who said she worked in a geriatric hospital) ran beside me, as she said she could resuscitate. But she looked and knew it was death.

The gum tree's trunk was white against the green grass, cars whizzed by. The radio played softly. Together we waited for the ambulance. Two young men got out, boiling with life, their cheeks rosey, with pink lips, laughing, drawing on plastic gloves. 'Yep, he's gone,' one said. They kept talking. I can understand why. How could they bear it otherwise?

The day bore down, the sun shone, the gum leaves moved in the wind, golfers strode across the road. It was as if a feather had fallen from a bird, it seemed to have so little significance to the world. Yet his mother had not been told, nor his father.

A station wagon drove past and stopped, and a boy called out the window, 'We saw him there at eight o'clock last night, how is he?' I said, 'He's dead.'

'Old chap is he?'

'No, he's young.' And they drove on, fishing rods poking out the back. The woman and I walked back towards the clubhouse. We parted and I walked home.

I can't think why that boy died. He was about nineteen, parked there just as if he was tired. Nothing at all to give any idea of trouble or illness. He was clean-shaven, short-haired, fit, just a lad driving somewhere in his old yellow car. I wondered if he'd had epilepsy and suffocated with his face on the seat. It seemed so innocent and just halted somehow, alive and then pulled over, and dead. Many things have happened while I've been at the farm, but this is the strangest.

I keep thinking of the boy's parents. All afternoon I thought of the moment the police went to their door. I hope to God he wasn't married. They marry young here sometimes.

Thursday, 17th August

I saw the hare darting through the orchard two days ago. The white peacock is here, displaying to me like a pale fan of lace. Sometimes, when they sit on the post down at the orchard, I think they are a fall of white water rushing. The tail frothing down like a cascade. When they fly out of the mango tree in the morning, it surely is like an angel landing. I could have visions like Blake. You would know you had seen angels if you saw this bird in flight, streaming down like a hail of white stones from the sky.

I have been down in the avenue of native trees thinking over this dead boy. Blue wrens flit around. The hare bounded out again and ran through the orchard.

I wonder if anybody will find my bunch of flowers and note within them and let the parents know. They have avenues to walk down.

Another strange thing happened today as I walked back from the coast. Again, a car was parked by the creek near where the other car had been. I walked up to it gingerly, because no parked car will ever again seem benign, and from underneath it a duck walked out with a trail of eight ducklings in a line. They wobbled down to the creek and suddenly it seemed a wonderful thing. Life abundant. This enchanting family, innocently sheltering under the car. I wish I could speak to that boy's mother.

Friday, 18th August

This morning, at six, a bush turkey was stalking around the lawn, pecking. I took out some old pasta and threw it over the verandah railing. The peacocks came with the turkey, which seemed almost tame, and they ate together. This is unusual, I think, to have a wild bird come and eat. The bush turkey is a protected bird, although it is an Aboriginal food. There has been difficulty in the courts from the Indigenous tradition of hunting. I saw similar complexities in Tanzania and Uganda.

On the matter of bush tucker, there is a book here on its history called *The Edna's Table Cookbook*, with recipes from the restaurant with that name in Sydney. At night I read it over and over.

Julie is here, spreading Nutririch 180, a black dust, on the orchard. She has a lawnmower she rides, with a cart full of this soil improver, which is new to me. It is made, she says, from coal. A bag of it hangs from the giant weeping fig, *Ficus benjamina*, in front of the house. As Julie was bailing the dust out of the cart she said, 'There's a tonne in here so if it falls on me, I won't get up.' The crown has fallen back from her straw hat and lolls like a tongue in the sun. She's just blasted off down the drive to the trees near the gate. The geese came up from the dam and walked around hissing, hooting and snuffling as I sat typing here, under the mango tree. They seemed satisfied and walked back down to the shed, waiting for Julie to feed them. Now there are five goose eggs on the nest. Last year a dog took four, but the remaining seven hatched. There were so many goslings Julie had to sell six for five dollars each. Peri hates to sell them, but there were too many.

There is a recipe for magpie goose salad in *Edna's Table* which, if I could have my way, I would make here. But the truth is, it is not only bush turkeys that are protected. Peri's law won't let a goose be killed. They are a kind of pet.

Saturday, 19th August

Floods at home in the south. Two years ago I was staying here when I heard the same news. While I was blithely writing to friends saying the news on the radio was of floods at Wollongong, I had no idea, sitting here in the sun, how serious they were. Cars piled on top of each other, swept up by the water. Hundreds of millimetres of rain fell in three days. Wollongong was declared a disaster area. In one night, for those who, like me, still think this way, thirty inches fell. This year the floods are not so extreme. It is raining, though not as heavily. I left white tulips swaying, creamy white, almost pale green. I'm glad I took the hyacinths in to Daphne and did not leave them for the rain. White hyacinths flowers are much more strongly scented than blue or pink. I learnt that this winter.

Crows are here with a great din. I throw small blocks of wood from the woodpile at them. They fly off when they see something picked up.

Julie is out in the vegetable garden planting dwarf French beans. She built a small shed there and put in the chooks to clean out the weeds. Now the earth is covered in newspaper, the chooks are gone and cabbage and beetroot seedlings are growing there. I cut some lemongrass to make tea and picked some curry leaves. I will dry some to take home. This crow is getting on my nerves. I threw a brush up and suddenly it flew off across the river. Peace.

I have just heard one of the reasons for the crow plague. Fish are being poisoned in rivers as sulfuric acid has been washed down in heavy rain from the canefields. At Tweed Heads, the pH of Cobaki Lake was over 3.5, which is as strong as vinegar or battery acid. Thousands of bream and whiting are lying on the shore while pelicans and crows feast.

I am having an enormous read. This morning I read some of *One Straw Revolution* by Masanobu Fukuoka: 'Now there is no one in this village with enough time to write poetry.' Fukuoka blames television: 'This is what I mean when I say that agriculture has become poor and weak spiritually; it is concerning itself only with material development.'

Lao Tzu, the Taoist sage, says that a whole and decent life can be lived in a small village. He also says that Bodhidharma, the founder of Zen, spent nine years living in a cave without bustling about. But who brought in the food?

'Extravagance of desire is the fundamental cause which has led the world into its present predicament', and 'The life of small-scale may appear to be primitive, but living such a life, it becomes possible to contemplate the Great Way.' This is defined as: 'The path of spiritual awareness which involves attentiveness to and care for the ordinary activities of daily life.'

These are beautiful ideas. But I saw my parents struggle to rear four children, working seven days a week, thirteen hours a day, and they weren't writing poetry between gathering eggs and washing them.

This farm is run on many of Fukuoka's principles. As a result there are piles of big branches left from the new road-widening placed around trees in the orchard. These will rot. I love this philosopher's method of growing cucumbers and pumpkins. Branches are laid around so, when the vines spread, the fruit is kept off the earth and doesn't rot. He says to let tomatoes sprawl as they then put down roots where they touch the ground. Ease is always beguiling.

I am trying to discover how to grow cumin. This is now my favourite spice. When it is stale, it smells of armpits; but when it is fresh, it is wonderful and goes with almost anything. Grilled chicken thighs sprinkled with cumin, served with mashed potatoes and a chopped, not torn, lettuce salad covered in garlic mixed with fresh lime juice and oil is very good.

Tuesday, 22nd August

A blue wren darted around when I walked among the avenue of trees I planted years ago. I cut a big bunch of grevillea flowers to take to the roadside where I found the boy. I've been doing this every third day to pay respect and also in the hope that his parents might see it, find the note and contact me. I could tell them how peaceful he seemed — how the music played around him.

Julie is here in her gumboots, making a fence around a goose's nest. The bush turkey is near her, striding about, picking grain the other poultry have left. It is now tame. I wish it had a mate. They are rare here — although once on a walk at Burleigh Heads, on a wild hillside, Peri and I saw a great mound of leaves. It was the nest of a bush turkey. It buries its eggs and lets them hatch in the heat that comes from rotting vegetation.

I have been collecting lemons and oranges that lie under the trees. Fruit fly breed in these so they must be put into plastic bags to dry out in the sun. The crows make holes in the oranges, sucking up the juice.

Standing beside Julie while she was making the fence, I asked her something I have wanted to know: 'How do you rear a turkey?' She said in exasperation, 'What am I going to do with this gate when I've made it? How am I going to get it to swing?' I didn't have any ideas. Then Julie answered me: 'The most important thing with baby turkeys is that they're kept warm with a light above them when they are little. Also, that there's always fresh food and water. They get raised on a medicated starter or turkey starter, if you can get it. Also, they must have medication in their water. Emtryl is its name. You get it from some vets.'

Julie knelt down beside me while I took notes. The sun shone down and the goose that owned the nest honked on and on at a rooster.

'You need to keep the Emtryl up to the baby turkeys for about six months,' Julie continued. 'They're susceptible to black-head disease and another problem I forget the name of. They get various problems and the Emtryl stops all of them.'

A wild duck waddled over to peck at the grain left on the ground. Its beak was curled upwards in a sweet way.

'They know they're all safe here, you see,' Julie said, nodding her chin at the duck. Then she went on answering my question good-naturedly.

'I put the chicks in a box under a light bulb for about six weeks. Depending on how big the box is, probably a forty-watt globe. I wouldn't put a hundred-watt in. It is good to give the baby turkeys boiled mashed-up egg — that's very good for them.'

'While this is going on, where is their mother, Julie?'

'Well, of course, this is if I am raising them. If the mother does it, she just does it. You lose about ninety per cent of the chicks to crows. And if it rains and they get wet, well you lose them. I mean, somebody might read this and say, "What is she talking about?" But every place is different. This is what we find here.'

While talking, Julie climbed onto an upturned bucket, wired the fence to a tree branch and then went off saying, 'I need two more nails.' I was left to watch the comings and goings. The wild duck, gobbling up the pellets I flung to it as it cringed and fluttered, strode off and returned. A pair of topknot pigeons came to eat too, and a wild water hen with its red-topped head stood on one leg waiting. A finch flew into the shed beside us, small enough to fly through the wire netting.

Julie returned and began banging old nails into a post to make a new safe perch for the poultry. This is because the angry gander that guards the sitting goose is stopping all the other birds reaching their perches. We ended our talk about turkey-rearing and Julie gestured to a white peahen. 'I've locked this one in this cage all weekend because its wings were hanging down, drooping. That's often a sign they're sickening. So I put her in with medicated water and I was wrong. See, she's laid an egg. They droop their wings down when they're going to lay. So I misread you, didn't I, girl?'

I am more than usually glad that Julie is here today, as while she is the caretaker she doesn't need to come every day when I am here to feed the poultry. But yesterday I spent half the day waving a bucket at the gander, trying to help four peacocks from a perch where they were bailed up, too afraid to come down. They sat swaying and calling in a plaintive desperate way. No sooner had I got the gander away, and the peacocks down, than one returned to the predicament. It reminded me of the way some of us return to situations we swear we hate.

A flock of finches with faces like owls fluttered down to eat the grain. Abandoning the birds, I went indoors to make lunch for Julie and myself. The time one can spend with poultry, as you can see, is endless. All day and night there is something going on. Sometimes a peacock slides down the roof like a skier in the night. Other times the geese begin calling as if they are saving

Rome. I lie and wonder if it is a fox sniffing around. But I stay inside, afraid to walk around in the dark. There are worse things than foxes.

Tuesday, 19th September

Home. Today I rode to Corrimal nursery and bought the third pair of citruses for two big pots on the back deck. All the others, cumquat and Meyer lemon, have turned to sticks in those pots, no matter how much sun, water and fertiliser they got. I heard about the benefit of putting urine on citrus from a radio advice program, where the woman said that a sick lemon tree in Mosman had been resuscitated by a football team having a barbecue in her garden and urinating on the tree. But Terry, pondering these things in his heart and saying nothing, knew, but didn't like to tell me, that putting urine undiluted on citrus in pots fills the soil with salt. There's a lot of salt in urine. This has been going on for years, while I've been going round shaking my head, worrying about the yellowing, dropping leaves. The money I've wasted. Three of these old desiccated plants have been put into the garden and are sprouting slowly now. And nothing's what they'll get, as nothing's what they want.

A New Garden

THE LODGER

Sometimes at night I smell toast
and I know the old priest
is making breakfast.
He thinks I don't know he lives here
rising when I sleep, a shadow
shuffling round the kitchen
with the lights off.
From time to time a whiff from a cigarette
rises from beneath my room.
I imagine him down there crouched
on the old mattress.

He is my better half
the faith I fail in.
The discipline and modesty
of quiet rituals. His old black cassock
hangs on a hook behind the wardrobe
door:
he thinks it's hidden there.

His beret lies like a cat on the pantry shelf.
I ignore it. Why did he come?
When will he go? This sweet enigma
undemanding, shuffling through the house
with the faith of our fathers
his breath like violets.

I've begun another garden. One day, having asked at the railway station office window for months if we might have some trees, I took a spade and a barrow of geranium and daisy cuttings, walked over and began to dig.

For six months I gardened there before any of the staff spoke to me. By then the garden was an accomplished fact. A narrow, empty, fenced paddock lay on one side of the line with a locked gate. I managed to squeeze through two posts joining the cyclone fence and pass buckets of water, the spade and cuttings over.

Six times on the paddock side and eleven times on the street side the garden was dug up by electricians over the next months. The men, when they saw Tom, who was in charge of the station, apologised for digging up the garden. Some men put the plants to one side to save them, others turned them under. It didn't matter all that much because the plants had cost nothing, being mainly cuttings. Sometimes I got a rose or sick hibiscus for a couple of dollars at Woolworths.

One day at the Corrimal Nursery it struck me that they must have plants that they can't sell. Jim and Shirley had sold their nursery to Denis so I asked him if he had something I could use at the station. He did. Day after day trays of seedlings, pots of perennials and shrubs were left on my verandah. Chrysanthemums and pansies galore. When plants were dug up at the station, I just put more in. In this way I learnt where the main electrical and plumbing lines ran and planted small things there. Trees and bigger shrubs were planted in places I hoped were safer. I was always worried that the paddock would one day be turned into a car park. Peri told me to stop thinking like this and to plant furiously and widely. 'Once the garden is established,' she said, 'they won't dare to destroy it. Look at what's happened to my street garden. The council wouldn't dream of digging that up. There'd be an outcry.' I hope she's right. But it isn't much use being afraid of the future when making a garden, though it's not a bad idea to look upwards when planting a tree. I see now that gardening is really planting the sky.

After some months, I was lent the key to the gate of the paddock. I got to know George, who is in charge of four stations and who visits daily to see Tom and check up on things. To George I was a burden to be borne patiently, sometimes affectionately. Tom always offered me a cold drink of Coca-Cola or a plate of chips when he had lunch.

Growing in confidence, I decided to ask if the station would pay for some native trees to shade the paddock side of the platform. George agreed, so I asked Denis to deliver a range of trees. For the other street side, I ordered three *Flindersia eucalypti* because Tabitha, who along with Adam works for Denis, said they are hardy trees that will soon be too tall for vandals to damage. For a month these three trees sat on my verandah, as I couldn't face the idea of them being torn down. They needed wrapping and staking and barbed wire and I didn't like to ask George for the money, or to mention that sort of wire. One day I rang Bulli Hardware and they delivered the wire and six star pickets. I dug them in carefully and wrapped them in old chicken wire Terry had lent me. He wasn't going to see that wire again and I hoped he didn't want to. But it turned out he did want it. The trees looked beautiful, waving their leafy tops, and I felt sick leaving them, wondering how long they would last. Prayer came into it.

Inspired by the fact that the Railways had put up, within a week of my asking, the white iron railing fence to stop boys riding their bikes over the garden at the crossing, I asked George if we could also have a fence running along in front of the trees in the car park. He said, 'What's it called, Kate?'

'Well, a white railing fence, I suppose.'

'How long is it?'

'I'm not sure, George.' So he paced it in his big black shoes.

'Seventeen metres, one extra for luck, eh?' Then, 'Come with me.'

We walked to the office and he rang someone he knows who builds fences, saying: 'We need a fence. What are they called? Yes, seventeen metres long.'

'Okay, Kate, they're coming to measure.'

Two days later, as I was walking past, I saw George, a man and a white ute by the trees. But later George said that it would cost a thousand dollars and they couldn't afford it, so there would be no fence. However, the man with the ute, seeing the rusty chicken wire cobbled together with the barbed wire around it, took it all down and replaced it with black plastic wire netting. He threw the barbed wire into the bush by the line. George said they aren't allowed to have that wire because somebody might get hurt. I said that only a vandal would be hurt, because nobody else would put his hands inside to the leaves. Although I was depressed, I couldn't argue any more, because George is being kind and only doing his job.

A week later, Tom, on duty, said: 'You know Kate, you can have that barbed wire of yours back if you like. It's down there in the bush over the fence.'

I looked down from the platform where we were standing and saw it. I said, 'Look, don't tell George, Tom, but I am going to put it back onto the trees. They won't last a month unless they are protected, and even so, they may not be safe.' So I re-wrapped them.

George, seeing me a week later, said, 'You can have that barbed wire for your own use, if you like. That chap left it in the bush.'

I said, airily, 'Don't worry. I have seen it.'

'No, come with me, I'll show you where it is,' he replied.

'It's okay, George.'

He insisted. So I relented and told him what I'd done. George said he supposed it was alright and so we left the matter. I see hundreds of metres of barbed wire coiled around the top of fences on Railway property close to Sydney, when I am on the train, so it can't be entirely illegal. Whatever made that man throw the wire into the bush and not take it, I bless it, because it has given me much peace of mind. And if these trees survive, it's because a benevolent fate looks over them.

Later. It's fatal to speak of a tree flourishing. I rode past the car park, feeling a bit queasy, thinking that I had perhaps tempted fate. I noticed that the tallest tree had been almost stripped of leaves. I went over and saw that the leaves had not been torn off, but had fallen, and each long twig I touched fell too. It is the rain. The sheer amount in the last weeks, combined with the position beside that platform, where the water runs off and forms pools, has drowned the tree and begun to do the same to the other two. Now here's a conundrum. What's George going to say if I ask him if I can buy (as I can't ask Denis to give) three new advanced trees that can stand a lot of water? And now, so carefully wrapped, how am I going to get them out and put them in a drier place? Was there ever a tree I planted that didn't have to be moved? I am getting sick of it.

I planted white Marguerite daisies from cuttings along that side of the platform with two grafted passionfruit Denis gave me. The men who come to mow the grass have mowed this three times, but still the passionfruit keep sprouting from their sticks.

We have a compost heap now from grass clippings and I use that for mulch. People walking past as I weed say, 'You can come over to my place when you've finished here.' Naturally, I find this intensely amusing.

I was always in trouble with the nozzle of the heavy wide hose that Tom let me use, dragging it from a locked room and across the train line. Men love nozzles. I'd misplace the nozzle as I couldn't control the force of the water, and so took it off, letting the hose run and flood the plants, making rivulets to take the water farther than the hose could spray. I had a system going like the delta of the Nile.

It drove Tom mad when I lost the nozzle. We searched the long grass for many days.

In the end I bought another.

The handle of the tap beside the steps had to be removed after use so that it couldn't be stolen, or used to turn the tap on to perhaps run all night. Once I lost this as well. So to use that tap, we had to borrow a handle from Bulli Station. Tom got on the phone. The tap handle came up and down the line by train, in a brown paper bag with a note in biro on the bag: 'This tap is a boomerang.' It took six weeks to get another handle for our tap.

Nothing had prepared me for the way that a newly dug piece of land becomes fertile. Kikuyu and couch grass, with other weeds, grew exuberantly as if fertilised, which I suppose they were, having the old grasses and worms enriching the soil. For a while I tried to weed, but it was beyond me. The great thing in any garden, but most especially, I think, in a public one, is to be able to battle a feeling of defeat. Nothing that I've ever done has beaten down weeds. Planting so thickly that they can't grow is best, but the garden isn't that advanced yet.

Peri, seeing the weeds when she arrived with a station wagon full of pot-bound trees for it, said crisply:

'You'll never get rid of those weeds. You'll have to smother them. Get black plastic or newspaper and mulch.'

That same day we drove south to look at some country and gardens, and, seeing a sign outside Franklins, she drew up. I kept protesting that we couldn't carry the pine bark she'd seen advertised and I didn't want her to pay for it. She wouldn't listen, and got twenty bags along with some gum bark, and we drove back and unloaded them on the verandah of the station.

The local newsagent gave me old newspapers which I took to the station in my wheelbarrow, loaded high. A woman, seeing the spectacle, drew up in her car and offered me a lift. We loaded the lot into her car boot and she drove the few metres to the station gate and she unloaded while I wheeled the barrow.

I have struck up an acquaintance with David, my blind neighbour, and one day I asked him if he would help me weed. He proved to be very strong and now helps me often. When we were extending a bed by the steps, he threw wooden sleepers around like matchsticks. Weeding needs strength and he tore into the grasses like a bull. Waving a metre-wide daisy bush around at me, he said, 'Big weed, Kate.' I replied, 'Lord, David, that's a daisy bush.' It didn't matter as I stuck it back and took a few cuttings to spread around. These daisies have been a triumph. Some are more than two metres square. They flash white through the cyclone fence and wave beside the platform, never needing any attention, apart from the hosing Tom and Sinna, a young woman who has come to work there, give them. It shows the richness of the soil. Red geraniums, blue plumbago and some dying Iceberg roses, which had been thrown out cheaply at Woolworths, went in too. Somebody dug up one of these white roses, but I put another there along with a filthy note beginning, 'To the thief who stole the rose . . .' Tom took the note away, saying to me later, 'I hope you don't mind, Kate, but that person could turn nasty, you know.'

A red climbing rose has half-covered the fence and had its first blazing blooming.

Tom was upset one day when he told me, 'A young girl, you know, has given me some lip so I wouldn't let her get on the train without a ticket. She went over to that rose there and tore off some of the flowers.' On St Valentine's Day, a boy had taken some geraniums for his girlfriend. Tom sent him off with a flea in his ear. I've told Tom that in a private garden the flowers would be being picked and if somebody wants to take them from here, I am glad. He shrugged and said, 'Okay.'

Red bottlebrush from two big bushes that bend over the footpath further down in this street are on the table in a blue glass vase. Some of these bottlebrush have naturalised on the banks of the drain running along the vacant land that is fenced off beside the railway station. It is in this block of land that I am making the second part of the station garden. The first part is beside the steps that lead up to the ticket office and the platform for trains that run south to Wollongong. Nature abhors a vacuum, but for some reason, apart from some bulrushes, nothing grew in or beside that drain. Recently though, the bottlebrushes have begun and, most wonderfully, a cedar tree. It was probably sown by a bird, because I can't imagine the wind being able to drive such a heavy seed.

I was walking along the drain, peering to see if any of the nasturtium seeds I had thrown there had sprouted, when I saw that, finally, the third attempt at starting willow trees had worked. The dry sticks which were grey when I stuck them into the mud in late autumn had turned bright yellow and had green shoots. Six have struck. This will be beautiful. I know willows can be a weed, but this is a man-made drain and they will clean it. Also, they cannot get away, because all around are roads and a dry paddock and a small bare park near the shops.

I had asked Denis at the nursery why the first two lots of willow cuttings had not sprung. He said that one way to grow willows, if you don't want to buy them as trees, is to layer the bare cuttings in early winter into sawdust or damp newspaper in a box and then, in spring, plant out the sticks that should have green shoots. However, I had one last shot with the bare cuttings I had taken from willows growing in a creek on the way to Diana's, a new friend who lives in Woonona. Here they are, alive and set to go. There is something about plants that cost nothing that is deeply satisfying.

Saturday, 23rd September

A mighty day. My old friend from when I lived in Adelaide, Lynn Collins, came with his friend Jo. They are both curators with NSW Historic Houses Trust. They brought with them an old-fashioned pie melon striped with a green and cream wobble pattern from the garden at Vaucluse House. Also they had cuttings of nineteenth-century pelargoniums and irises for me to use at the station.

Earlier this week two cardboard boxes came by mail. Coffins full of life. They sat waiting in the pantry until today. One of these held twenty-three roses and the other seventy-six liliums. I had been idly riffling through garden catalogues one day and, being bored, stood up and went to the fax machine. The Treloar Roses Catalogue (from Portland, Victoria) had an offer of David Austin roses, ten for seventy-five dollars. The catch is all ten must be of the one kind.

I asked Diana and another friend, Dorothy, if they'd like to share some of the roses. Dorothy, a Professor of English, chose Jude The Obscure for its literary connections and because she likes yellow roses. So I ordered ten of those and then another ten of The Armitage rose, which is pale pink and named for 'The Archers', an English radio serial. Three gift roses came with this lot, a bonus for ordering twenty. One of the gift roses is Madame Gregoire Staechlin, a fabulous rose that Philippa swears by. She had it at Leura, and although it only blooms once a year it is worthwhile with colossal bunches of pink flowers; really fabulous blooms.

Lynn, Jo and I dug up some of the back lawn. There was no other room left for the roses and the liliums. They made a curving edge with bricks so sweet each time I look I smile. Lynn, seeing the old stones and bricks I'd used to make other edges, said, 'Do you want to keep it eccentric?' I realised it was a curator's term for make-do material. I told him I did. So towards the end he used a piece of slate and then tailed the whole thing off by sinking the bricks lower in the ground. All day they worked with stringlines, digging and building. It is enormously exhilarating to have people helping in the garden who do it just for love.

Inspired, these two dug up self-sown pale blue forget-me-nots and replanted them to soften the brick edging. We planted a dozen roses and among them liliums, also by the dozen. The liliums look like hands curled upwards with the fingers pointing inwards, clasping promise. These came from Windy Hill Flowers, which can be contacted through PO Box 420, Monbulk, Victoria.

Someone sent me a bunch of oriental liliums and it made me wonder why I didn't grow them. This thought led me to the Windy Hill catalogue and their LA Hybrid liliums, then to *Lilium longiflorum*, best known as Christmas lilies, and these led over the page to Asiatic liliums. There is a difference, I see from the pictures, between these latter and oriental liliums. As you may notice, I couldn't get enough, but stopped myself at seventy-six when my money ran out. Two pages on Peony roses began but they will have to wait.

Lynn, Jo, Dorothy, Diana and I had lunch on the back deck and then we walked to Sandon Point. The brides frolicking on the cliff made Dorothy especially exclaim, 'Oh how beautiful!' Especially when the flower girls were wearing lilac, which she always wanted to wear when she was a child but was not allowed. Funny how these things last a lifetime.

Back in the garden Jo and Lynn worked on until dusk and the job was done. There is still some lawn left, but what was called the meadow bed is now almost twice as big and bulging full.

The dawn lit the dew on the lawn. Its light cast long shadows and the clouds faded from pink and mother-of-pearl to puffs of oyster grey and white. The daffodils and narcissi were moving in a breeze, pale yellow and cream, full of scent, and around them the citrus trees gleamed with water on their leaves and fruit. The stars had just faded, retreating, leaving the moon alone, silvery white, enduring like a beacon of faith.

Sunday, 24th September

Whales. Today, while Sophia was sitting in the train, looking over the head of the big cloth doll she clutched with both arms round its stomach, she told me she had seen six whales. Daily my eyes rake the sea, searching for them. Terry has seen some as they are now coming down the coast to Antarctica to harvest the krill.

When I mentioned white horses at sea, meaning the waves, Sophia could see those too, galloping, she said, under the sea.

I heard a blind man say that, as a child, because he had never seen a bird, he imagined them as four-legged animals with wings. He only discovered his mistake when other children found this out and described them.

Imagination invents whatever we need. So, seeing six whales and horses galore is perfectly normal when a person has the authority of knowing the names. But I never saw a whale today.

'It is very hard to live without a horizon, when you have had one,' Sophia's father, Hugh, said. It's true. The horizon, although seldom mentioned, has more power than we give it credit for.

The man sitting opposite us on the train remarked to Sophia on the ships lined up waiting to enter the harbour. 'Where are they?' she asked, obviously thinking she didn't need to imagine a ship. 'On the horizon. It is there, that line where the sea meets the sky.'

'Oh, yes,' she said, seeing the ships, I assume. And what did the doll see?

What we saw as we came in the gate was the opium poppies, *Papaver somniferum*, tall and drooping, like grey suede gloves, some already forming buds. Dozens of these were self-sown this year. I shook the bursting dry heads last summer as I pulled them out. Where they lay, piles on the lawn, more came up and I have put them around in sunny places. Cosmos grew too, from last year's, and to make sure I had plenty of white ones, I shook out a dish of soaked seeds through the poppies. This will be a harvest like a meadow in a French painting.

It is odd how quickly these trees bud — the *Ailanthus* tree is greening. I was only away two days, but either I hadn't been looking, or it burst during those hours. I bless this tree, for its shade and its faithfulness. More faithful than I ever found a man. It's like my bed, reliable.

Thinking some more about horizons, have you ever noticed the eyes of people who live or work looking at the horizon? They are actually focused farther out, as if the long looking has given the eye a particular and beautiful length of vision. I married a sailor and it was in him I first noticed it.

The horizon is something rarely spoken of except in certain circles. But it has a big effect. When I go to the desert with my friend Ian North, he gets up at four in the morning to photograph the horizon. He doesn't take pictures of trees or kangaroos; it is that line he's after. And if it has a wobble, a few mesas or jump-ups as they're also called, he likes that too. But a long straight line in a photograph often seems like nothing at all to some. I see this when the travel editors return photographs I've sent with stories. I realise that they think it's a photograph of nothing. But the horizon is like an electric wire dragged along under the sky, holding to the land, full of streaming tension.

The garden now is lit by stars. The sea roars on and all the invisible things in the earth and above go on moving, worms, roots, hope, glee, the pull of the moon and the fish in the sea.

Friday, 29th September

Today, in a coincidence, Lynn, who dug up the lawn last Saturday while I planted liliums, has sent me some old letters of mine he found in a bag. In these letters, written over thirty years ago, I am talking to him about liliums and a few other things.

TO: Mr Lynn Collins
Kibbutz Eilon
West Galilee, Israel
Saturday, 12th February 1972

Dear Lynn,

This is rather wet from Burnside pool and an oozing pen. I lie in the sun and write to you. Heat, heat, it's the fifth day of it. I bring the children here each day after school in a taxi with their red faces.

Your mother is helping with our garden and I am looking at exotica in plants and asking her opinion. Liliums (Japanese lilies like Easter lilies) are my current favourite. I'd love it if your mother could find some. Last week we took the children to Clare Robertson's to see her studio and the paintings for our show. She gave Caroline two Italian puppets on strings.

The children woke us next day with a lovely puppet show in a real theatre they had cut with a Stanley knife from a great big cardboard box and had a script, roles for each of them. We lay and clapped and I wished we had been more awake and appreciative of their childishness.

Caroline insisted on taking the whole thing to school and she could barely carry it all but did and she said all the children stood up when she walked in for she was the first person to ever bring a puppet theatre to class. Bravo!

Monday

Your letter just came as I was sitting on the gallery steps cleaning two copper pots with lemon and salt. I was thrilled to read your letter. It is so taxing to write letters, all of oneself goes into it. I have about ten inside me to you.

I feel such a mix-up today, as so often lately. I am always wondering how I ought to be living.

Can it be that everyone finds it so tricky and complicated to be a housewife? For example, Lynn, advise me where I am going wrong. I like a clean house, but how to get one without becoming obsessive, that's the critical balance I search for. All of life is related to this balance, I know, and I long to reach it.

Well, this is how it went today. I got up and made the children Rice Bubbles by pouring them out. Easy. Then I made some poached eggs and toast and we all had that.

Then I made carrot and raisin sandwiches for their school lunch.

While I was doing that Caroline had to find some clothes that she was happy to wear to school. She has six, yes six, jumpers left at school and so dressed herself in her uniform and a fawn and green ugly cast-off cardigan somebody left here. Then she put on a red elastic headband and all her blonde hair stood around it like a shock victim.

I talked her into changing and she wore a pretty dress with two singlets as a compromise. Half an hour down the gurgler on that.

Then the lunch boxes had to be washed and we were out of cat food. Hugh went and bought Kitty Kat, which is against our rule for it contains kangaroo meat, but they had no Luv, which doesn't. Well, just this once won't hurt as I can't reason with this hungry cat.

Then I went back to bed and read the paper. Why? People are bashing their babies.

Got up and began the washing machine and accidentally let my bath run over. I couldn't hear it because of the machine. Bathed in half-cold water.

I dressed in my new pink suede shoes and went to pick some yellow daisies and Canterbury bells your mother has grown for us. The copper pot was dirty and I had to clean it.

Then I thought I had better put this oldish old chicken on for dinner. Did that and wrote a poem.

I put the flowers in the Milton Moon Pottery jug you helped Richard buy me one Christmas. Because of all the work entailed in getting the brass really clean, it put me off using it for the flowers. They are all in now but no beds made, mess everywhere, can't get into the pantry except by standing in a big dish of potatoes.

Now where did I go wrong?

Now, to think of something cheerful: the postman lost his balance on his bike when he was trying to see up the slit in the front of this new dress of mine.

I have finished *The Female Eunuch* and liked it and admired Germaine Greer for her courage. I do think though that it is cruel to desert children even for a revolution.

Because Hugh has been good I relented and have let him have two white mice. He was overjoyed. He called them Simon & Garfunkel. But Simon died next morning. Hugh came home from school ill with grief. He is better today. I wrote a note saying he had stomach ache; heartache is not so easily excusable.

Keep away from evil and bombs, Lynn. Love from Kate.

Butterflies and Bombs

GHAZAL 12

Looking round the garden
means there's always an ideal
which spoils what is.
Planting delphiniums, rhubarb, gypsophila
beside pink poppies are optimistic
dreams — there's always an ideal
which spoils what is.
Playing hopscotch, praying, teaching,
writing — everything's a struggle.
Racing yourself on the beach, counting steps
where the sea creams — there's always
an ideal
which spoils what is.
In the sky weeping horses slide away
fire tinges the horizon as darkness pales.
The bay curves round the reef
where Cook and Flinders found
by scraping beams — there's always an ideal
which spoils what is.

Every day solitude
a white crown of flowers rots.
Covering the table made of glass
is poetry a grail
in reams — there's always an ideal
which spoils what is.
In fever crawling to the bath in darkness
I got stuck behind the door.
A labyrinth of rooms I couldn't see
up, up away from helplessness crawling.
Water, the world's poetry.
Stand behind a waterfall and it
no longer seems — there's always an
ideal
that spoils what is.
Kate, hide your rejoicing, let the frog
reach the cleaned-out pond.
Lie quietly while his call
redeems — there's always an ideal
that spoils what is.

Monday, 16th October

$\mathcal{A}$ very old neighbour came into this garden some months ago. 'Oh!' she said, looking around in shock. 'You've got the job ahead of you, haven't you?' I was hurt by this because to me it was, as Auden said of his lover, entirely beautiful. I didn't say that, to me, a garden clipped and mowed, with only one small trimmed tree, no shade, no wantonness, is not entirely beautiful at all. But to the owner it is and that's the lesson for me. But, by God, as I walk by those gardens, I long to plant a dozen trees, and in my mind I do. So now, unbeknown to the owners, the street is full of trees; they scrape the sky with their lovely branches, birds call and swoop from tree to tree. Children walking to school walk in cool shade, and sometimes they reach up and take down an orange, and at other times they sit in the shade in the gutter waiting for a parent in a car.

It can tangle with the others: the thought came to me as I dug a hole for the English rose. And that weird tangle surprised me, because in the past I've tried to keep air around the roses, thinking them the asthmatics of the garden. But now I see they can grow and tangle, reaching upwards in chaos. When Peri came to stay a fortnight ago, she kept saying, as she always does, 'You've got such growth! You've got more growth here than I've got on the farm.' She means in Queensland at 'Bend of the River', where she pours on organic fertilisers. Then she said, 'I can't get things to grow over paths. No man will ever let me have things run wild. They are drawn towards the tidy. It drives me mad.' So I cheered up, having thought she might think the wildness a sign of neglect, which, of course, it is.

Tuesday, 17th October

If you want to write a book, stay home. There is nothing like getting on trains or planes or hopping into cars for delay.

I was muttering this to myself as I stood up, rubbing my back which was sore from tearing up weeds that morning. In the last few months I have hardly been home. The Olympics had something to do with it, though not entirely. But today I planted basil, radicchio and lettuce. Terry had been thinning out his plants and tossing away what he didn't need. The idea upsets me, the waste of it. For years I wouldn't eat bean sprouts because it seemed cruel to stop the plant having a chance at life. But I don't have the same trouble with weeds. All of life seems 'yes' and 'no'. I think one thing and immediately another seems true. Is this the beginning of wisdom?

Basil, the king of herbs, has self-sown all through Terry's vegetable garden. Yet I have taken the dried heads of his basil, shaken them on the earth and nothing has happened. Perhaps it was too early in the spring.

Today I am making yoghurt and also yeast tart bases. There is something thrilling about turning one thing into another and having it grow within hours. The yoghurt is easy and two or three litres grow in the sun within six hours. The trick is not to pollute it by stirring with an unsterilised spoon. If you bring as much milk as you want yoghurt to the boil, it will sterilise the pan and the milk. Even though the milk is already sterilised, boiling it serves two purposes. First, it heats the milk to begin the bacterial changes, and second, it sterilises the pan. Then, when the milk has cooled and reached blood temperature, tip in about five hundred millilitres of good shop-bought plain yoghurt, trying all the while to make it pour in blobs or drips, to mix better with the milk. Nothing more need be done except keep it warm for six hours. You can swill the pan around from time to time to help the blending, if you wish. If it is not a sunny day, the pot can be put over a pan of warm or hot water and checked for temperature from time to time. And that's it — yoghurt.

When taking yoghurt from the pan, it is best to pour, not spoon it out, and so keep the mass sterile. You can make labna cheese from this by simply pouring the cooled yoghurt into a sieve lined with muslin and leave it to drip above a dish overnight. In the morning the result is labna, a white cheese that can be made into little balls with a sterile spoon and kept in olive oil in the fridge for two or three days. Again, don't pollute the jar by using anything unsterilised to take out the balls. They can be rolled in chopped chives or other herbs and served as part of an antipasto platter.

Now here is a coincidence. Wondering how to spell a word, I have just now idly turned to a magazine on the table and opened it at the recipe for labna. I had no idea there was a recipe for that in those pages. Sometimes I think that simply speaking or writing of a thing makes it appear. From talk comes action. I've made it a motto. That, along with 'Put things in envelopes' has proved useful.

'I'll make that woman some shortbread,' my mother used to say, tying on her apron. She was acting on one of her strongest mottos: 'A little help is worth a ton of sympathy.' It would be for some woman whose child had drowned in a dam or whose husband had been rolled on by a tractor, or some other tragedy.

Wednesday, 18th October

There is a pool of apricot nasturtiums outside the French windows on the back deck, they are climbing through the mandarin tree and the tall fronds of the Claire rose. I did not know that nasturtiums will climb metres if left alone and will decorate trees, just as roses can.

The great thing is, I now see, to let things be. Some of the best effects come from neglect. Tidiness is a form of death. But what is love but the paying of attention? Yet, in the garden, it is often the thing that is not noticed that, left alone, finally gives the deepest pleasure. That is a paradox.

Then there is the moral question of snails. Is it better to poison them, to drown them in dishes of beer, to squash them? Unless a swirl of snail pellets is left around a magnolia late in August or early in September, there will only be leaves of lace left. And then, after two weeks, the job needs repeating. Squashing mating snails seems vicious. Sometimes I wonder if there isn't an element of envy. Or perhaps that miserable impulse, deeply hidden but the more powerful for that, of pleasure in the destruction of innocence.

And then the phone rang. It was Nan Evatt, my friend from Leura. She said in passing, 'You know, plants are healthy and happier when they are grown close together. You can see it, their leaves are greener; it is as if they like the company of others.' I said that she ought to know that this would go straight onto the page and she laughed.

Mulch as love. That's a new idea. A man on the radio, speaking about the development of character in people and using nature to illustrate this, said that if a plant is left to grow naturally, without extra water or fertiliser, it will develop a strength rather like character in a person. However, if fertilised or watered too much, the plant will be weakened into keeping shallow roots that allow it to fall in wind. So, he reckons, if you really care for a plant, you will not spoil it by such indulgences, but merely give it mulch.

Later. I have been out looking. I was wondering how the roses I transplanted two days ago were faring. Yesterday, one had wilted. But today the plant has lifted its head. In the night I decided to dig up the big orange hibiscus called Surfrider. Too many discussions and too much time has been spent on it for too little effect. I decided in the night that if I put in the pink robinia, which is five metres high, pot-bound and not wanted by Peri for whom I got it, the hole from the hibiscus will be filled well and the pink flowers will mingle with the tallest olive tree. Now, of course, I can hardly wait to start digging. But it's a big job and must wait.

Peri rang a week ago and asked if the Corrimal nursery might have an advanced yellow robinia as they are very expensive in Sydney. Things in the country are sometimes cheaper. So when Tabitha at the nursery dragged out the huge plant, I didn't care that it was pink and took it anyway. But it's not what Peri wants. And I now do. The pink robinia Nan gave me years ago in a pot at Leura is in bloom near the front verandah. When I told Nan this today, she gave a happy cry, as she thought it had died long ago.

Cold and wet in the mountains today, damp here. Which is why I came.

On my brother Tucker's desk is a sign which reads: 'The best fertiliser for land is the owner's feet.' So when I was out on matron's round today, I remembered to dead-head the roses. I always thought this was done to stop the rose putting its energy into seeds rather than growth. But in *Botanica's Roses* I read that it is to trick the plant into making more blooms. It used to be thought that cutting the stem of the bloom back hard was best, but now it's thought that just taking the head at a small swelling below is best. Lieutenant Colonel Ken Grapes writes in his chapter in this book, 'Recent trials, however, have clearly established that the more foliage a rose plant bears, the better its performance, and it is now recommended that the dead flower heads be snapped off at the abscission layer . . . This is a revolutionary new method that applies to all large-flowered roses. Not only does the rose come back into flower between flushes more quickly, but with appreciably more flowers.' He goes on to say that this principle should be used when dead-heading cluster-flowering roses. He has an impatient attitude to roses that are not performing well, rather as an inefficient new soldier might be viewed: 'If a rose performs poorly and continually gets disease, it is a pain in the neck and should be thrown on the bonfire. In some countries, this is called "shovel pruning".' So, in the good soldier's ideal rose garden, if you are out of step, you're out of line and you've got to go. But soldiers and nurses are trained differently. On hatching day, it was my obsession to run around behind my father's back, peeling shells from emerging chickens to save them from the dreadful bin. This was because all the chicks not fully emerged by an hour decreed by a clock, some human convenience and a date went into the bin. I couldn't bear it. Half out, covered in wet black feathers like commas, squawking and thrusting towards life, why shouldn't they be given a chance?

However, my father was acting on a healthy, honest, survival-of-the-fittest ethic which all farmers need to practise, especially if they are going to sell the young.

But there's many a chook alive today that owes its life to a fourteen-year-old girl saving an ancestor long ago on a Gawler poultry farm.

The idea of the bonfire of roses is interesting. Maybe it's still done in the English countryside but garden fires are banned here. But, my God, this soldier knows about roses. For twenty years he has been Secretary-General of the Royal National Rose Society. He runs the world-famous 'Gardens of the Rose' at St Albans, where international trials for new roses are held, aimed at testing the truth of many widely held ideas.

Butterflies concealing bombs. It's such an original idea that I keep laughing when I think of it and I laugh also because I was told of it in such a way. Yesterday at the station, on the way back from the shops, I was leaning over the fence, staring at the weeds and thinking about them, when an elegant old woman paused and said, 'Pansies, are they?' I said that, yes, there were pansies there as well as other flowers. 'They blow in on the wind,' she said. I replied that these were actually planted, feeling a vague sense of pride, I suppose, and not wanting her to think the whole garden had been an act of nature.

'Do you have children?' she asked.

'Well, mine are grown, but I have grandchildren.'

'Well,' she said, as we walked across the train line together, 'you must warn them that if there is a war, they are hiding bombs underneath butterflies and flowers. You warn them.' I said I would and came home thinking of the strange ways of madness, its beautiful and terrifying originality. She was not an unhappy old woman, not at all. She was alone, and seemed well. In fact, she was so normal, I am beginning to think she might be on to something that's been kept from me. But they'd have to be very small bombs. What would it be like to be the only sane person in a world full of the mad?

Thursday, 19th October

On the matter of weeds: I feel for the first time since Philippa stopped working in this garden, because she moved, that I am managing them. For a long time I was worried because I could not see how I could ever keep them at a certain level. There were more and more because, although weeding was done, it wasn't enough. A simple bit of arithmetic. I keep thinking of what my brother Tucker said, when I asked him after a small rain during the eight-year drought they've had, how, if the cattle eat the new grass, there can be enough seeds left when this goes on for years. He said, 'Nature always provides more than enough.' Like sperm, I thought, thinking of the population of the world. Now I think, when weeding, I must stop this abundance. So as I walk

I snatch at seed heads. At least if the roots aren't out, and they may come out later, that abundance can be quelled a little.

I think too of what another man said: 'A weed is a plant that likes being disturbed.' This thought drives me mad sometimes and makes me tug and dig with more vigour so that not a bit of root remains. Disturbance. What is a garden, but disturbance. Yet the effect of a garden is to give serenity. If you have disturbed things enough, you'll get a serene vision. Another paradox.

The blue flowering *Thunbergia grandiflora* is climbing up the verandah post again. Each year it wears the house as veil does a hat. It blocks the gutters too and that makes bubbles on the new cream paint in the living room. But I say nothing of that when Phil, who lives on the northern side, tells me to dig it out and get a canvas blind. I know he's got a point but still. I cut it down in autumn and let it come again in spring. Because I love it.

Friday, 20th October

Parrots screeching over this morning. There must be plants seeding that they like. They only come occasionally. They're gone before I can see what kind they are, but I think they are green. On the train two days ago I saw a flock of white Major Mitchell cockatoos in some bush, feeding with the busyness of birds when they find what they want. They remind me of French housewives at a vegetable market. Perfect attention is being paid.

To my mind, love is the paying of attention. I read the other day that it is easily seen whom you really love. It is those people whom, if you can, you put yourself near or you contact often. What the writer said was, it's no use saying you care for somebody if, for instance, when they are sick, you don't visit them. A simple ruthless test. If you love your silver teapot, you polish it. If you love your garden, you weed it, unless you're half-dead.

I have just heard while writing that people have been shot while gathering olives. The news announced this as a breaking of the cease-fire in the Middle East. And here, in peace, I am hoping that before this book is ended I will have bottled olives from my own trees.

The olive tree in the back garden is now matched in height by the coastal banksia I put near it. The olive has got into the old septic tank, I think. It is more than twice as big as those outside the front gate. All that talk about the Ancient Greeks and it taking about fifteen years for an olive to bear fruit, and on this depended something like the funding of war, is interesting. No doubt it is true in a hard climate with poor soil and no fertiliser, but the soil of Ancient Greece wasn't then what it is today. Erosion from the cutting down of trees to build ships and for firewood and housing has ruined much of the soil. But once it was rich.

This olive is ten metres high and it was a small sapling, probably three years old, when it was planted two years ago.

Grey plants near pink flowers look wonderful. The olive has a pink trumpet vine growing through it, as the vine came across from the other side, where it was put in, along with the blue potato vine, to disguise the shed. These are happy accidents, born from chance out of ignorance.

Monday, 23rd October

'I've got mulberries in my garden and I love them,' Diana said on the phone this morning. When I put the phone down I remembered that two weeks ago, walking down Darling Street in Balmain, I saw a small boy on a bike trying to jump up to get mulberries. I drew down a branch for him and together we ate some.

Also, at church, the priest had said while giving out the parish news, 'Please help yourselves to the mulberries on our tree.' It seemed medieval that news of the harvest and an invitation was spoken by a man standing there wearing gothic garments.

'Work, for the night is coming when a man's work is done.' That old hymn goes through my head often.

Plants are models of work: they never stop unless the cold makes them rest.

A fortnight ago a friend, Gem Flood, gave me iris rhizomes and together we dug them into the bed at the back step. Only one golden iris from earlier plantings has bloomed among the artichokes. I've heard that an iris won't flower unless the rhizome has some sun on it and that is why most of mine don't. So we stuck the rhizomes up and let the roots below go into the soil. Even when an iris is planted high, it seems to soon sink down and soil or mulch covers it, even if you don't mean this to happen.

Speaking of artichokes: Sarah Day gave me two plants when she came to stay last autumn. Yesterday Terry, looking over the fence, pointed to one of these plants which has an artichoke on top. This is a surprise and I am waiting for it to get a bit bigger before I cut it. Terry said that if I wait the artichoke will come into flower. We had one of those tangled conversations where neither person wants to offend the other but cannot quite make themselves clear. I said that I thought this *was* a flower, as it has green petals and is shaped like a tulip. He said, nonetheless, that it *will* flower. Does a flower flower? Obviously I am not going to wait to find out, as I will eat it. I admit there are no seeds inside an artichoke unless the choke itself, the best part, is a big seed perhaps. On reflection, I think Terry must be right. But how?

It is one of the things I like about a cottage garden (an over-worked term which has come to mean mainly a mess), that vegetables and herbs grow among flowers.

Wednesday, 25th October

I've been asking that old question: how does one live well, especially alone in middle age? A life of contemplation and then hectic activity has always attracted me. Dates and meetings get things done but I prefer to think of them as frivolous. If you elevated digging, planting and staring out the window to the most valued acts, life would take a form that gives a certain amount of peace.

There's no point in envy or a feeling of importance; they're just beguiling traps. Few things can make as much trouble for a person as working in the arts. There's always someone else who the sun shines on. Sometimes I forget all this and become frantic, ridden with nightmares and there's no laughter anywhere. At other times peace rises, as if a pair of blue cranes lifted up from a creek, and the day unrolls like a cream silk scroll. Most of the time I think what I work hardest for and long for most is simply the approval of my children. I can't decide if that's a fool's errand or the better part of wisdom. Perhaps for that, it's just too late.

Farmers and gardeners, although both people of extreme action, are also among the most contemplative. The farmer driving to the shearing shed, the water troughs or cattle yards looks out the window of his ute and sees the grass waving, the horizon and the vault of sky. The gardener walking among the weeds and plants looks at the ants, last week's sprouting seeds and the birds in the greening trees.

People who live the life of the religious in convents and monasteries have always known how to balance their lives with physical work and contemplation. In one of my favourite travel books, *From the Holy Mountain*, William Dalrymple says that St Anthony invented the idea of the monastery. The saint was hounded by his admirers, rather like a Hollywood star, and when he fled to the desert they followed. No doubt feeling harassed, the idea dawned that setting the men up in separate cells or hermitages would leave him in peace. St Anthony began what soon became a rage for monasteries. Within two centuries, there were monasteries as far away as Scotland. He'd hit a nerve.

Thursday, 26th October

A wonderful day. Nine pot-bound advanced Lilly Pilly trees went in at the railway station. So too did some pot-bound pink poinsettias and a Yesterday, Today and

Tomorrow bush. Tom dragged the heavy hose over the line and turned it on at the tap by the passengers' shed for me to use. I flooded the annuals planted there last autumn, the pansies and others. Digging a hole for a tree beside the platform, which stood three metres above, I heard a voice. A man on the platform, who looked like a priest in mufti — black trousers, white shirt, gold badge that I couldn't read — said, 'On your own, are you?'

'As you see,' I said. He wished me luck and said he'd noticed the Flinders Ranges eucalypts on the other side of the line had been wrapped in barbed wire. He said, 'I hope it cuts them to pieces.' Meaning the vandals.

Taking Peri's trees over to the station, I was just going out the gate when I noticed my old barrow had a loose wooden handle that made it veer crazily. Four girls about twelve years old were passing. I asked for help and gave them a tree each to lug over. Amused at this, they walked ahead laughing among themselves, and the youngest lifted, dropped and dragged her tree while I wheeled unsteadily behind them, wanting to ask her not to damage the roots which, with every dump and drag, I could feel breaking. But I didn't. One tree was a big robinia that Peri had donated. The girl who took that had it waving above her almost to the electricity wires. They left the trees at the steps of the station and went off to the beach, still laughing.

Sunday, 29th October

Silence, except for the faint drone of a plane and the sizzle of some skate cooking. Diana is coming and we are going to walk on the beach to Bulli. I picked the artichoke and I think I will give it to her.

Violets are blooming under the *Ailanthus* tree. The ground covers, with the violets among them, have flourished. I didn't know that violets fly into other parts of the garden and grow easily.

There is one green fig hanging on the tree. I saw it as I threw Yates fruit and citrus fertiliser around. A bag of Yates rose food didn't go far. I will get more this week as Woolworths at Corrimal have it as a bargain. It is extremely satisfying to slit open the bag with a knife and let fall the white grain. Like cheating without dishonour. Seems like a secret short-cut. I do not know, and possibly don't want to know, what Fukuoka would say about this.

Margaret O'Hara gave me a dozen clivias from her garden at Mount Ousley. They still sit piled in the barrow. I can't dig; too worn out. It is always like this, a flurry where weed and plants are dealt with, as if a bomb is about to go off. (No, not one hidden by a butterfly.) Then nothing for days, weeks or months. In these flurries as I look down and often notice I am wearing my best Stephan Kelian shoes, or other unsuitable things, I think often of my first editor, Barbara Ker-Wilson, who told me that she could never make herself go in and change her clothes, even when she picked up a paint brush full of paint and began on a wall.

Later, as I stood outside in the sun, eating the skate, I noticed what an amazing sense of smell seagulls have. Two arrived within moments of my stepping out with the fish. It can only be smell that directs them. When I put meat on the lawn, seagulls come in a shrieking flock within a few minutes. They are not sitting in the trees waiting; no, they are away elsewhere and, with one whiff, they fly in. I think it may be that other birds can actually smell seeds.

As Diana and I walked on the beach, she told me that she's had an article accepted by a Greek archaeological journal and so she said, 'I suppose this means I can call myself an archaeologist.'

Jane, in Adelaide, wants us to join a dig at Paphos in Cyprus, where Diana goes most summers, to excavate a fourth century BC Greek theatre. But washing shards in a cold wind or hot sun isn't appealing to me. Hundreds of volunteers go to the dig each year. Diana curated an exhibition of drawings and photographs of fragments found at the site, for Sydney University.

As we walked she said that the ficus trees I had planted at the station are the kind farmers plant to shelter a mob of cattle. I see now that it is the same giant tree in front of the farmhouse at 'Bend of the River. And that tree could shelter about fifty cattle as it is as wide as and taller than the house.

Speaking of animals, Diana brought me back from Turkey, where she took her art students last year, a silk mat decorated with animals and birds. It looks a bit Egyptian, with cats standing in cream squares with burnt orange and purple peacocks. It tells a story, but what it is I don't know. Diana is a tapestry artist, so she told me how the mat was made and says that each knot on the back is one stitch. Among all this colour, pale turquoise deer stand, their antlers like question marks in the story.

The clivias are in. The soil is rich and soft down there in what I call the badlands, an ugly neglected spot. And now, with a dozen clivias, some spare arum lilies and tall cuttings of tree begonias Peri brought, it's starting to look better. And then I saw a frog.

Six months ago, Jack and I rode to Diana's with jars and plastic bags. Five times we brought back tadpoles and put them into buckets with plants and water from Diana's pond. But never a frog was seen. Lacking a pond of my own, I decided to dig the buckets into the earth and plant ground covers around them. With stepping stones inside and ramps to travel on, the tadpoles thrived. I can't wait to tell Jack. Frogs at last.

When a house down the street had a green iron bath removed, because the daughter was afraid her elderly mother might slip in it, I asked for it. Day after day I moved it around on the owner's lawn, trying to stop the grass being killed, until some men carried it down here for me. They brought it in, though it was no feather, even for them. One, looking around, said, 'I used to play in this garden when I was a kid. You've certainly filled it up.'

One day when I was away and Hugh was here with his daughters, as a surprise he dug the bath into the soil under a gum tree. Then he made a wall around it of geraniums in big pots, so that Claudia, his youngest, couldn't crawl into it. I was glad when I saw what he had finished, but a book I'd read said a pond for frogs ought not to be entirely under a tree. I didn't tell Hugh this, as the job was done and it was too hard to undo. But no frogs ever called or ruffled the surface. Week after week I gave the frog report over the phone to Jack.

Tonight, discussing this with Diana on our walk, I said as we parted, 'Well, that's it. It's no good, the bath has to be dug up. They can't live under the tree.' Then I walked down and saw the surface rippling, although there was no breeze. No leaf above stirred. I thought perhaps it was mosquitoes landing. Then I saw legs swimming. It's frogs alright.

Harry, the pet duck (which has begun laying eggs) belonging to Phil's son Brett will have to be kept away, because ducks like to eat frogs. Margaret O'Hara gave me a printout of a web page on frogs and how to bring them into a garden. It says it is unwise to take frogs from other places. You are advised to make the environment and they ought to come. But Diana's frogs are close by and so I am not removing an animal from its true locality by using her tadpoles. Perhaps these are not Diana's stock, but fresh ones from the old drain over at the station, where the willows are springing. I heard frogs there after recent rain. I heard them, with some chagrin, thinking that in this filthy drain they thrive, but never in our waiting green bath. And now this. Success. Every now and then I run out, creep up and look for ripples and legs kicking like a foetus. I keep wondering why I am so happy, so jubilant. It must be that they are my first pets. Frogs are perfect for me, as you can leave a frog, but you can't leave a dog and you can't leave a cat.

Tomorrow Ghilly, my old friend from Newcastle, is coming to stay overnight. She's driving to Melbourne to sing in *Die Fledermaus* for six weeks. An opera singer's lot. Six weeks in lodgings, away from husband and children. There might be a few stage-door johnnies, but it's not the glamour it's cracked up to be. But then, what is. Take a look at a writer in full throttle at a literary lunch. You'd never think of them wandering around in their dressing-gown, looking distraught at a publisher's letter asking for the money back. And not a cent to spare. Quaking with fear and worry. There they are, hair shining, laughing, flowers on the table, everybody drinking but them, signing books and looking as good as they possibly can. It's a living, that's what it is. But don't let the glamour fool you. That's just a charade. Once I saw a photograph of myself sitting in a car, the door open, with my arms full of purple *Cattleya* orchids after a signing. I looked like Maria Callas. All I needed was a fur coat. Yet I'd been three hours on a train with dirty windows which the cleaner had refused to clean when I asked him to rub his filthy rag over them, so that I could see. I had hardly two cents to rub together. Somebody at the lunch had given me the orchids. I laugh every time I look at that photograph.

Monday, 30th October

As I rode south to the nursery, a white heron stood in a lagoon, its reflection like the open white pages of a book. So still, it was as if it were reading itself.

At the nursery I had a long consultation with Denis and Tabitha. Denis gave me some old tomato plants he was throwing out, along with white salvia, Shirley poppies and two punnets of old lettuces. I bought some French sorrel plants. Tabitha, seeing this, said that her Lithuanian grandmother used to make sorrel soup, so she would take some plants home too and look up the recipe. She advised me on the mess the two big pots on the verandah have become. The *Dracaenas* took the cold, hard winds very badly, even though I thought they were sheltered there. They are tattered and brown. I will put them with the clivias down among the shelter of the fences. Tabitha showed me new weeping spreading Lilly Pillys which are also available in an advanced state. She also said port-wine magnolias might fill the pots and thrive there. I would very much like to have scent at the front door, and these, she says, are in bloom for a long time. I ordered two and one of the Lilly Pilly.

Denis sold me his second to last pair of green French rubber clogs. The pair I had from him are wonderful in mud so, in case they wear out, I took the others. A shoe you can hose is a good thing.

So much to tell, so little time. One of my favourite singers, Andrea Marcovicci, is playing and the song, 'The Kind of Love You Never Recover From', has a sharpness that I like even though I ought not to be playing a song with weakening lyrics. It doesn't make me unhappy, merely thoughtful. The song goes on and lingers like smoke.

Ghilly is bringing me jacarandas dug up from a bit of vacant land near her home, where they've become weeds. No, it isn't a National Park. Even if it were, it would be a good thing to dig them out as, along with willows, they've become a true weed. I have such plans for the station. South, south I am going. With any luck, I could get to Bellambi along the railway line. And there never was such a place as Bellambi for need of trees. As Peri and I passed over the line on one of her visits, I said, 'Isn't this the most desolate place? Can you imagine coming down here to have a drink at your local pub?'

She said, 'No, it isn't as desolate as around the Guggenheim Museum Frank Gehry's built at Bilbao in Spain. That's a lot worse and it's got a polluted river besides.'

Today, coming back from Corrimal, I saw a pencil pine dumped in a trailer with rubbish from a renovated house. These are hardy trees. I put it on top of the fish and groceries in my bike basket and even though it fell off a couple of times, it's now in a bucket of water. The roots are mainly intact. Everything wants to live. I can hear the tomato seedlings in punnets that I left in the dump at the nursery calling: 'You should have chosen me. Choose me. Choose me.' Grosse Lisses wailing and calling. A small high call for such a large fruit.

Here is Peri's beautiful pear cake recipe.

Peri's Upside-down Pear Cake

½ cup of brown sugar
1 cup of butter

½ cup of caster sugar

¼ cup of ground almonds

2 large eggs

4 or 5 pieces of chopped preserved ginger

1 cup of self-raising flour

1 teaspoon of baking powder

quartered pears or apples or both

Method:

Butter a cake tin. Preferably not spring-form as they can leak.

For the base:

Melt ½ cup of brown sugar with ½ cup of butter and boil for 5 minutes. Do not burn.

Pour this caramel into the cake tin. Place on this, very neatly if possible, quartered fresh pears or apples or a mixture of both.

Pour onto the fruit the following mixture:

½ cup of caster sugar mixed with ½ cup of soft butter.

Add ¼ cup of ground almonds, 2 large eggs and 4 or 5 pieces of chopped preserved ginger (the type that comes in syrup, or if you have none use crystallised ginger). Gently fold in 4 tablespoons of the ginger-preserving syrup, or milk.

Add 1 scant cup of self-raising flour sifted with 1 teaspoon of baking powder. If you have plenty of fruit, you can double this recipe for the cake mixture.

Bake the cake for at least 45 minutes in a moderate oven. The cake must be baked right through and can take 1 hour or more depending on the amount of fruit, as it is this that slows the cooking.

When the cake is done (test with a knife), remove from the oven and stand to cool. Turn out upside-down onto a plate and serve with thick cream.

Bees and Bonfires

THE HIRED HAND

Would I hire me
to look after me?
This rosy bag of excuses
for the half swept floor, unmade bed
late flu injection
crowded wardrobes
shed of spiders, leaves
and tax returns, unwritten poems
lines lost in the bike's breeze.

Would I like the meals
I cook for me?
I don't think so.
With no union for me
I would harry myself
lying in the sun on the couch
legs up reading.

(In this harrying I remind me
of my mother who could never bear
to see an idle hand, her own
or anybody else's.)

Would I let me rear my children?
Lord, no. And yet
who else would I trust?
I can't be hired
I can't be fired
arguing with myself all day
watching the wind blow the leaves
those mortal warnings
that I love to scuff through.

Wednesday, 1st November

*S*ix jacarandas standing in a row. Dug, Ghilly said, from a neighbour's garden and their own where they grew wild. They've come in good condition. Ghilly is asleep, with the long drive ahead. I am making tea and waiting to take her for a walk around the garden. Then we are walking to Bulli along the beach.

The first cornflowers are in a vase on the table with mock orange (*Philadelphus*) and pink roses.

Sometimes in the night the sound of the sea — familiar in childhood, an ancient memory — knocks through my dreams so that the bed is in a sleep-out with glass louvres open to the night.

The air, laden with the sound and scent of the sea, fills the blackness with its vague softness, soothing and beating like the patting hand of a parent.

When I wake with the hazy light of early summer outlined through the white wooden shutters, the garden wet with dew opens like a hand as I walk out onto the deck through the French windows and lean on the railing looking out towards the distant sea as the house sails through the garden to the harbour of the day.

The sweet and utter freedom to be able to decide what to plant and how to spend the day is something that seems so rare that when I think of having it as I do, day after day, year in year out, leaning there, staring out, I can hardly believe that I have reached a place and a time where the burdens and the privilege of work, routines and slog have faded away and are now just a memory. I could paw the ground like a horse, so eager to begin the day.

Thursday, 2nd November

Suddenly, rain. Last week I sowed Italian parsley seed and later, while Ghilly was here, some coriander, the slow non-bolting type. I have been out looking for parsley seedlings and also killing snails. The lemon tree is sagging under the weight of lemons. Well, not exactly the whole tree, the lower branches, so that the lemons rest on the earth.

I took a jar of salted lemons to Jenny Gribble in Balmain. Recently I have been staying with her on Tuesday nights when I teach in Sydney. For days the jars of lemons had sat on the lawn in the sun, after they had been cut into halves and slit, filled with salt, and set upside down, one upon the other, with the jar topped with lemon juice on the second day. When they have released juice of their own, they must be put into the sun for about a fortnight. Sometimes I leave them a month to be sure they are pickled and I like the look of all this bricolage standing in the garden.

Sunday, 5th November

Today, the fifth, is Guy Fawkes Day. When my brothers and I were children we burnt guys on bonfires, but I didn't know why. And now, after reading Antonia Fraser's *The Gunpowder Plot*, I know and I wouldn't burn an effigy again. When you read of the persecution of Roman Catholics in England, about their horrific suppression, it puts a different light on trying to blow up Parliament.

I'm making cheese sandwiches for lunch with Grandmother Shemmald's Pickles. Here is the recipe:

Grandmother Shemmald's Pickles

3 cauliflowers cut into medium flowerets, stems cut finely

2 kilos of onions, peeled and sliced

2 cucumbers (optional)

Cover these vegetables with cold water and a cup of salt. Stir to blend and then leave overnight.

Bring this mixture to the boil and cook only until the onion looks clear. Strain it.

Mix the following ingredients together to make a smooth paste:

1½ kilograms of sugar

1 cup of plain flour (or more if needed)

6 flat tablespoons of dry mustard

1½ tablespoons of turmeric

¼ teaspoon of cayenne pepper

1.25 litres of vinegar

Now pour this yellow mixture over the vegetables and bring gently to the boil. Simmer for 1 minute, being careful not to let it burn. If it does not thicken enough — mix extra flour and extra vinegar and add until it does.

(Cauliflowers seventy years ago may have been smaller.)

Pour into sterilised jars and seal. Keeps well.

If the cauliflowers are very large, you can use one less or make extra of the sauce in which it is boiled.

Monday, 6th November

Bees like poppies. Pink poppies up to my chest have bees ducking and weaving in and out. After admiring the bees and the poppies, I came inside. On the radio a man was singing 'Where the Bee Sucks, There Suck I'.

Two more jacarandas are sitting in the drive, waiting to be planted at the station. I tell myself that even if one tree a day goes in, eventually, if vandals don't come, it will be enough to make a difference. This torment for getting things done, in beating the chaos of nature, goes on every day. Tearing at weeds as I pass by, I wonder if these handfuls are enough to keep the balance at least level with what is growing silently elsewhere in this garden. Then, when I am at the station, I look at the thin line of trees, so vulnerable yet full of promise, and wonder if I can keep them alive for the first summer. While these thoughts are anxieties, they are the anxieties of luxury. No prisoner is thinking of this in their cell. No unhappy person, full of grief, is staring at a thin line of trees, full of plans and longing.

'Never without a cause,' as a friend said of me. I know he's right. These invented anxieties are part of a lifelong characteristic of inventing urgency. Those who lean on the fence discussing the garden seem calm. Do they toss and turn, half-dreaming of slitting bags of red-gum bark, pouring it out onto layers of newspaper smothering weeds, or do they think, when they flop down to read, that trees are waiting to be planted, or that those put in last week are probably wilting. I have invented all this to please myself. To live with a sting to my days, as if bees come nightly with horticultural messages of urgency. My dream, the honey, will be the avenue going to Bellambi, shading the platform and feeding the birds.

Tuesday, 7th November

A card has come from Diana telling how a particular 19th Century cannon ball came to her family. Her father got it when he trained at Holdsworthy Army Base as part of the University Field Battery in 1939. 'He brought it home — a very heavy object the size of a head. My mother and grandma sensibly used it for pressing tongue.'

This reminds me that my father had a brass shell case gathered by his father in World War I, which my mother used for flowers in what she called 'autumn colours'.

Diana wove a tapestry quoting her father's diary from before the Battle of El Alamein. She said it was incredibly moving to weave her father's words. This is what she wove above a pattern of a Roman tiled path: 'The regiment marched all night.'

Watching a bee enter a pale nasturtium, as I am now, reminds me of Margaret O'Hara's hive in her bedroom wall. A local beekeeper is willing to remove the hive, but he is hard to pin down and she is worried that the bees will multiply. My brother Tucker had to burn down a perfectly good house on his land, as bees got in and took over a billiard table, and in the end it was easier to burn the house than to save it.

There is something very unlucky about poisoning bees. The American poets Raymond Carver and Tess Gallagher had a hive in their home poisoned and then he got lung cancer and died. There are many stories about bees and illness. Bees know when you are sick.

The writer Nancy Phelan told me when I asked about her hives that bees need to be told when somebody dies in the house. If you don't, they leave. It's an old country-folk thing. I don't know if it is in Australia, but it certainly is in England.

When Nancy's husband died, she said, 'The bees went. I didn't have time to go and tell them, so they left. I can only assume that they were offended.'

Nancy also told me, on the matter of poisoning bees: 'They travel far, you know, and they take the poison with them, so if something eats them it is poisoned too. So it spreads it.'

At Peel, Barbara and Ruth have beehives and now Barbara has sent a parcel of soap she's made from the wax, as well as furniture polish. Those hundreds of trees we planted will feed the bees, because they were native trees. There's a pot of their honey on a shelf in the pantry. Christmas is coming and I am going to make a panforte with it.

Oh, these sweet sparrows. A flock have come down to peck among the blue flowering vine and the nasturtiums, eating some insect or other. I love their alert busyness, their darting ardour.

In the shade of the big tree, the arum lilies are raising their pale flowers like the upturned, soft, lustrous palms of saints. As if to say, 'See, I have nothing. I am a lily of the field and I want for nothing. Behold my beauty.' And when the plant has two lilies, it looks like a white benediction.

Here comes a pigeon to drink at the dish.

Now here comes a horse race to make you some money. Yes, a horse called Brew (its mother was called Horlicks) has won the Melbourne Cup.

Saturday, 11th November

Three loaves are about to go into the oven. It is the River Cafe recipe for sourdough bread. There never was a more complicated recipe. It has taken two weeks to get to this stage and about five different actions. Three more to go. Spraying the oven with water, turning the loaves, reducing the head, spraying again — it's four. Then cool the bread on a wire rack. And nothing makes me sure it will work. The recipe is for two loaves but I have made three big ones. How did two turn into three? Who can say. I was telling my friend Patricia Harry that I was making this bread and she said, 'You'll only make it once.'

I am reading *One Art* the letters of Elizabeth Bishop, the American poet, who lived a long time in South America. She wrote the poem 'The Fish'. She also has the bread-making bug, as she says in one of her letters. There is something very attractive about work that involves many processes. It means the kitchen becomes a sort of boiler room and there is no time at which something is not being prepared. One thing I hate is a house where nobody knows what the next meal will be. In fact, in some households a person must get into a car and bring home some ingredients for almost every meal. People might have lived like that (without the car) before the invention of agriculture, but I can't see the point of getting out your bow and arrow for every meal. What if you came home with nothing? Makes life miserable.

Well, the oven is at 230°C, so in they go. It's a lottery. It might work. And if it doesn't, there's merely a colossal mess to clean up: flour on everything. But it's still a thrill.

'Can you water that new rose, please, Tom?' I called as I ran up the platform to catch the train one hot day this week.

'What one is that?' he replied.

'It's the one with yellow flowers, the new one, Tom, the one that's drooping. I didn't have time to water it.' (He didn't know what a rose was.) He walked down to the tap with a bucket while I watched from the other side of the line. Then he tipped the bucket from the high platform and missed most of the rose.

'Oh, Tom, do you think you could give it another bucket, please? That lot didn't really hit it.'

Again, he took the bucket and poured, this time with better aim. Then I knew no more of the fate of the rose because my train came. It is not that the people who work at the station are not helpful, they are quite the opposite, it is just that they do not know about gardens. A coastal banksia died last month because I saw, too late, it was wilting and the water then didn't save it. The problem is that they do not notice wilt, or, if they do, they do not realise its meaning. If I am away a few days, plants can die.

Sunday, 12th November

This morning when I visited my neighbour, David, for the first time, an enormous magnolia tree (*Magnolia grandiflora*) amazed me, growing behind his house. David, of course, has not seen the tree because of his blindness. We walked over and I brought down a branch to show him. At first he held the leaves, thinking he held the flower, but then I put the petals into his hand and he felt the circumference of the flower and smelt it. He said, 'They're white, aren't they, with a yellow centre?'

I said that they are really cream, with a slightly darker cream centre. He felt the pistils, standing as they do in a small cone.

When I arrived at David's and got off my bike, I saw that all the blinds and curtains were drawn and thought perhaps nobody was at home. Then I realised that there would never be any reason to open them, day being the same as night for him.

Standing beside this amazing tree, the most beautiful tree in the town, hidden away from everybody, including the owner, we had a talk in the sun. David was speaking about the lawn and mowing. I realised that he mows the lawn himself. He bent down and said: 'See, even now I could get a catcher full.'

We spoke about the station garden. One day over there, when I showed David where the red geraniums had begun to bloom he bent down and felt them. I described the rest and we walked along as he felt the edges that lead up to the rail crossing with his cane. I showed him the new white steel railing the Railway people erected when I asked. It is to stop the boys riding their bikes over the garden for the pleasure of a leaping bump.

We were talking about vandals because recently David fell on a log on the bike path walking to Bulli. The fence protecting the dune plantings has been burnt in a big bonfire on the beach. Other logs were left strewn about on the path. Now he doesn't walk on the path, he walks on the edge of the road, which is unpaved and full of its own surprises.

I rode away, more thoughtful than when I set off, leaving him to his music and books.

I would have liked to take David a loaf of the bread, but, although full of the right sourdough flavour, it's a rock. I am going to chew my way through it, just so as not to waste the work. The bread will be alright soaked in water, squeezed out and mixed with sliced ripe tomatoes, basil and olive oil for panzanella. Patricia's right, this *is* the only time I'll do it.

Why is it that there is so much pleasure in all this bricolage? Barbara and her soap and furniture polish, me with the bread. The tracklements I love to make. The pickled oranges, the salted lemons and now the lemon chutney I'm about to make. I think it's really a form of play. It has a deep ancient connection to creativity. To change one thing into another is to make a person happy. There are some people who can barely take a look at a thing without having an impulse to change it into another. It may be that gardening is part of this impulse. Nothing is the same once a person has begun a garden. And nothing beats planting and sowing for helping allay depression. It's up there with swimming with dolphins, and is a lot easier to implement.

Have you seen a mouse spider? I was standing beside Terry, who was about to bend to turn on his tap to rinse off a bunch of onions he had pulled for me, along with some silver beet, when he said, 'Have you ever seen a spider this big?' I hadn't. He said, 'It looks like a mouse. Maybe it is a mouse spider.' And truly it did look like a mouse, a sort of eerie, benign mouse, as if a spider went to a party in a mask, just for fun. It must be spider season, because there are several daddy-long-leg spiders indoors. My mother said that spiders are lucky, but I think that was to stop her children being afraid.

A letter came last week from Adelaide. It was from Ian North, who had just rung to invite me to Lake Mungo. We did a desert trip to Lake Salvador and covered three thousand kilometres in two weeks. Madness. We howled with laughter, collapsed on motel beds or swags, helpless, suffocating, drowning in laughter. He drew in my writing book. First a tree on a dry creek's bank.

'See,' he said, 'draw it as it grows — from the roots.' He draws those fine accurate lines like Ruskin. He drew a dingo running and then the kettle on some flaming sticks. While he drew, the kettle's carved wooden handle caught fire. The drawing had distracted him so he let it burn.

His letter says:

Whales! We two [Mirna, his wife, and he] saw two large ones, blowing and wallowing about five hundred metres off Moana yesterday.

I was (predictably?) moved to see so many people staring out to sea. I felt a jolt of something like religiosity. Before sighting the animals I asked an Aussie couple in their sixties if they had seen anything yet. 'No,' they replied. I said: 'It's good to see so many people interested.' 'Yes,' said the man, 'Mary was just saying that a moment ago. There is still a little bit of hope,' he added. 'Yes, exactly,' I said, and we parted the best of friends . . .

A letter also came from Betty, my neighbour at Leura, on holiday at a shack at Valla Beach. (Bill, her 85-year-old husband, wrote last week that he was reading her *War and Peace*.)

This afternoon, we sat for a while on a high headland [Betty wrote]. A calm sea sent low curling rollers towards the beach in rows of white frills. One day last week we were sheltering among the dunes, eating sandy sandwiches. The wind was strong and the sea wild, beating the shore with thumping great waves — the pounding heart of the ocean. An old fisherman hailed us. He wore a close-fitting beanie, knitted in broad bands of blue and white, the exact colours of foam and sea. The fine ivory sand was a perfect mount for such a picture.

And yesterday it was different again, no wind at all. We walked for an hour northwards, sloshing along in the water, watching sea hawks circling high overhead. No other creature at all to be seen anywhere. We sat on a rotten sea-soaked log and peeled oranges and prayed aloud for my brother Vincent in hospital emergency, a double by-pass. We walked back noting the strange patterns in the sky — fine white shreds, as if the frayed ends of a silk tassel were brush-stroking the indigo sky. And again, whilst still on sky scenes and such — each early waking morning I lie in bed and look out through the arch formed by two giant old paperbarks and know it's time for the birds to commence wheeling over the distant sky towards the dark mountains, out to sea and around again, over and over. They keep it up for ages and remind me of Bill out in the kitchen stirring the porridge. Do not give up on your book. Remember we are all clowns.

This letter is written by a woman married to the same man for fifty years.

Tuesday, 14th November

It's pouring and I must go to town and teach. A pink foxglove has bloomed overnight, and beside it a taller hollyhock is in bud. The garden is drenched. A few drops of water ran down one of the wooden crosses that hold the railing on the deck and stained it like a sudden blush. It is warm. The rose on the green steel arch Jack and I assembled two years ago has bloomed. It is Albertine. No rose blooms more than this, but it is not remontant, so this flush is the only one until next spring. Would you plant a rose that blooms only once a year? I suppose it depends on how big your plot is.

I am waiting for the port-wine magnolias for the front pots to be delivered, along with half-a-dozen small pelargoniums, which I knew only as geraniums. I read an article in *Gardens Illustrated* on pelargoniums. The photographs of the tiny flowers were beautiful.

The magazine says that there are about two hundred and fifty species of pelargoniums, succulents, evergreen perennials and shrubs commonly (but incorrectly) known as geraniums:

> But the species themselves, many of which grow in the wild in South Africa, are not often seen in cultivation. Since the seventeenth century, when the first pelargoniums appeared in Europe from South Africa, debate has raged over their relationship to the

geranium. The fact is, however, that although they are part of the same family (*Geraniaceae*), geraniums and pelargoniums are two distinct genera.

Now I am mad to have some.

While I wait, I'd like the owl to come too. I still remember the thrill as it flew down from the *Ailanthus* tree. What brought it and what will bring it back?

Saturday, 18th November

Yesterday I got out of bed, where I'd been for thirty-six hours. Diana, her friend Jon, who like her is a tapestry artist, and Margaret O'Hara came to lunch. Not having been shopping for a week, I opened the freezer to find something to cook and luckily an ox tongue fell out on my foot. This struck me as the reverse of Homer's saying, 'An ox stood on his tongue.' I boiled it and, with a jar of pickled oranges and some mashed potatoes and salad, it made a main course. Ian was intrigued by the oranges, which, as Diana said, are a type of Elizabethan dish, so I showed him the recipe in a book. He copied it out. These oranges keep a long time. That jar had been in the pantry for three years and was still good, even perhaps better than earlier.

After lunch we walked around the garden. One day, Diana says, she will come and draw one or two of the big pink poppies. Often last summer, as we sat at the table at dusk, having a drink after a swim, she would comment that the white *Datura* in bloom would be a wonderful flower to draw. (Yes, they did finally grow.) This summer I will make sure to ask her to draw all three. The *Datura* flower crumples by dawn the next day, as if it had bad news overnight. It falls into a white slump but even then would make a good drawing.

Drawing dead flowers reminds me of Keats' death mask. I have just finished reading a biography of him by Andrew Motion. The death mask brings Keats to us, as if asleep. If only, I kept thinking as I read, he had never gone near a doctor he would have lived a little longer. And then, if Keats had practised medicine, as he'd been trained, he'd have done the same harm to others.

The lives of dead artists are intriguing. Shelley and his small boat. There is a drawing of Shelley's boat on the cover of a book I've been given. It is Mary Oliver's *Winter Hours.* I don't remember a book that gave me more pleasure. As I kept reading, I was thinking, oh God, oh God, I am going to read this one hundred times. She teaches so much. Her stillness, her detail, her profound attention to the natural world.

I was thinking when I looked at the picture of the small yacht drawn by Shelley's friend and sailing companion, Edward Williams, that this friend, drawing that vessel, drew his own coffin.

He and Shelley were sailing the *Don Juan* from Lerici to Livorno, Italy, when a storm came up. The captain of a passing boat, seeing he said 'that they could not long contend with such tremendous waves', offered to take them on board. A shrill voice, which is supposed to have been Shelley's, was distinctly heard to say, 'No.' The waves were running mountains high — a tremendous surf dashed over the boat which, to the rejected captain's astonishment, was still crowded with sail.

'If you will not come on board, for God's sake reef your sails or you are sold,' cried the sailor through a speaking trumpet. One of the gentlemen (Williams, it is believed) was seen to make an effort to lower the sails, but his companion seized him by the arm, as if in anger.

So it was that Shelley and Williams sailed down into the Gulf of Spezia, ten miles west of Viaggio, under full sail. We are left with a mystery. Was it Shelley, impetuous to get home to Mary, who had just had a miscarriage, or perhaps resenting anybody trying to prevent him sailing in the manner he wished to, who refused help? Or is it all a tale told later, exaggerated or untrue? I can't imagine a sailor, for instance, using such words through a megaphone, during a storm.

Ten days later, when the bodies were washed up, Shelley was identifiable by his nankeen trousers, white silk socks and his friend Hunt's copy of Keats' poems doubled back in his jacket pocket. This is a true story. This part we know. He went down with his compatriot's poems in his pocket. Who will I have in my pocket when I go down?

Later. I have been out planting tomato and basil seedlings. My friend Paula, on the telephone from Mornington, said when I explained why I was puffing when I answered the phone, 'Oh, this is the right time, you know. Tomatoes and basil are supposed to go in by Melbourne Cup Day.'

The plants are those rejects from the nursery — Grosse Lisse, Roma and Apollo Improved, along with basil self-sown from Terry's plot. A punnet of lettuce went in also. Vegetables are much more difficult to grow than flowers. A great meticulousness is needed and I don't have it. But having been given the seedlings, it seemed wrong not to use them. None of the parsley or coriander have come up yet. I go out and stare at the ground, pulling up seedlings of impatiens to make room.

As I ran to answer Paula's call, I dropped the hose which slumped onto the back deck and quickly filled half the kitchen with water while I spoke, my back turned. So now the floor is uniformly clean. I remember a friend saying years ago that he would like to have a house that could be hosed out. He could see no reason why one couldn't be so designed, but, as yet, as far as I know, there never has been such a one. It would only need cement floors done on a slope with cement edging instead of skirting boards.

The first gardenia is out. It is now here in a sliver of a glass vase beside me. Smelling strongly. This summer I hope to have hundreds of gardenias. Months ago I planted twenty along the side path in the gaps between the blocks that form the diamond shapes. I meant to have all the same kind to give a uniformity to the edging. But I have never managed uniformity in anything. (This book is an example of that, as it was meant to be only about plants and building a garden.) When I ordered the gardenias, Denis had two kinds that he sent and then, there not being enough to finish off the path, and finding it hard to get others the same, I accepted different kinds and shrugged with another bit of uniformity lost.

A grey pigeon is drinking from one of the bird bowls. And now that it has flown away, a small wind ruffles the silver reflections of the sky in the water. A bee has disappeared inside the throat of an apricot nasturtium. There is no moment when something is not happening in the garden. Snails, worms, stink bugs clinging to the cumquat leaves, poppies bursting out silently when I am never looking. I have always wanted to watch a poppy burst.

THE MERMAID

No, I wasn't surprised
when I hauled her in
gleaming rose and emerald,
opalescent in the net.
She smiled at me and that I see now
is why I would risk everything
for the mermaid.
For weeks I'd been trying to catch
one or more of her kind
out there with the flap of the sails,
the slap of the prow on the waves.
I knew the weather was right —
there are some things experience tells —
you can't have been fishing so long
without an inkling of how to catch
a deck full of scales. The miracle of it.
Her smile and her elegant tail
hitting the deck in a rhythm
as strong as a poem.
Her hair wasn't seaweed at all
though it did have a green bow
tying a clump behind one of her ears.
On a breast an oyster had settled
a natural beautiful brooch
which I wouldn't have dreamt of disturbing.

Why did I want the mermaid so badly
having given up most of the trappings?
I wanted her
as a horse wants to run.
To some I know she's a myth
they've never seen her
and what they don't see they don't
believe
yet, like radio, the mermaid exists
sleekly ravishing, gasping and smiling
knowing that I'd write this
and then let her go
watching her swim away
in her own muse the water.

Sunday, 19th November

Clunk. Clunk. The frog has sung. Riding to Thirroul last week, frogs were calling, sounding like trucks running over a wooden bridge. Next day, David and I walked there, and again the rumble. In my heart dark doubts were rising like bubbles. I thought, how can I tell the reader I am mistaken? No frog is in my pond, there has never been a croak and, surely by now, there would be. The legs I saw must have been those of something else.

That night I heard it. At first I thought it was Harry, the duck next door, calling. Then I thought it was his owner,

Brett, chopping wood. And then I knew it, I knew it, and ran down to the pond. I stealthily bent among the white geraniums and papyrus grass. A rustle, and the frog stopped. I knew it was a frog. I came back and lay on my bed, listening to the lovely noise. It has taken two years and now victory is mine. All doubts have gone. Frogs in the pond and it's still raining. It has rained for almost a week. The barrow is no longer the rain gauge because it is full of rusted holes. Buckets are more than half full. I love gathering rain water. There's never a bucket standing upside down. All stand waiting. It is not that I do anything in particular with the water, it just goes onto plants. But I think they like this better than any other.

Oh, go on, frog. Croak now, so I can put you here on the page. Perhaps in answer to this rainy day, so soft and mild, it has sunk under the water and pulled it like a crinkled quilt over its head.

Two days ago I took the two big dracaenas from the pots on the front verandah and put them into the Badlands. They had been savaged by wind, as already mentioned. The two port-wine magnolias have arrived, and Tabitha has sent these, along with six different miniature pelargoniums, which trail sweetly. There is nowhere to put them as they are most subtle plants, unlike the others in the garden, hardly noticeable at first, their effect almost nil. Nonetheless, like a mother, I love them.

The rain is soft, the air warm. I lay under the mosquito net on my bed, watching through the open French windows the rain coming like drifts of veil. A great circular spider web hangs from the back eaves, catching the rain. Its symmetry glistens and shines, sagging and wafting like a drenched bride.

Every day these gifts. Sometimes I lie between moments of thinking, lulling in happiness.

Yesterday, old friends who used to share my house at Leura, Gordon and Woolfie, came to lunch with their daughter, Kitty. Diana and Margaret came too. Margaret now has two possums in her chimney as well as the bees in the wall. It was too wet to go for a beach walk, so we sat and talked. I got out some Peter Levi books to show Woolfie, because Diana was talking about Greece and the dig she does in Cyprus. She has written a book on her archaelogical travels called *The Fabric of Ancient Theatre*. Diana had been in Greece with Levi when she was twenty, before he left the Jesuits. He's recently died, and I found his biography of Milton called *Eden Renewed* at Gleebooks last week. Levi wrote of a walking trip in the Peloponnese with another poet, his friend Georgis Pavlopoulos, called *A Bottle In The Shade*. This is one of my favourite travel books. I read it with a map of Greece on my stomach.

On the matter of wheelbarrows, Margaret said if she won the sweep at the Melbourne Cup lunch, she'd buy me one. Terry's, which I now use as he no longer uses it to carry manure, has the bottom replaced with a piece of wood. This I cover with a hessian bag and I have moved loads of compost onto plants and taken many things to the station in it. People peer but go about their business. Live and let live. My own barrow collapsed at the station; the tray fell off, along with the weakened wooden handle. I brought it home in Terry's barrow, a teetering palace of broken barrows.

Later. I have been out gathering snails. As Woolfie came in the gate yesterday, she called, 'Look, Kitty,' pointing to nasturtium leaves each holding a single drop of shining water. The drop, when the leaf was picked, rolled like mercury on a green plate. She opened my eyes to this, as I had neglected to see it. Now I do. And the voice of the frog called, not from the pond but somewhere near the jacaranda. Only twice, then it heard my step.

Watching a wet mynah bird on the neighbours' roof, preening itself and shaking out the moisture, I saw that it too, like the owl in the book I am reading (*Wolf Willow* by Wallace Stegner), can turn its head around and peer out between its shoulder blades. Maybe all birds can do this. But until I read of the owl, I had never noticed.

As I stand looking out into the garden, I feel myself a coat hanger with a dress of flesh wafting at the window.

The tall poppies have fallen under the weight of rain. I prop them up among the cornflowers, each limp but helping the other. The roses remain stalwart and on them I lean the others.

Tuesday, 21st November

Floods in the north. Gunnedah, Taree and Muswellbrook have roofs poking through water. Here, heavy rain keeps pouring down. It couldn't be better, in a way, for me. Yesterday I finally dug up the yellow Surfrider hibiscus beside the shed. This had been on my mind and I waited, thinking Hugh might come and I would ask him to dig. Then I decided to try it and it was not all that difficult. I lugged it over to the station and put it beside the ramp where it will hide a gap. George, the stationmaster of Bulli, Bellambi, Woonona and Corrimal, arrived and said, 'What are you up to today, Kate?' I showed him the hibiscus and then asked him for an extra dozen bags of gum bark to more perfectly cover the newspaper and bark I have put down to kill the weeds. The paper shows through, so it looks bad. A mad woman's breakfast. I saw two women pointing down at it on Saturday, and they were not approving. I think people believe that when a job is done by a public authority, they have a right to perfection. That's understandable. I am possibly adding to the poor reputation of the Railways by this imperfection. One day, though, when these trees are grown, the roses are climbing on the fences, the plumbago, daisies and hibiscus are in bloom, it will be beautiful.

Although making a garden puts one in a state of perpetual longing, a sort of long slow ache, the fulfilment can never give the energy or happiness that the longing created.

I am not morbid, thinking of the Lilly Pillys dropping fruit on the ramps, nor the giant figs pushing against the railings, but it's on my mind. I know they must all be moved. At the moment they are safe and can be left a while until I get enough energy to do it.

When I asked George if I might buy the bags of bark, he said, 'Well, $40, eh?'

I said, 'Well, possibly $50, George.' He said I could go ahead, buy them and bring the receipt and he will pay me.

The last jacaranda went in yesterday with a small hibiscus I had dug self-sown from here. Being wet, I took a spade to the weeds and, in a flurry, cut a swathe. Then the rain came back and at home I dug the pink robinia into the hole left by the hibiscus next to the shed. Now I stand watching the rain, with my forehead against the glass of the back door, looking at the robinia. It is not as tall as the big olive beside it, but almost.

Neck and neck I will watch them race. Next spring, what a sight. Pink against the grey. But nothing is certain in gardening or in much else either.

Patricia, when I last called on her at Woolloomooloo, gave me a sandwich of meat left from a standing rib roast and lemon chutney. I have been making the chutney which comes from her fifty-year-old book full of much older recipes. The recipes are Edwardian in the main, unusual and good. All written in pounds and pints.

Lemon Chutney

4 large lemons

½ kilo of onions

600 ml or 2½ cups of good wine vinegar

½ cup of salt

1 cup of raisins (optional)

30 grams of mustard seed

500 grams of sugar

(I double or quadruple this recipe adding plenty of mustard seeds)

Method:

Wash and slice the lemons. Chop the onions and put in a china or glass bowl with the lemons and sprinkle with the salt. Leave for 24 hours. Put all the

ingredients in a non-reactive pot. Boil and then simmer until tender and thick, stirring occasionally. Place in sterile jars and seal.

Saturday, 25th November

I am making my friend Annie Guthleben's recipe for slow-baked stone fruits. This is how she told me to do it. On an oven tray, spread baking paper. Cut peaches, nectarines, plums and apricots in halves. Allow one piece per person. Sprinkle with caster sugar. Set the plums in the centre as they are the juiciest. Bake at 169°C for one hour. Leave in the oven to keep warm. Serve with cream straight from the tray to the table so as to keep the shape of the fruit.

The Premier, having flown over the floods, has been presented with a bouquet of grey and black wheat, damaged from the rain. Farmers have lost an estimated over half a billion dollars, the radio says.

Monday, 27th November

White November lilies are blooming. I never see them without thinking of Margaret Sharpen, in whose memory I planted the bulbs. The lilies, I see now, are like her veil. Nobody who wafted down the hospital corridors at Gawler ever had a more perfect veil. Before the phrase 'role model' was invented, she was mine. She taught me to lay out the dead and to help a baby emerge with serenity. When I flooded the Sisters' Home by overflowing my bath, she merely suggested I take a dustpan and scoop up the water. It is a strange thing, but it is when you know you have done wrong and are in trouble, that the person who is mild with you, when they could be harsh, stays with you forever.

Once I gave a woman two injections of morphine within the same hour. I told Sister Hansbury, thinking I might have killed the woman, and even if I hadn't, I would be dismissed. She, too, whom I was frightened of, was mild with me.

The nurses then were from fifteen years old to about twenty-five when they enrolled. It was nothing that we crushed tablets of morphine in a teaspoon, mixed it with sterile water and drew it up in a syringe, then administered it to someone in pain. It never occurred to any of us to plunge the thing into our own vein. The very thought of it would have made us laugh. Every time I see a heroin addict on television using a teaspoon in this way, I remember nursing.

One day Sister Sharpen showed me all her frocks, long and short, lined up in matching colours in her wardrobe. After that, not only did I want a veil like hers, I wanted my clothes to be matched like that too. I thought of her big floating organza veil folded into four layers as a layer for each year of training. (If you trained in a country hospital, you went after two years to the city and did two more years. Whereas in the city the training was three years.)

Immaculate and serene, the lilies remind me of Margaret. A royalist, she once went, while in London, to a royal garden party. She had bought in Rome a sensational wide straw hat covered in roses. On the day of the party it rained continually and her hat got drenched. She did see, though, a hand waving as a car went past. She put the sodden hat into a bin as she left the party.

If I had known Margaret was sick I'd have gone to see her in Tasmania before she died. As it is, we never met again after I left Gawler. She was thirty and I was twenty and her effect was simply immense. When this nurse came into a room, somehow the atmosphere grew calmer and, subtly, healing seemed possible.

Oh, you should see the big bunch of lilies I lashed out and picked in this vase with the pink hollyhock, lavender and roses. It looks like a wedding. My daughter's being married in March and I wonder if there will be roses in the garden then. I once heard Tammy Fraser say she was told by an elderly woman that if she pruned her roses in January or some time like that (don't try this, I'm uncertain of the detail) the roses will bloom in a big flush very early. This proved to be true and hundreds of roses were there for her daughter's wedding. But you'd feel pretty silly if it didn't work.

Hugh has been using Seasol, a seaweed solution, on his foxgloves and all else. His biggest cream foxglove is three times the size of my pink one. Next to my foxglove, the tall hollyhock is about to bloom.

My friend Clare, in Adelaide, has a front garden full of self-sown hollyhocks which have never had anything done to them. Neither water nor fertiliser; nothing but sun and the little summer rain Adelaide gets. Each time I stay, I plan to dig some seedlings. This one came from a punnet from Denis's nursery and only three have survived. Hollyhocks, once established, seem to be easy to grow and they give that middle-linking height that gardens need. I couldn't see this myself until a garden designer from Plum Tree Cottage in Wentworth Falls came to help with my front patch at Leura. Suddenly, when it was pointed out, I saw it, and once seen, this sort of thing can't be forgotten. It is like throwing a rope up from the ground to lasso the trees visually.

Yesterday ten of my students came to lunch, which is why I brought in the flowers. We sat around and had a reading of our work. It is everlastingly marvellous to see how people learn to write. It is like riding a bike. One day, after all the trembling, wobbling and falls, a steady pace comes, direction and off they go. It's heartening and whoever scoffs and asks, as one academic did, if I really do think writing can be taught, I know it can. Every year I see it happen. Not to everybody, I admit, but then not everybody learns to ride a bike, or learns to swim either. Not everybody wants to enough.

Today, the first swim down at the sea pool. I wish I had begun earlier. When I got in it seemed hard, I thought I'd get out after five laps, but then it seemed easier, so I stayed in for twenty.

Have you ever smelt sweet osmanthus? Yesterday, at lunch, Jan gave me a plant and, as she put it into my hands, she said its name. I remembered we had spoken of it in class when she'd brought a sprig with her. We all smelt the perfume that day, surprised that such an unremarkable little creamy flower could send out such a strong scent. Today I dug the green glossy bush in beside the side path facing north against the wall of the house. There were pots of osmanthus Denis showed me at his nursery this morning and I thought of buying more because, as Peri says, a woman can't have too much of a good thing. I got into serious trouble with that little homily of hers which she'd embroidered on a cushion. I'm more careful nowadays. You need to live a bit less close to the edge than I do to act for long on that.

Thursday, 30th November

Tomorrow, the first day of summer. Hooray. It's hot and the bees were out early. The tall pink poppies are flagging. I want to pull them up, but I need to make sure the seed pods are nourished enough to be fertile. They've got about two more days to go. I want some tall summer thing to go in the tiny meadow plot. Not sure what. More white cosmos perhaps. I'll ask Denis. Tabitha is not at work. She's on her honeymoon. Last week over two thousand dollars worth of plants had to be thrown out at the nursery because of spoilage from the rain. I stood beside Denis in the sun, with the green shade cloth thrown back to air the plants, everything steamy and drying, almost shaking themselves like dogs.

We were discussing a deal on pine bark to finish mulching the station garden. Today it is due to be delivered and I must run over, slit the bags and spread it at once so the vandals don't get it. It's twenty-nine degrees, five past eleven, and I have just picked the first two tomatoes. Glory hallelujah, it's going to be a tomato summer.

Dozens of tomato seedlings have sprung from compost around plants this week. These two small tomatoes are from another self-seeded plant beside the lemon tree which I only saw after it reached maturity.

They are the size of golf balls, but what kind they are I don't know. Terry probably could say.

Friday, 1st December

I have been round planting tomatoes with David in his back garden. Watching him work, feeling the earth, circling his hands like an elephant's trunk. A storm was coming and big slow drops fell in the warm air, so we worked fast. I was bursting with excitement. Denis gave me two grafted Apollo plants and one pot, which were being thrown out and were perfectly good to my eye. I rode to David's, hoping to find him home, because if I left the plants without saying he could trip on them. He was at the post box. I called and he turned in the wrong direction. At first I thought he was avoiding me. He wasn't. He felt the plants in their little pots, saying that one had a curious stem, and he was right as the leaves grew thickly up the stem.

I rode home to bring in the washing before the storm.

While the storm held off, I hurried back to David's with a bag of mushroom compost and a bottle of Seasol in the barrow. He had already placed the little pots beside his four tall staked tomatoes. But there, by the fence they would be shaded. I suggested he plant them out in line with the others, away from the fence, so he did. He has white plastic tubes that he puts around the plants, as I thought, to keep weeds away. But he said it's to stop him treading on them. Together we piled up the warm compost around the plants and he weeded. Then we went to the tap with his watering-can to put on the Seasol, which I gave him a whiff of.

'Smells like the sea,' he said. The can leaked, as I showed him, so we used a bucket. Again and again I saw how detail matters. A fine hole that you can't see could let out all the fertiliser before you have reached the plants.

I stand beside my friend and try to see the garden his way. The world as shape and sound and scent and feeling. As a result of this, I am now mad on scented plants. Keen before, now besotted.

Today I planted two pineapple lilies (*Eucomis autumnalis*) and ten tuberoses. In the third pot on the verandah, having taken out the weeping Lilly Pilly, I put in a Madagascar jasmine (also called *Stephanotis*). This smell is always at Peri's Christmas party because she has it growing up the back verandah posts. Traditionally it's used in wedding bouquets for the scent of the small white bells. And what else can I lay my hands on? Oh yes, *Nicotiana*. I put in a punnet of the annuals and asked Tabitha, back from her honeymoon, about a tall one. Colette writes of tobacco plants scenting her mother's garden at dusk as Colette laid her head in her mother's lap. The annuals I bought are not that kind, so Tabitha is ordering in the tall perennial. Three punnets of petunias went in too, as their smell at dusk reminds me of Adelaide and drinking beer under the grapevine outside our house at Dulwich.

When David finally comes to lunch, he is going to be swept away. But how to negotiate the diamond-shaped cement blocks of the curving path down the side? He says he used to have a dog, but now he prefers 'stick work'.

Peri has sent a box of mangoes from the farm. She rang and said: 'There are so many mangoes, we are almost up to our knees in them. My brother Frank, who is eighty, has spent all afternoon up a ladder, bringing them down. He's worked like a dog for hours.'

Tomorrow I will make mango chutney.

In her back garden, I heard Peri speaking with her daughter Skye recently. They have written a book together called *Bend of the River*. Peri said: 'You've got to live your values. If you don't live your values, part of you dies. So you might as well die anyway. You've got to live your values.' I walked inside and got an old envelope from a wastepaper basket and wrote it down while it was ringing in my ears.

Stitches in the Earth

THE RIM

I was running on the silver rim
of an old blue plate. From time
to time pink clouds were reflected
as my footprints marred the surface
and were swept away.
I turned to run again
on the restored and perfect rim
as if at dawn the seagulls called
to greet another day.
And then I saw the dog.
It was Funny Face our dog
from Tumby Bay.
Our father brought it home
sixty years ago and Muttee said 'What a
funny dog!'
He barked and ran beside me
then tore off to chase a gull.
Here he was triumphant while the waves
rushed in and out as generations'
blow across the sand
and disappear replaced
in endless waves.

Saturday, 27th January

*P*ink hibiscus flowers almost cover the side path in places. This is the glorious month for hibiscus. The Wilder's White I planted to block the neighbour's kitchen window is taller than the gutter and in full bloom. It has a faint scent of something familiar. Going out and sniffing some, and then bringing them inside to describe them, hasn't helped me work out what it is.

Last week, on a picnic to a bay with Diana and her friends, we snorkelled above a reef. After lunch I walked around to the headland over the rocks and lay in the sun while the others swam. Salt crystals sat in dry ponds, shining white. I gathered about three cups of salt in my hat and brought it home. This place is an Aboriginal site of immense age where Diana brings her students to teach them history and archaeology. It seemed, when I bent, scraping up the salt, that I was part of a history of this work. Salt could have been traded for thousands of years from this bay. Big colourful fish swam among the coral and oysters grew on the rocks. I had a strong wish to bring a swag and to camp here with Diana some time, because there was a feeling here, like the white hibiscus smell, not easy to describe but nonetheless real, of happiness. This is a feeling, perhaps it's called spirituality, that people, not only myself, get at Lake Mungo near Mildura, where new dating of human remains found there has placed them at about seventy thousand years old. When all around us there are signs of human habitation going back thousands of years, it's not unreasonable to imagine that these people, their bones and their lives, had an effect.

Silence has fallen. The wind is moving the blue flowering vine outside the window and I can hear only a fly.

Sunday, 28th January

Yesterday, hearing a story about people on an island where they make flowering fences by cutting long branches of hibiscus and sticking them side by side into the ground, I decided to try it. Pruning the bushes down the side path to make room to walk, I stuck the cuttings in the ground and will wait to see if this can make a hedge of pink and white flowers.

I took a barrowload of pink hibiscus cuttings, a jacaranda thriving in a pot which Ghilly brought me last week and some *Ailanthus* seedlings from my garden to the station. Staggering around in the mud, I planted them down the side of the platform towards Bellambi. The barrow stuck. It is thrilling to see that about five of the jacarandas and *Ailanthus* trees David and I planted have taken. Now they must make their own way, because unless it is a true drought, it is too far down the line for us to carry buckets. The amount of water that falls from the platform makes a bog at times, which will help all the trees to get established. Tom hoses down the platform daily and a waterfall results. Perhaps it will keep a deep-down tide of water for their roots even when above it is dry.

I mulch as I go, as best I can, with whatever is around: stones, bits of old wood, weeds, iron bars, anything at all. Sloshing around in the mud with buckets of tree seedlings and cuttings makes me immensely happy.

Last week I put half-a-dozen cuttings of frangipani into the mud and they are all thriving. One day, this may be the prettiest bit of line on the coast. I am heading towards Bellambi and now have almost reached the last of the platform and head off like an explorer into the vacant land stretching as far as the eye can see.

Mung beans. I was proudly showing Terry my crop of mung beans, which I had sown to fortify my blood orange, and said I was planning to dig them in almost at once. Terry said in his cryptic way, 'You need to wait until they flower.' So I thought I had better wait.

Thursday, 15th February

My youngest brother, Peter, came with his wife, Helen, and took me to lunch at a new Indian restaurant in Corrimal. We sat talking about his crops and I told him about planting the mung beans to fortify the blood orange tree. Peter said that it is probably about time I dug them in, because before the beans are formed the nitrogen level will be high. What shall I do?

My back has made me lie on the floor to ease it. This is the only place where it doesn't hurt. Gingerly walking around the garden shows the weeds quickly growing, but I don't bend and pull.

David brought me round two bags of mushroom compost, along with the two he gave me last week to take home in my barrow. But they sit on the verandah, unspread. Whenever I see manure or fertiliser in bags waiting in a garden, I think of Peri saying to Frank the gardener, 'Frank, that manure there is not doing any good sitting in bags.' To get here, David carried these big bags down three streets, coming through the gate between the roses.

Geoff Wilson, an old friend from Adelaide, came to stay and at Fairy Meadow nursery we found a big pot-bound Lisbon lemon tree. We brought it home in Geoff's van and the next day wheeled it round to David. While it wasn't a gift he really wanted, it was accepted. Every tree David plants is another obstacle for him to avoid when he is mowing the lawn. Each time we discuss planting a tree, David says he will put it down the side of the house. This amused and puzzled me for a while, until he said that it keeps it out of the way of his mower. The mowing is done with the help of two white painted plumbing pipes which he lays on the lawn and can somehow see enough of their light or shape to know where he is heading. Yet, as far as I can tell, David has no other sight, because, when we talk or I introduce him to somebody, he sometimes turns in the wrong direction.

The lemon tree is now planted in a spot where we strode out the measurements to get enough sun and space, away from the fence and the fig tree he's just planted. David lugged over a big log to save the lemon from the mower and himself from falling over the tree.

Sunday, 18th February

Gardenias are blooming so that Daphne next door and I have fresh ones in glasses of water continually.

Weeding under the Mutabilis rose out the front I got stung on the chest by a wasp. I thought of Cleopatra and the asp. Only the letter 'W' stood between us. It's a coincidence because I had been thinking about Cleopatra lately, as somebody said to me that we are inhaling her exhalations to this day. They said this because I told them that, although I know it's stupid, when I pass somebody who looks ill in the street I am afraid to breathe. All air is used over and over. Take any small thought and multiply it to infinity (which is what holds everything in its grip) and you have a thought to keep you astonished all day. Sometimes one of these thoughts can last a lifetime.

I think I have had about three new ideas in my life. One of them was when I was about ten years old: lying in my bed, I suddenly realised, hearing children playing in the street, that if the wall fell down we would all be visible. And the same with gardens. All gardens would merge if our fences fell. So it is a natural thing for me to dig at the station, because, in some ways, that garden adjoins my own and all others in the street. In fact, it joins all those here on the coast, and goes to Sydney, north to Cairns, around to Darwin and then down to

Broome and Perth. A bird, for instance, would not be noticing the definitions of each garden; all of them would be a mass of trees and water bowls, flowers and nesting places. Streets are really only paths in gardens. It is only when we walk in the front gate we begin thinking, in the odd way we mainly do, that this plot is ours and is unique, separate and individual. It may be individual, but it is joined, as a patchwork quilt is joined, by roots — those stitches in the earth.

Peri has made a garden behind her house in Mosman, on the council's nature strip. It is full of flowering trees, begonias, citrus, herbs, annuals, lawn, hibiscus and other shrubs. She's built a stone path and steps to her back gate and the whole thing is serene and green. I remember Peri squatting under a hibiscus, trowel in hand, on the footpath of Moruben Road about twenty years ago. I was startled to find her there, and saw that she was busy and did not really want to stop for me. This was the first time I became aware of street gardening and I couldn't understand why she was so gripped by the work. She was wearing a yellow jumper and I can still feel the force of her energy.

I have begun to read Richard Mabey's *Home Country*. It is a classic of nature writing. Gilbert White's book, *The Natural History of Selborne*, is, the Corrimal librarian tells me, only available to read in Wollongong Library. So this week I am going to ride down and read it. I am trying to learn about nature and, as ever, one of these books leads to another.

Richard Mabey tells of that moment when you can feel the season change. A slip of wind and a sudden breath and spring stood there. I love his description of how spring came to England one May day:

> I saw the actual beginning of spring here, and felt for a moment like a witch-doctor whose spell had worked. There had been nearly 24 hours of cool, heavy rain, and I had driven down to the Chess to try to get beyond it. I sat on a log by the side of the river and watched the cloud begin to lift. Small bands of swifts and martins appeared, drifting in high from the south. Then — it seemed to happen in the space of a few seconds — the wind veered round to the southeast. It was like an oxygen mask being clamped to my face, so sudden and inspiriting that I looked at my watch for the time. It went down in my diary: '6th May, 1978. Spring quickening, 4 p.m. exactly.'

Last week I had a similar experience. I didn't write the day in my diary, because I wanted to deny that summer's ending. Yet the change coming can't be wholly denied because three days ago the water in the sea pool was colder. I will keep on going to the pool, but it will be harder. The cold tides come up early from Antarctica here and whales begin to come north. Last year I swam until the middle of May, but it was so cold that, when spring came, the water wasn't as appealing as it had been so I waited weeks to swim. One elderly man swims at the same time all year round. Reliable as the dawn, he is there at 2 p.m., going up and down. Speaking to nobody, he walks along the beach, bringing his towel, and, with little ado, he undresses, strides in and begins his laps. His back is brown, his hair short and white, he gives a sweet wave, as if wiping a windscreen of air, when we meet.

Yesterday Hugh mowed my lawn and spread the mushroom compost David gave me. I have been too timid to lift anything, to weed or to dig since my back began to hurt. Afterwards we went to the pool with Sophia and Claudia, who are learning to swim. Coming home in the car, in wet bathers, both girls began a sort of thrumming, like pigeons in the afternoon. It may have been to get warm. It's not a noise I know how to make: a blowing through the lips that makes them tremble and gives the pigeon's noise. The car was filled with the sound of satisfied pigeons.

Thursday, 22nd February

Yesterday David and I walked to Thirroul for me to pay a bill to Tony at Beach Art for framing some paintings.

As we walked with the sea crashing on one side, high clouds moving slowly in a blue sky, and, from time to time, soft warm rain, we held a broken black umbrella above us. Occasionally the sun came out, and then finally it stayed and we folded the umbrella into David's yellow backpack.

Between Bulli and Thirroul, where three creeks come down to the sea among sedge and reeds, about twenty tents had been erected. Two Aboriginal flags fly above the sea. We walked down a muddy track to investigate. There had been some signs on the track earlier, protesting about housing that is planned for this green place. White Easter lilies bloom on the low green hillside and, behind, the mountains rise in a long dark arm.

Two men came out to greet us. It began to rain again, so they invited us into the biggest tent, where there were two chairs, a table and boxes of food, bread and cans. We were given chairs, and while the two young men told us that their people were buried on the side of the hill, and that one skeleton had been dated at sixty thousand years, I signed the visitors' book. Two young women with children arrived and asked what they could do to help. They had walked along the beach from Austinmer, but neither of the men seemed to be able to say what was needed, apart from candles. The women made many suggestions and to all of these — meat, camp beds, hot-water bottles — the men agreed modestly they would be acceptable. As we left, Glen, the taller of the two men, showed David a smooth wooden tool like a boomerang but without the curve. He held David's arm and showed him how to throw it with a flick of the wrist. I stood directly behind David. After a flick, and then a flop into the sand, Glen threw the tool and it spun like a helicopter's blades, high into the sky, and landed on the sand.

David and I had lunch at Oskars Wild bookshop cafe in Thirroul and discussed planting a hedge of either *Murraya*, hibiscus or sasanqua down David's drive. I see now that I have been too ardent in suggesting this, because it is not convenient and will need pruning. Because I see the bareness, it does not mean David should have suggestions made that will probably give him little pleasure — unless the hedge is scented *Murraya* — but will just make work. I need to learn to hold my tongue. And yet, if he had a sasanqua hedge, how beautiful it would be.

Friday, 23rd February

The sound of chainsaws made me run out into the back garden. Men were cutting branches of the camphor laurel hanging over from my garden into Phil's. The circle of the neighbours' washing, sheds and roofs were revealed and the scent of the wood filled the air. There was nothing I could do so I have come indoors.

Nothing can be taken for granted. I had been thinking that now, after almost four years, my garden was enclosed: the trellises made from the doors of the house are covered in white potato vines and Terry's shed is screened by the old pink cottage rose. Now there is a gap where the branches hung. I will save up and get a man to erect twelve metres of trellis. Tabitha, at the nursery, will know the name of a shade-loving vine to cover the screen. It is a way of thinking about trees that I find hard to endure. Nature harnessed, trees pruned, lawns trimmed; neatness the ideal, and trees seen as threatening.

This is not uncommon and I often puzzle over its origins. All attitudes come and go according to fashions but are sometimes hard to fathom. I am out of kilter here, although there are some people who would like to have trees, surely. This is a street Howard Arkley would have liked to paint.

When I letterboxed this street, asking if people would allow the council to plant any trees of the residents' choice, nobody replied in favour of the trees. The general opinion was that it would be difficult to drive out into the street with a tree blocking the view. But I could not see how, if the trees were planted up close to the front fence, and if they had a slim trunk with foliage branching out above, there would be much interference. I didn't persevere, because I didn't want to stand out or become unpopular. This was one of the reasons I began planting at the station. Desperate for trees and some gardens, I thought that nobody would mind as it would not block a view if the garden grew there. Already there was a pink and white bauhinia tree and a tall banksia thriving beside the steps leading up from this street. Stymied as I was, the frustration and pressure led to this explosion of tree planting elsewhere.

Sunday, 25th February

There have been many coincidences in the last week. Wondering what vine would grow in the shade, within the hour I saw in the newspaper that the star jasmine thrives in shade. Reading Richard Mabey and idly listening at the same time to the radio, I heard his name spoken. They were talking about the great storm in Britain in 1987, and Mabey's belief that tremendous storms such as this are not unnatural: they are, in fact, nature, and the trees respond in their own way, left to lie in woods, creating habitat for hundreds of animals and plants. Sawing fallen trees, unless they are in the way of roads, paths and so on, is more unnatural than a storm, Mabey says. His own wood, Harding's Wood, which he bought in 1981, had adapted to the storm and the light let in from fallen trees has been good for many plants. The radio began a program about trees and nature as I read, and I was glad of these coincidences, meaningless perhaps, yet they felt benign.

I try to think of myself as an animal, because it helps me see my place in nature and to think of people in a different, wider, even richer way. Now that the Human Genome has been discovered, we know that mice and corn have similar numbers of genomes as we do.

Yesterday was the day of the barrow. Margaret O'Hara, having tried to win the money for my barrow on a horse, and failing, has been paid for teaching poetry, which she views as a pleasure. We have been to Warrawong and there, in an enormous new shed, were almost a hundred barrows of ten or so different types. Marg told me to choose any one I liked. Now a scarlet and dark-green barrow with a thick plastic bowl is leaning up against my shed. The bowl won't rust. There's no room in the shed because of the family's bikes.

Now people won't stare at the old barrow with the bottom rusted out and the wooden handles wobbling when I am at the station. But I'm keeping it.

Out in the hot sultry day, small butterflies, like the hands of children, flutter above plants, drifting and mating, their dance celebrating the fading summer.

Sunday, 11th March

Two tuberoses are flowering, bent under the weight of the rain in the hot air. I have never grown tuberoses successfully before and, from time to time, I run out to smell them. Now I have found a third, bending forward unseen before, and it is in full bloom so I have brought it in. Now and again I reach forward and take a sniff.

Why is it that they did not grow for me before? Perhaps in Leura it was too cold. These bulbs were planted late in summer yet they ought to go in before Christmas. Warmth, water and good soil is all.

Cutting back the big pink hibiscus down at the back fence, I saw a plague of snails making a beach of shells. I dipped some of the cuttings into hormone powder and planted them outside the bathroom, because I fancy lying in the bath and looking out on hibiscus as if on a tropical island.

In Melbourne last week, for a reunion of friends, I saw Paula's new garden by the sea at Mornington. It was professionally designed, and it shows. I will never get the harmony of a balanced structure in this garden that a landscape designer could. I wonder if it is too late. Embedded in the design I have made, which seemed logical at the time, I have grown fond of it. Yet I know that if the garden were to be redesigned to a better form I would be happy and wonder why I hesitated.

Monday, 12th March

Prince Potemkin, whose biography by Simon Sebag Montefiore I am reading, inspected his gardens in a dressing-gown lined with fur, worn open to the waist, and a pink bandanna. Walking this morning around the garden in my own version of this, I saw that a small avenue of gardenias alongside the curved path have been almost completely overgrown. Another idea that didn't work. They must all come out and be put on the other side of the path, where plants do not reach out for the sun as if drowning in shade.

Prince Potemkin introduced potatoes to Russia, created the cities of Odessa and Sebastopol, and loved English gardens. He brought in Capability Brown's protégé William Gould, among a host of other gardeners. Gould travelled ahead of the prince, making gardens overnight for his arrival. How a garden is made overnight is, I suppose, a bit like a garden festival. An army of workers and, in this case, instead of trees in pots, they were brought holus-bolus on sledges. Money is a great help in this. I am also reading George Eliot's *Silas Marner* which gives balance to any longing to bring in the experts here, dig up the lawn and hurl money at the plot. The pleasure this garden gives me, day by day. Bending among the dew to pull a few weeds first thing in the morning, smelling a gardenia that has bloomed overnight, throwing out food for the birds and seeing how the robinia tree has grown gives point and anchor to a day. Only those who have done it can know its pleasures. A pot of tomatoes on a verandah may not look significant, but to the owner it can be a consolation.

There are times in a life when a sight, sound or an idea springs up that never vanishes. One in mine was when I was about twelve, reading about the life of people who had been released from a German concentration camp. An old man, seeing an idle plough, was given the handles and his triumph and joy were all over his face. It struck me as strange that anybody would be happy to begin hard work again after its loss. It was then I saw the importance and privilege of work. That was when illumination came.

It is not that the person growing tomatoes on the balcony cannot buy them at the shop or eat them in the communal dining room, if there is one, although the flavour may be different; it is the pleasure of this mystery of growing plants. They give more than they take.

Tuesday, 13th March

Down at the birdbaths, a crow has taken a bread roll to soak and soften. Having eaten half it left the rest, and now sparrows and a bigger brown bird have come to eat. If this isn't a recipe and a restaurant, I don't know what is.

Today David and I walked into Woonona to look at flowerpots because we are both keen to plant bulbs. David knew of a place and had said, when I suggested a fresh planting of pansies at his back door, that he would rather plant bulbs as they are easier to differentiate from weeds.

I took around the Windy Hills bulb catalogue and together we sat in the new shade of the *Melaleuca* trees which he cut back so hard that two died, but three are now sprouting. I read out the descriptions of split daffodils, which have a trumpet made of separate petals and of mixed lots. After about five groups being read, I barely could remember the difference myself, with the pictures before me, so I wondered how David was going. I lay on the grass while he squatted, and read about Christmas lilies and freesias, choosing, you see, my own favourites. So today we looked at pots but came home with none. For myself, it's a matter of my daughter's wedding coming, and for David, I am not sure. Sometimes a sort of Zen state overcomes the two of us and we stride around, feeling the pots and me looking, and then we drift away.

On the long walk home I saw aloe vera plants growing wild on the side of the road. I went over and pulled out three, leaving about six, so that we can have them in our gardens to use for burns and rashes. The leaf is broken off and opened. A clear viscous fluid comes out, which is cooling and calming to skin. I have wanted aloe vera for a while and now I have it and it was free.

Free like that dish of soaked bread the birds are eating in a small flock with fluttering pleasure.

When I got home, I reheated a Chinese dish in a wok and, taking some chopsticks to the table on the back deck, tried to eat it with my eyes closed so that I could feel something of what David does. Only the birds could see, but I felt a fool and soon gave up.

Champion of Camellias

LIPS

Loyal workers in the factory
of language.
All have one pair to do with as we wish.
I thought of my father's excoriated lips
burnt and blistered after auctioneering
sheep in dusty yards. And my own used
then
only for whispered secrets, laughter
shrieks and questions.
The sieve of language through which
we can only say certain things
to certain friends beyond
'Help me', 'Pass the salt. Please,'
'Get out'. Just the bolts and screws
of language in the wood of the everyday.
But lips! Sweet pink doors
on the wardrobe of our teeth.
This sublime ordinary pair, soft tissue
of sighs, the shy muscle of the kiss.
Little bow of sorrow, perfect hollow
for the flight of our last breath
and our first.

Monday, 16th July
'Bend of the River', Peri's farm

The bauhinia tree drops its purplish-pink petals onto the balcony of the upstairs bathroom. Sometimes they fly into the shower and float around my feet. The white peacock flies down from the big mango like a bride falling from a cliff, veil streaming.

This morning, as I sat talking on the telephone, a blue peacock flew past at eye level. A low comet with a long green tail.

The wind, that great caresser, arranger and boss, flows over everything. The orchard rustles, the pink petals fly and the crows, black, fleet and shining, sweep past. Their bleak cries echo. We are related, the crows and I. We want the same things: the eggs, the fruit, the right to speak our minds.

The giant bay tree down in the horse paddock by the river where I am sitting on a log spreads like a hand of green cards. Its beautiful grey roots rise up like the gnarled fingers of an ancient bridge player. Nothing stays the same, yet every year that I come here this tree stands as if it will last a thousand years.

All around new houses spill over the bowl of hills and they make it all seem more ephemeral. The fall of a leaf is a message to the living.

The geese that live among all this have their own concerns: their loyalty to each other, their nests and eggs, goslings, the foxes circling and their own flock's striding events onto the golf course or into the dam. Everything is essentially individual but connected. Why else would we love the sight of this noisy white flock, and why else would they run to Julie flapping their wings and honking as she pours the grain onto the ground?

Tuesday, 17th July

Julie caught a crow. She put it in a box and said, 'I am going to kill you!' and wagged her finger. Next day she came and said, 'I am going to kill you!' On the third day she said, 'What right have I to take your life?' and she let the crow go.

We have been down in the new pen containing eight chooks Julie and Peri bought on point of lay. One is dead, caught in the branches of a curry tree in which they perch at night. Julie and I buried it in the orchard beside a banana plant and laid a log and a bale of lucerne on top, to keep it from the fox.

The fox took all eight of the last lot of hens two months ago, because the pen was old and had begun to sag.

This new batch came home from the breeder in a small cardboard box on a hot day. They sat in the station wagon an hour or two while the new pen was being completed. Suddenly Julie saw a hen flapping in the car and she ran over to it. One hen was dead, the rest collapsed. The breeder had put two bags of compost on top of the box and the lid had fallen in and begun to suffocate the chooks. They recovered and are laying four eggs a day. Death tangles through life.

'It is never the one you are looking at,' my friend Clare said one day in Adelaide, when we were each worried about one of our brothers. 'You are always looking in the wrong direction,' she added. It proved true not only for brothers.

This afternoon Anton drove me down the Pacific Highway looking for a shop that sold typewriter ribbons. I said, 'Anton, you could find a wigwam for a goose's bridle.' He said, 'You know, there is such a thing. Did you know that?' He told me a wigwam is a wire that they put on posts above grapes or hops and from which they used to drop a leader down for the new plant to climb up. That leader of string was the goose's bridle.

Julie, sitting here drinking coffee, began to tell me the names of the trees in the orchard because I have forgotten many. I know the mango, lime, orange, lemon and mandarin and black sapote but forget the rest. 'Grumachana, ramonche, ndea, Brazilian cherry, Barbados cherry, inga beans, Davidson plum, mulberries, sea grapes, jackfruit, giant lau lau, Fiji apples, macadamia, custard apples, rollinia, iaboticaba, carambola (star fruit), canistel, monkey pod, pecans, Indian almonds, abiu, and I forget the rest. It's time I went back to work.'

Saturday, 11th August
Home

Laid out on trestle tables were dozens of individual pink and white camellia blooms attended by three elderly men in cardigans. This happens every year in a local shopping mall.

It seems more Oriental than Australasian, this business of men involved with flowers. Yet I think there is a long history to it in this country and that we got it from the British. It is hard for Australian men to be involved with making beauty and yet here is one of the quite radical ways they can be. Men pass this love of flower-growing and flower-showing to their sons. Men who love dahlias have been known to dig up their entire backyards to give the whole lot over to competitive dahlia-growing. Plants so tall that they are tied to thick wooden stakes, and with heads so enormous they are in danger of breaking off, fill these men's gardens. Almost the entire year is occupied for the grower: feeding, watering, staking and then showing the blooms. The tubers are dug up, powdered with insecticide and put away in sheds for winter. There is something wonderfully obsessional about it, in that the growers rarely specialise in more than one type of flower. A camellia grower, for instance, doesn't as a rule grow dahlias for competition nor does a rose grower plant dahlias.

Last year among the hundreds of camellia flowers laid out on the trestle tables was a great pink frilly one called Laska Beauty. I said to one of the men at the stall, 'I don't suppose I could buy a plant of that camellia?' William Walker said that he would grow one for me and that it would be ready in about a year. I left and almost forgot about it, until last week in Wollongong Library when I saw some men putting camellia flowers into an empty glass bookcase. These men belonged to the same group of camellia fanciers as William so I asked if they knew anything about how he was going with my Laska Beauty.

A few days later I had a phone call from Brad, William's son, who said that he had struck the plant for me and he would bring it round along with a few other types if I was interested in them as well.

Brad came with three plants and sold them to me for fifty dollars the lot. He brought with him four saucer-sized flowers to show what the plants were. We walked around the garden and, pointing to the Brushfield's yellow camellia, he said, 'That's too close to your sasanqua and you'll get a few flowers for a while but in the end it will stop flowering because they need some sun you know.'

I explained that I had tried to move the plant but it had a deep tap root and rather than risk killing it, I'd left it where it was.

'I'll move it for you. No trouble. I moved one last year a lot bigger than that. I took out eighteen barrow loads of soil from around it before I could move it.'

I asked how it has done since.

'Won Grand Championship at the show last year,' he replied. That was good enough for me so I accepted the offer.

Two nights later he arrived from his work as a fitter at Bulli, carrying a pointed shovel. We decided to move the plant to full sun beside the path that leads down along the northern side of the house. He dug the way those log-choppers who race each other tear into logs, swaying from side to side, sweat spraying out. Roots were cut while I watched anxiously, but a big root ball was left. The plant toppled over once freed from its bed and I ran to get the barrow.

Brad said, pointing to the hole he'd dug where the camellia was to go, 'Have you got any boiler ash?' Surprised, as I knew that camellias like acid soil not alkaline and that ash makes soil alkaline, I said I had none as this house has no fireplace. 'It's not wood ash I mean, it's boiler ash.' He went off to the ute and got a bag of it, explaining that he bought it from a soil company at a garden centre because camellias thrive in it and that is partly why he wins prizes. The secret at last.

As the plant was lowered into the hole Brad said, 'You know that's a Paradise camellia you've got over there.' Pointing to one in the shade by the fence. 'Bob Cherry bred it. It's a chance seedling from the bees. He collects the seed from his sasanquas and he grows them on until they produce a worthy flower. He spends a lot of money to distribute his new flower, about a hundred thousand dollars. He just can't grow it and get it out to nurseries. He's only got one plant you see, and from that he's got to get thousands of plants, so it takes a while — years.'

'How many camellias has he bred?'

'He's only done Paradise as far as I know. Laska Beauty, the one I got you, is also Australian. That was a controlled cross. That's when you take an unopened flower on a bush that produces seed. Then you wait for the right time before it opens so that the bees don't get in. You remove the petals before it opens by cutting them and then you take your fresh pollen from another flower and put it on the actual stigma — that's the little bit in the middle. Then you take a paper bag and cover the controlled cross. And, if you're lucky, it will produce a capsule with seed or seeds in it. You wait for it to mature — several months — and then it splits. You take the seed and label it, of course, and put it in moist, not wet, peat moss in a plastic bag.'

He puffed and worked, dig dig dig, enlarging the hole as he spoke. 'Then what?' I said. While he was digging I'd dragged up a chair, brought out pen and paper and started to write down what he was saying. 'Leave that and wait for it to germinate.' More digging. Then he went on, 'What we do is, after we've got an inch of growth or a bit more, we nip the tap root off and then it puts out feeder roots. Then you put that into a mix of sand and peat moss. By this time it's into the growing season and you've got a little plant — we like to get them early — if you leave them in the bag you get a twisted camellia.'

Brad began to sound like a human fertility expert explaining the finer points of embryo implantation and I wondered if it was all too complicated to be useful. Yet I felt that here was an expert, even a champion, and that I ought to take the chance to wrest from him (all this was gathered over more time than it takes to tell, with many questions pressed) the knowledge from generations of breeders who had developed all the finest skills. It was up to me to take it down and to spread the news, although no doubt much of what I was told would be in some botanical book . . . somewhere.

Father and son are in competition but not, it seems, mother and daughter. 'Do any women come into the camellia-showing business, Brad?'

'Well, my mother shows miniatures.' But as far as I can see, it is wives and daughters who sell the tickets and make tea and scones for the visitors to exhibitions.

As Brad had been on his way to buy material to make his own special camellia potting mix when he'd brought the plants to me a few days ago, I asked what it comprises.

'I get this boiler ash. It's Australian Paper Mills' product from their steam boilers. I get sand from a soil company at Nowra or Unanderra. This mix is made of one-fifth coarse river sand, one and a half of boiler ash and two and a half of decomposed pine bark.'

I enquired who told him of the mixture.

'Charlie Cowell, a retired nurseryman. Going to get some more ash. Back in a minute.'

While he was pouring the ash into the hole, I asked about the red camellia plant he'd sold me.

'Dr Clifford Parkes, grows like a weed. Hardy, likes the sun. It's what I won the Championship with, you know. I'll give you one for the railway station garden if you like and I'll give you a gardenia too. Get the hose, will you. This thing needs a big drink. Now you'll need to give it some Seasol once a fortnight and a deep watering once a week.'

Darkness was falling so we walked together to the gate, the man sweating yet seeming as exhilarated as if he'd ridden a horse. The woman impressed, grateful and slightly astonished at all she'd heard and seen.

Saturday, 15th September

While in the garden crushing snails, I set fire to the kettle. I came in to see flames eating it like greedy yellow birds.

The sea is still, only the top branches of a gum tree by the fence move slowly.

This morning I took a bucket of Thrive around to the poppies I moved yesterday. Some are stalwart, sword-shaped leaves upright; some are flagging like grey velvet gloves dropped on the soil. Yes, yes, I know — never try to move a poppy.

It is my new plan to weed daily. Ha ha ha. The earth is so moist, everything comes away easily. A small flock of sparrows has flown up from the feeder, like the wave of a hand. Below, pigeons are strutting around, eating some pea and barley stew I threw out.

A bulbul with its black topknot, like an Oriental husband's, has come down to drink.

I watch for a while and think of the sacredness of food.

In the freezer there were leftover ciabatta bread rolls bought for lunch with a friend before I went away. I ate them with tea to wash them down and watched the television. I saw an old woman, probably not sixty but looking eighty, in Moscow, saying, because of Russia's lack of heating, 'What will I do in winter?'

Two-thirds of Bangladesh is under water. I remember the little girl who wrote a poem in the Dorothea MacKellar Poetry Competition I once judged. She wrote: *My Beautiful Bangladesh*. Until then, because of my Western hubris, I had not thought that anybody would want to do anything but flee that country.

The first blowflies have arrived. The crepe myrtle tree looked dead, but when I peered closely there were tiny reddish-green buds.

I wonder how the five geese sitting on eggs on Peri's farm are going?

Thursday, 20th September

Dusk. Pigeons are on the lawn. Everything is quiet.

Today Terry leant over the fence and asked if I had any land to spare. Puzzled at first, I found he wanted to sow some sweetcorn seeds in a bare patch of my land.

'The rain has leached out all the goodness from my patch,' he said. 'And I've been planting vegetables for too long. I have to give it a rest.' He's worked that plot for forty-eight years. He said we could share the crop. I thought it was a wonderful idea. He came straight over with his spade and dug a patch about two metres long and one metre wide. Sweat flew from his head. He just turns the weeds in, no throwing out or shaking soil from the roots, in they go, for fertiliser. Three rows were made and he planted more than would be good to grow if they all came up. Now we are share-farming.

After he'd dug, Terry told me that when the corn has formed flowers, it is best to wait till a sunny day comes and then to fertilise the heads, to shower them gently with the hose from directly above. 'Sweetcorn needs to be closely planted,' he said, 'to ensure fertilisation.' When these seeds sprout, I can't imagine pulling some up and throwing them out. If they are too thick, I won't be able to waste them. I will just put some in another spot to grow. I have never understood how people can throw out living plants. Weeds, yes, but flowers and vegetables, no.

Friday, 21st September

Have you heard of the boy at Geelong Grammar School who mapped wombat burrows by creeping out at night and crawling down to investigate the holes? To this day that man, as he now is, is footnoted in scientific journals, as nobody has ever superseded his work.

I know a girl who tamed a praying mantis. I first met Rosanna at the Sofala Cafe, which her parents own. Rosie, who is ten, sat beside me at a table in the cafe in her bottle-green school uniform, sucking a rainbow-coloured iceblock and said, 'I found him on the windowsill. He was sitting there and he just started living with me. He started living on a vase of flowers on the kitchen table and then he just wouldn't leave. So I called him Mate and I would share my breakfast with him. He really loved Weetbix. I'd get it on my fingers and I'd hold it up like this [she pointed her index finger down towards the table] and he'd just sip it from my finger. And he really liked arrowroot biscuits dunked in tea.'

'How did he eat them, Rosie?'

'Um — he just, I just got a bit of arrowroot on my finger and I'd hold it up and he'd [throwing her head backwards] go like that and eat it.'

'How long did you have him?'

'For a fair while, I can't remember. Mum will know. Well, then I met Godzilla, she was a female praying mantis, and they mated. I didn't see that. Then Godzilla ate Mate. I found wings and feelers and legs on the table, that's how I knew. Then I found one more praying mantis outside and another on my kitchen table. And Godzilla ate them as well. Then Godzilla laid some eggs. We've got a blind with a pelmet on the top and she laid them in between the blind and the pelmet. Then she came back down onto the vase of flowers and Mum saw her die. Mum said she just wound down like a clock. Her eyes, which were light green, changed to black when she was dying. Now we've got a nest and I'll watch to see if they hatch.

'Mate used to stroke me on the nose with his hand. He really knew me. We had a really big relationship. He was a really nice praying mantis and I was very upset when he was eaten. I knew it was nature and that's how it had to be.'

My friend Laurel, who is Rosie's grandmother, told me that you can tame a thrush. She also lives at Sofala and has an apple, pear, peach and apricot orchard. There are deep frosts in Sofala and Laurel said this morning, 'As the sun comes up after a heavy frost it shines on the bare branches of the pear tree and it all glitters like diamonds. Sometimes the red and green king parrots perch in it and they look like ornaments on a Christmas tree. I stand there on my deck and revel in it.'

There were blue wrens pecking at the French windows as we sat by the fire this morning in her living room. Laurel said, 'They are gathering spiders' webs for their nests. And that one is becoming fixated on its reflection. It thinks it's another wren. It's attacking it. You can hear its beak and it's chirping at it.' We sat and watched and then Laurel told me she had an elderly aunt who, as a girl sleeping on the verandah in the country, had tamed a thrush. 'In the mornings it would come and perch on her pillow and run its beak through her hair. She had the most gorgeous hair, beautiful, chestnut, thick, curly hair.'

Lisa, who is Laurel's daughter and Rosie's mother, has inherited her great-aunt's hair. She has the thickest, lush ringlets. Lisa gave me a recipe for one of the most popular desserts she makes in the cafe. Here is the recipe which she wrote by hand on a scrap of paper from Rosie's exercise book:

Spotted Dick

Serves 4
½ cup of brandy
¾ cup of currants
80 grams of butter
½ cup of caster sugar
3 eggs, beaten
1⅔ cups of self-raising flour
1 teaspoon of baking powder
2 large tablespoons of golden syrup

Method:

Soak currants in brandy, preferably overnight. Grease four dariole moulds or teacups. Cream together butter and sugar then add the beaten eggs and golden syrup. Fold in sifted flour and baking powder. Stir in currants and brandy. Divide the mixture between the moulds. Cover with foil, leaving a space at the top for rising to occur. Place the moulds in a baking dish half full of hot water. Bake at 180°C for about 45 minutes or until puffed and golden. Serve with a large dollop of whipped cream on top and drizzle generously with warmed golden syrup. The cream and syrup form a delicious caramel. Very popular in winter.

Saturday, 20th October

Here is the *Ailanthus* tree now in full leaf. A long drift of pink, red, cerise and white impatiens has flung itself the whole length of the garden. It is drowning a white, or perhaps it was a green, arum lily under the tree.

The geraniums in twenty pots are in full bloom. A burning red that it hurts to stare at, and also pink and white. They cover some cement paving by the lawn. I was never sure if I could dig up all that cement, so left it. When Dave (the tree man I hired to dig) pulled up the side drive of cement blocks, the sweat spun out from his red face in silver drops, showing what hard work it was to dig this. (Why doesn't this happen when women work?) He rolled the squares of cement onto steel pipes and manoeuvred them into position. Placing them tip to tip made the path I am so happy to have. It was a case of necessity being the mother of invention, leading us to use the blocks this way. There weren't enough to make a curving path. Children love to run on this path, jumping from one diamond-shaped block to the next. Among them now, small blue Agathea daisies are blooming, stretching down, almost throttling the big creamy Edelweiss rose that flowered for five months in its first year. I love that rose. It's so much better than Iceberg, as my friend Toni's daughter, Sarah, said. How right she was. I'd never heard of it but got eight just in case, from Ross Roses at Port Willunga in South Australia, posted in sawdust.

Sunday, 21st October

A hot north wind is blowing. The garden is flattened. Foxgloves and poppy leaves are laid out, gasping. I went round with buckets of bathwater trying to revive the plants.

Earlier, in a fit of energy, and in spite of the heat, I decided to dig up two red geraniums by the side path as they are too bright there. Also a yellow-leafed pink-flowered geranium was dug out. I dragged these in a bucket of water down near where the potatoes once grew in a neglected place, worn out from the trellis of potato vine falling in wind. The white dahlia that I'd meant to move weeks ago, before it grew too big, was dug out. It went outside the front gate, near the magnolia tree. Terry has a theory that the more that is planted there, the more normal it will look, and the plants will be less tempting to vandals. He has read research on it. I think there could be something in it. Once planted, I propped a newspaper over the dahlia to shade the wilting leaves. I would like to use a wet towel, but you and I know, from past experience that it would probably not be left there long.

And now, as I have been out to see, the paper is gone too, blown away, I suppose.

While I was standing there, pondering the lost newspaper, a young woman passing with a boy who was sucking a big red iceblock on a stick said, 'Can I put my banana peel on your garden?'

I said, 'Yes, please do.'

The woman, who seemed strange, disturbed, drunk or under some duress, then asked if I would go and fetch a cream labrador dog which she had found at the corner shop, looking lost, with a bite mark on its neck. She said the woman in the shop had given the dog a drink, but did not seem to care much that it looked lost.

As the dog was resting there and had water, there was nothing I could do to be useful, as the pound wasn't open and I wasn't going to give it a home. I told her I would see what has happened to the dog in the morning. All this from a white dahlia being moved.

Monday, 22nd October

A still, quiet, wet day. Misty rain. This will probably save the dahlia and those geraniums. This is the month of geraniums. There are dozens — pink, red, white, cerise, apricot and crimson. The crimson one is climbing up one side of the shed. It will meet the blue potato vine coming up the other side, over the roof and window. All I need now is some white potato vine to cover the roof of the shed and I'll have a flag.

It is time to pull up the nasturtiums. They are waning, though still full of flowers. But if there is to be space for the cosmos seedlings, now almost ready to move from among the cornflowers, the nasturtiums must go. The cornflowers are in bloom. The stocks are full of flowers and the smell is at the gate. All that scent from a one-dollar packet of seeds from Bi-Lo. This place has a big seed stand and all packets are only a dollar each.

I am waiting for the moon to be in its right phase. Terry told me he is waiting a few more days before sowing. I can never remember if it is on a waning or a waxing moon that seeds should go in. I will ask him again today.

Not much luck at all with our share-farming of the sweetcorn. I sowed two more batches, after the first Terry sowed came up so sparsely. But the last packet was a different kind, called Terrific, and I put in the whole lot. No point in sowing a few at a time to spread the harvest when so few sprout.

The beans are a puzzle too. The first sowing of dwarf French beans are doing well, leafy, the length of a hand in height, but none of the next two lots came up. What is the matter? Terry said his friends have had no luck with seeds this year. I read a long article in the *Henry Doubleday Newsletter* on seeds. Now, staring at the bare earth, I think of the turmoil below: the breaking of the seed case, the sprout and then the death. For three weeks, whenever I have been home, I have gone to stare at the earth two or three times a day, anxious as a war bride waiting for a ship.

Sunday, 28th October

Now that the new moon has come, I had a long talk to Terry on the method of planting by phases of the moon. I came away a bit wiser, but also confused. He said it is best to plant seeds of root vegetables on the waning moon, and to plant those whose leaves we eat on the waxing one. As if the moon were to pull down the root vegetables and draw up the leaf vegetables. But what then of flowers? I suppose it is on the waxing moon they get planted, and the same for grain.

Our share-farmed sweetcorn definitely went in on the wrong phase and must be why it has been poor, because the third lot are up and thriving — there are now about fifty plants. But they will be overwhelmed by the six or so that grew from the first sowing. I must move the smaller ones. And is it worth it? Well, it is for the moment, because I am intrigued. How long this will last, I don't know. There is always a limit to my ardour. It is more like a wave of the sea than a mountain. Ephemeral but ruthless.

Children are coming so I'm making another of Belinda Jeffery's recipes.

Sweetcorn Fritters with Spicy Tomato Sauce

60 grams of butter, melted and cooled until lukewarm
1 cup of milk
1½ cups of creamed corn
½ cup of corn kernels
2 eggs, beaten
1 teaspoon of curry powder

1¼ cups of plain flour

2 teaspoons of fresh baking powder

pinch of salt

olive oil or vegetable oil

For the sauce:

2 tablespoons of olive oil

2 large onions, chopped

1 heaped tablespoon of curry powder

2 cloves of garlic, chopped

2½ teaspoons of grated fresh ginger

3 teaspoons of turmeric

2 teaspoons of ground cumin

2 tablespoons of sugar

1 x 800 gram can of diced tomatoes with its liquid

salt and pepper

Method for the sauce:

Heat the oil in a large pan. Add the onion and cook until soft. Stir in garlic, ginger and spices. Add the sugar and tomatoes. Simmer for ten minutes, stirring, until thickened. Add salt and pepper to taste.

Method for fritters:

Heat oven to 100°C. Mix together the butter, milk, creamed corn and corn kernels. Add the eggs and curry powder. Sift the flour, baking powder and salt into the mixture. Mix and leave to sit for 30 minutes. The longer it is left the lighter the fritters will be.

> Heat the oil in a pan. Drop in tablespoons of the corn mixture. Leave some space between them as they will spread. Cook until golden on the base and bubbles appear on the top. Turn and cook the same on the other side. Place in the oven on a plate lined with kitchen paper to keep warm until all fritters are cooked.
>
> Serve with the sauce and sour cream and lemon or lime wedges with parsley. Belinda says they can also be made very small with a dollop of sour cream on top with smoked salmon for a party.

Daily now, there is a bunch of sweet peas, roses and stocks on the table by my bed. It is the first thing I notice when I wake. It is said that hearing is the last thing to go when we are dying. I think smell must be close behind. It would be worth playing music and having good scents and words for the dying, even if they seem to be far away and on the first part of the journey.

I have never believed the unconscious can't hear. Rolling people in a coma over and having a chat with someone else while doing it, about the dance, the matron, the boyfriend or other gossip, has always seemed to me a big mistake. It seems so rude to act as if no one else is there. I suppose I have done it, but I can only remember being upset when I saw it happening, as we two in our white aprons, pink frocks and white ice-cream-cone starched hats washed and turned somebody who seemed so departed from their presence.

Sophia is watering the garden and herself with the hose. Her mother, Cathy, is under the *Ailanthus* tree, reading, and her father is in here on a couch. He is reading his Uncle Tucker's diary of a walk in Botswana.

After the walk, Tucker and his son, Angus, went hunting buffalo with a local hunter. There are camp-fire agreements between the people, the government and the hunters in Botswana. The people get the meat and a fee; the hunter, who takes the visitors around, looks after them and provides everything, also gets a fee; and the visitor gets the horns. I'm not sure what the government gets, but I am sure it is something.

Every society has taboo topics, which spring from ideology full of denial of facts. Hunting fills this role. One day, perhaps, a person will be able to say that hunting increases habitat without being considered an unthinking, callous wretch.

While I don't really wish to go hunting myself, I don't feel superior, much as I'd like to, when my brother tells me he's shot an old buffalo bull. A breeding pair of wild ducks have about eighteen offspring annually. Left to nature, without increase in habitat, all these but the fittest two will die.

Tuesday, 30th October

Ages ago I poisoned Belle Story. An English rose with pink cupped flowers named after a nurse, it stood in a sunny part of my garden at Leura. It flowered a long time and profusely too. One day I gave it too rich a mixture of Thrive and it died within days. I've had to have a plague of cats poisoned once, and this rose and the cats are hard to forget among a few other matters.

When I lived in Adelaide I started feeding two or three feral cats because I felt sorry for them. Soon there were ten or more. There is a service there, and I suppose in other places, that will come and catch wild cats and have them humanely put to death. With so many cats I thought this was the kindest thing to do, so I called. But the man couldn't catch the cats. One fled inside the house, ran through a roasting pan of cool fat, and then slid around with us chasing it as it skidded through the bathroom, the bedroom and kitchen and out the back door. That was when the cat-catcher said there was only one thing left to do, and that was to poison them.

Today, with Philippa's book, *Old Roses and English Roses* by David Austin, open beside me, I saw a picture of Belle Story and began remembering. In both cases, I had upset a balance.

To try and move on from dead cats and poisoned roses, I read the book more carefully. English roses are bred to be repeat-flowering with some of the best attributes of Old Roses, Modern Hybrid Teas and Floribundas. 'They combine the unique character and beauty of Old Roses with their more graceful shrubby growth, and the ability to flower for a long time, both at Christmas and again in autumn,' Austin declares. English roses are really new Old Roses. They also have a stronger scent than Old Roses, if that can be believed. Possibly this is because they have always been bred from fragrant roses.

Here the Claire rose now has more than two dozen blooms. The wind is scattering the petals like pink feathers on the wooden deck. The book says the shrub grows to about four feet by three feet. Yet this bush, planted eighteen months ago, is well over four metres tall.

On the front fence the Ophelia rose is blooming and so is one called Honour. What is really needed is about three more planted on the street side to make a really big tangle of cream and white abundance. Now that there are more shrubs outside the gate, and more lavender planted to fill gaps to make a good hedge, I think it's fairly safe to put more roses there.

Outside the small town of Peel, which has no shops, post office or any facilities at all, there is a derelict house. Ruth, Barbara and I stopped there one day and took cuttings from a rose. After various mishaps, the cuttings came here. They had been out of water for four days. Stuck into dirt in a greengrocer's white plastic box, they have grown leaves. I put one of these outside the gate, near the neighbours' fence, hoping it will grow into the wild big bush which was at Peel. Some of these roses may be rare, perhaps the only one left in the world. I planted another cutting, which has leaves now, into the back garden to take its chances.

A Different Geometry

DIRT

Then, just when I thought
for me it was all over,
I fell in love with dirt.
Mr Right at last.
Wife of Dirt.

I slaved over him,
fed, shaved and was ravished,
year in year out. Not just Spring
and Summer when he can escape
his wife, but other seasons too.

Camellias are our winter quilt
and in autumn, I know he's true
when his face is striped in shadows
of the trees.

At last, a faithful lover
solemn, silent, majesterial,
profound and mysterious
all the things I like in a man.
I've always been a bolter
but this time
I'll go to my grave with him.

Monday, 3rd December

*P*icking gardenias and squashing snails at dawn, I saw how high snails can climb. Out the front, the burgundy hollyhock is two-and-a-half metres tall and has only just escaped the snails. In the lemon tree by the shed, the snails climb taller than my head. It must be the long rains. Now the taller gardenias are out, the creamier ones that turn yellow as they age. Twice as big as the others, their pale petals spread like wings. If this book doesn't smell good, it won't be my fault.

Yesterday Diana and I went to lunch at her friend Liz's at Mount Kembla. We walked around the new vegetable garden Liz has made next to her enormous new studio, which is fifty metres long. They say every man loves a shed and so do some women. On the farm at Peel, Barbara and Ruth were always being asked by men, 'But what will you do with the shed?' It got filled fast. Friends store things there. Barbara has her honey extractor there, and all those other things that go in sheds. But no cars, trucks or tractors.

I am about to make mayonnaise and am waiting for the eggs to reach room temperature. Last time the eggs were cold, and I didn't know that was the reason the mayonnaise wouldn't thicken. I made four lots. All failures. The mayonnaise is to go on a chicken salad which Peri taught me how to make. She used to serve it in her bistro, Scoffs, which is now the Macleay Street Bistro in Potts Point. I gave the recipe in my book *The Waterlily*, but forgot the fried onions. Peri made hundreds of gallons of that salad. I am making it because friends are coming to lunch. All you do is cut up some cooked chicken with the skin removed. Fry three onions for one medium-sized chicken. Add two tablespoons of mild curry powder and cook a minute. Cool and add a cup or two of mango chutney. Stir this into a cup or two of mayonnaise, then mix in the chicken. Serve on a platter on a bed of lettuce with parsley, salt and pepper sprinkled on top. You can use takeaway chicken if you are in a hurry, but not the stuffing. Or use a boiled chicken, as it is more luscious, cooled in the jelly.

Tuesday, 4th December

I love days when you can get into your bathers when you get out of bed. Pity I didn't today, as I could have and meant to. I went out to bring in a bucket for kitchen scraps and saw a drooping branch tip on the biggest lemon tree. Stink beetles had sucked it dry. I took a bucket of water and knocked them off into it. Then I saw a big lemon had dropped and, when kneeling down to pick it up, saw hundreds of snails on the underside of the lower fence railing. I half-filled a bucket with them and then tore out the weed *Tradescantia*. In my favourite white pyjamas, I had the bit between my teeth. I wonder if it was the fact I was wearing these that made the work feel slightly forbidden and therefore more appealing? It added a frisson. All the time I was on my knees, tearing out the weeds, I thought of Barbara Ker-Wilson and her habit of painting in good clothes.

Now all I must do is work out how to kill the bucket of snails. I watched Stefano de Pieri on television as he cooked a snail and pasta dish, using a box of snails a woman had gathered and cleaned by feeding them flour and bran for a few days. When I told Hugh you can eat garden snails, he, like his father before him, doubted me. I once had a bet with his father that the snails we ate at a local French restaurant in Hyde Park, Adelaide, were not imported but gathered from a garden. I won that bet. When Hugh heard the story he decided to cook himself some snails, but they made him ill. He didn't know you must fast them. Now my pyjamas have black knees.

I'd like a dozen more white hydrangeas. Looking at the shady corner where the new clivias, tree begonias and Happy Plants (dracaenas) have gone in, I saw that the two pink hydrangeas I planted last week would be better if they were white. The orange clivia flowers bloom in winter and all this greenery could do with something to light it up — hydrangeas, like white candles in the shade.

Ghilly rang. When she finishes work in Melbourne, she's bringing her girls to have a few days with Jack, who will come as soon as school is ended. She might bring some more jacarandas for the station, if there's room with the bikes in her station wagon. All but two of the jacarandas she gave me have survived. One small one got hit by the poison the council used to kill weeds near the fence. The other was too small, I think, to survive. But it is true that smaller trees do better as a rule than larger ones in transplanting. The poison also killed the willows in the drain, but I have planted more.

I must go over and move the Lilly Pilly, which is planted too close to the platform, so that people don't slip on the fruit. Also, those ficus trees need to be moved to allow them to grow to their full thirty-metre width. I heard a garden expert on radio once saying that she often has to move plants three or four times, until she finds the right position. That was a comfort.

Wednesday, 5th December

I rode to Bulli and ordered the Christmas tree. Caro, my daughter, is coming earlier than planned. She lost a week in the rush that is December. The mat is covered with presents to be wrapped and there is nothing among them that looks suitable for anybody. Tomorrow, I will get on the telephone. I rebuilt this house using the *Yellow Pages* and maybe Christmas can be done the same way. There are no gift shops for ten kilometres and a hard ride. Sounds like the Highwayman.

Yesterday David and I swam in the sea pool. He had not known it was there. We paced out the length and breadth to start. Seventy metres long, thirty wide. The pool had two swimmers in it as we went down the wide steps to enter. Then a class from the high school came and began a game of water polo at one end. We were swimming the length along the wall, when suddenly David veered out diagonally. I was unable to make him hear, as he'd taken out his hearing aid. So he entered the water polo game. We laughed later. The world has another geometry when I am with him.

I borrowed David's Akubra hat, as I had left in a hurry to go to his house wearing my yellow bike helmet, but decided not to ride as I was taking a piece of long white plumbing pipe with me. I was halfway down the street when I realised I must have looked like a medieval jouster. The piping is like those David uses as a gauge when he mows. He said he'd like more. When I held the piping up before him, he did not know what it was, so I still don't know how it helps him to mow. Perhaps it has a glow in the sun against the green lawn.

Thursday, 6th December

Today I went to swim in the pool, but it was empty as it was being cleaned. Suddenly there dawned the possibility of David going swimming alone (as he now says he will) and him not knowing there's no water. Yet the day is cooler and windy, so I think he won't want to swim.

Daphne, Terry's wife, and I have Mr Pooterish conversations about rubbish bins. Today, she said, 'Kate, our bin was taken out last night. I got up (Terry was dead to the world) and brought it in. I thought it was you. Marion's was out too. But yours wasn't. Now I think it must have been Ron coming home from a meeting of Neighbourhood Watch at the school.'

'No, it wasn't me. I only put my bin out early on Tuesdays because I have been teaching. But now I'm not teaching until January I might take yours in, but wouldn't put it out because I know you're afraid of vandals.'

I walked inside and thought, this is what life comes to. Forget the life of the mind, or growing a line of jacaranda, it all comes down to rubbish bins.

I keep thinking of a glimpse I caught of a lyrebird's tail. Perhaps it's because yesterday I had a long talk to Peri, who is on her farm. Peacocks were screaming in the background. We could not believe our luck the day we saw a lyrebird. We had taken a wrong turn and saw a glimpse of the curving tail, like a musical instrument, disappearing in the bush. A flurry and it was gone, like a bird diving into a river. It was as if the lyrebird entered the car and came back with us.

One of David's big magnolia flowers is beside me in a square whisky bottle, looking like some famous drawing I have seen somewhere. Not Leonardo. But like him. Not Holbein (the Elder, not the Younger) either, but that sort of drawing.

Diana said she would come and draw the white *Datura* lilies last summer. The first *Datura* lily is out in a pot on the back deck, so I will remind her. There are two pots of white petunias and two of *Daturas*, which wilt quickly. So far, most nights we have a small rain.

When I began the garden, I initially intended to plant a *Magnolia grandiflora* where the Hills hoist clothes line was dug out. But Peri explained that it would shade everything, so I put in the *Magnolia stellata* instead. The fig tree down at the end of the garden has twenty figs, and sometimes I wonder if I ought to have put a *grandiflora* there. The breathtaking sight of David's magnolia shows that one tree, well planted, is better than half a dozen smaller trees.

The *Gordonia* tree at my gate will soon grow too big and shade the whole front. So I offered it to David. He has dug a hole as big as one of those old rubbish bins behind his shed and put the soil into the bin and then replaced it in the hole so nobody can fall in. Today, he is coming to take the *Gordonia* to his garden in my old wheelbarrow. I can't help thinking, this will be interesting. Little does he know the condition of the barrow. Though if the board forming the base moves, he will find out soon enough. I suppose the flat tyre's a giveaway. In fact, apart from the handles, which are still attached, there is nothing I see now that is as it once was. My new one has been borrowed and not yet returned.

Dolphins, a pod of about twenty, frolicked, going north, as I rode home after buying the turkey and ham at Corrimal this afternoon. It was three o'clock.

'Dolphins!' I crowed to a man. 'Five of them.'

'No, more like twenty,' he said.

'I hardly ever seen dolphins here,' I answered. Then he told me, 'They come past here almost every afternoon.' The way a dolphin swims seems to imply happiness. Such loping ease, it lifts the spirit to watch.

As I was pulling snails from the lemon tree, I remembered another bet I won (besides the bet the snails were from the garden). I've won a few bets over the years. This one was, 'I didn't kiss the waitress.'

'Oh, yes, you did!' I said to my husband, when he asked the day after a lunch why I had given such a large tip.

'Well,' I said, 'since you kissed the waitress and gave me your wallet to pay for everybody, I didn't want to seem resentful, so I dealt it out plentifully.'

'I did not kiss the waitress,' he stated. So the bet was made. A day or so later, he remembered. But so sure that he had not, he bet me a thousand dollars. That was a lot of money then. I still think it is. In the end I relented and said I'd buy a pair of Pierre Cardin shoes instead and he could keep the change. I have a feeling he is still kissing waitresses, but I bet he doesn't bet his new wife that he hasn't.

Saturday, 8th December

On happiness: a chair in the garden; a table in the shade. Is it possible for a married woman to tell a friend that she is happy? Does a woman sitting in her garden annoy a husband? Who do I blame that I don't sit in the iron chair under the big tree reading? Wherever I look when I walk out the back door I see work. Work is like the poor, it will always be with you. Bending down this morning on this beautiful day, dew on the grass, trying to pull wet weeds, slurping tea into the saucer and onto my dressing-gown, I wondered why it is I could not simply sit down and take a good look. Does happiness lie in weeding? The moments when one can forget the self? As you weed, all you see are more weeds farther in, under the camellia, around the hydrangeas, weeds creeping up through the straw mulch and eager as a hungry rabbit, farther and farther in you go until, drenched in dew and tea, you back out and stand in the sun, suddenly aware of yourself. But for a few moments you have been without self-consciousness.

You remember that your friend is coming, you are going to town with her, you must dress. Inside the front gate I see that the two box plants are now too big and block the view, making the garden even smaller than it is. They must be put down the back in the shade, where there are still gaps. It will be a big job. Retreating inside, I think that I was happy walking around in a slightly tormented way, seeing what must be done. Is happiness simply planning? I want to live in the moment. But I think my nature is against it. My brother doesn't like his wife to sit in a rocking chair on the verandah. I saw that when I dragged chairs out one day so we could drink tea and talk. His daughter said, 'Dad won't like this.' Perhaps it's genetic, this greed to improve things. Or perhaps it's universal. Yet happiness was with me in those moments this morning when I stood looking at the lemon tree weighed down with fruit. Looking up at the pure blue sky can seem a balm, a gift. My friend Anthea, who has less in this world than most, says that every morning as she drinks her first cup of tea she gives thanks and says to somebody, she doesn't know who, 'Thank you for this tea and this lovely warm bed.' Sometimes I think melancholy can be an addiction. A certain wistfulness can permeate every hour. I wonder if it is, in fact, a form of happiness, as the person who has this sadness clings to it against all evidence, while all around there is abundance, stacks of grace, like paddocks in summer. I spent years like that. Here, my work is to learn to live with vulnerability, nose to nose with the world, unprotected by melancholy, not letting the weeds give me anything but the pleasure of the dignity of work. And to sit, from time to time, in the garden with nothing in my hand or head but pleasure.

Flash Point

GHAZAL 1

Again, we entered the old gate
in the glorious green gardens.
Under our umbrellas it's impossible to hate
in the glorious green gardens.
hoop and Wollemi pine, fig and ginkgo,
each symmetrical as algebra.

On the path, mud oozing from bats' droppings
there's talk of bait
in the glorious green gardens.
The pyramids of glasshouses hold jungles
of leaves dripping into pools.
You'd almost expect to see lyrebirds mate
in the glorious green gardens.

Two old friends talk of past mistakes,
the trees and what we plan to plant.
Consoled, we strolled in the pitter patter rain
while it grew dark and late
in the glorious green gardens.

everything seems fragile after shock —
I could venerate a worm.
Somehow these ibis seem an authentic
Egyptian frieze
something left by fate
in the glorious green gardens.

'Those purple flowers, Peri, glowing in
that shade
remind me of a bridesmaid's dress I wore.'
'Kate, what we must face is we're heading
to that final date
in the glorious green garden.'

Tuesday, 25th December
Christmas Day, Mosman

*P*eri came into the room saying, 'That was Servio in Brazil. He was ringing to see if we were alright. He says we are surrounded by bushfires.' We walked outside and could smell the smoke. The sky was darker and we had noticed nothing. The fires had been on Brazilian television.

At dusk, the full moon, a boiled rose, hung above the street. The sky was purple and ash fell. We went inside, closed the windows, and twenty of us pulled bonbons and ate Christmas dinner. After the turkey, I slipped away and had a quiet swim in the dark pool in the garden. The eerie malevolent moon stuck to the black wall of sky as if it had been spat there. I swam below, feeling a strange combination of foreboding and being blessed.

On the south coast, my house, uninsured, is safe so far.

Wednesday, 26th December

Thousands have fled firestorms. There are seventy-five fires burning in the state, some lit by arsonists. Five thousand people are fighting the fires.

Bob, Peri's husband, was giving me a lift to the train on his way to work at the radio station, when I had a thought to ring and check the timetable. All trains to the south coast are cancelled and all roads blocked because of the fire. So I will stay longer.

Sleeping on Peri's studio floor, I wake and look out at the Heads with the Manly ferry trailing backwards and forwards. Only the ferries are not affected by the fires.

Nonetheless, the blue jacarandas are blooming. I hop in and out of the pool all day and pray my house is safe.

Christmas dinners were abandoned on tables yesterday as people ran. Decorated with tinsel, fire engines fought fires.

Saturday, 29th December

Still stuck at Peri's, the fires are worse than before. Fifteen thousand people are ready to fight the flames because the winds are strong and it is very hot. Arsonists light more fires, and fires join each other. The ash falls on the back lawn day and night and the beautiful poisoned moon hangs as if filled with rotting rose petals. It feels like war and, in a way, it is. Our oldest, and the world's second oldest, National Park, north of Wollongong, has been burnt out.

Peri and Bob's granddaughter, Natali, is a State Emergency Volunteer, so at least one of us is able to do something. The sales are on and we are watering the garden. Peri and Bob play Scrabble at night on a table on the back lawn. Bob won't play with me because the first time we ever did, I knocked the table over. He said, 'You might be my wife's friend, but I'm never playing Scrabble with you again.' And he hasn't.

Ghilly arrived and we drove to her home at Newcastle. Before we left she sang Musetta in the dress rehearsal of *La Boheme* at the Opera House, and I sat in the audience. We drank tea in the Green Room and read more about the fires. The road north was still open, so we could go.

Sunday, 30th December

It's Ghilly's birthday lunch in an hour, for ten friends. I looked out at Blackbutt Park and thought, what would happen if the fire reached there? Nothing would save the houses beside the park in Ridgeway Avenue, but nobody seems worried. I think maybe we should check the gutters, but don't like to say so. The fires at Leura, when I lived there, made me aware. I remember pouring potatoes into the downpipe, when I had no tennis balls to block the pipes as was suggested, and filling the gutter with water. The sound of chainsaws and helicopters went on day after day. The memory of the pile of branches cut from my trees on my back lawn, almost as tall as my house, stays with me. Now we raise our glasses to Ghilly and the New Year. And to the firefighters.

Tuesday, 1st January

Happy New Year! The fires burn on. Black gum leaves fall everywhere. The train home from Newcastle went through blackened bush on both sides. I'll never travel on a train on New Year's Day again. While a teenage girl quietly vomited and her wild drunken boyfriend ran up and down the carriage, a young Chinese man, possibly a student going down to Wollongong University, put his video camera to the window and filmed the blackened trees. I wondered what his family back in China would make of this scene their boy had entered. Luckily they couldn't see what was going on in the train itself. Bedlam.

My house is safe and still, as yet, uninsured. Understandably, insurance companies don't accept people ringing up for insurance when the house has a bushfire coming towards it.

All's well. Daphne and Terry watered my garden while I was stuck in town. Terry gave me his home-grown tomatoes and cucumbers and my mail. Blackened gum leaves have blown inside the shed. At first I couldn't think what this substance was. Then I deciphered the shape. I ate panzanella with basil and went for a swim in the sea pool. The black leaves litter the beach. It's starting to feel like Pompeii.

Thursday, 3rd January

Thousands of people have been evacuated to the beach south of here, at Sussex Inlet. The smoke has reached New Zealand. Our ash is falling there. Jack, Caro and Peter are here from a holiday at South West Rocks. Caro drove from 7 a.m. and got here at 2 p.m., exhausted. We had a swim and they all slept. Helicopters are dropping water on the fires. Jack and I, floating in the sea, watched as two helicopters flew over, each with a dangling umbilicus waving over the water.

Wednesday, 9th January

Jack and I caught the train to Sydney. Fire was burning exactly beside the track on both sides. The train went slowly through the bush and we expected to be turned back at any moment. Smoke rose through the black trees and flames snickered beside the line for half an hour. We saw plumes of smoke from new fires rising through green bush, in many places on unapproachable hillsides, silhouetted against the calm sea.

Sunday, 13th January

Heavy rain, thank heaven. Dressed like a firefighter, with big shears, I tackled the wild tangled roses in the back garden. It is no good waiting for autumn; the Albertine doesn't bloom then, not being remontant, and the pink Lorraine Lee has collapsed onto the dirt, with two cottage roses making something like a barbed-wire blockage suitable to protect a beach in war. My clothes were in shreds at the end of the job, but the fence is clear now and Terry no longer has to worry about his shed's gutters being blocked with my roses. I took cold baths all day and ran in and out, ragged and happy.

Monday, 14th January

The fires are becoming controlled. Hundreds of firefighters who came from interstate are going home. My sister-in-law, Patricia, from Kingston SA, said two of the men who work for them drove over. She turned on the television one evening, having wondered if they had arrived safely, and saw them in the Willalooka fire engine spraying water. That must be over two thousand kilometres those men drove to help, and all done voluntarily.

The local paper, *The Mercury*, says that everything has a flash point at which it will burst into flames. Conifers ignite at fifty degrees celsius. Eucalyptus trees ignite at between sixty and ninety degrees Celsius.

David has offered to cut up the branches of roses left on the lawn, so they will fit into the bins. He says he enjoys it. But without seeing the thorns, and not using gloves because they make it too hard to sense things, it must be painful. He seems impervious or just stoical to the prickles.

The aftermath of the fires leaves a sad feeling, so much lost and yet so much saved. Lives and houses gone. The beach is still littered with black gum leaves. At night, the sky turns red and now we fold our fear away.

Wednesday, 23rd January

Mung beans. It's something Terry told me over the fence again. 'If you have a tree or plant that's sick,' nodding towards the blood orange, more wilted than before, 'plant mung beans. Then you turn them in and that's the best nitrogen and the plant will love it.'

It rained in the night. One of the loveliest sentences in the language. For hours the sound on the roof was there between the shifting screens of dreaming, turning or just sleeping. At dawn the rain stopped. I walked out in bare feet to look at the new rain gauge, which had overflowed into its container and even out of that onto the red camellia below. As I emptied and poured the water into the measuring tube, it looked so pure and enticing that I lifted the bowl and drank. Suddenly I saw that I had spoilt the measurement by this lavish gulping. As the water went down my throat I remembered an old grey iron pump on an underground tank we had in childhood, and how the water streamed out as the handle was pumped up and down. I remembered the pleasure of making the water rush after its first thin reluctant stream. One by one, my brothers and I cupped our hands and drank the sweet water. Sometimes we used an iron dipper, a lipless jug, which altered the taste of the water, or seemed to, and made it slightly metallic as our teeth hit on the dipper's cold edge. Gulping water is one of life's deepest pleasures. Wells, dams, rivers, ponds and lakes; the way light loves water. As I raised a glass to my mouth the other day, I saw reflected on the surface the sky and branches of trees.

Thursday, 24th January

I want summer to never end. The frangipani is in full bloom, gardenias too. The purple bougainvillea spraying through the back fence is reaching farther up into the jacaranda, which has grown tall. Everything is abundant. But the opium poppies are done for. I shook their seed pods hard as I pulled them out. This has led to something I've never had here before and that is bareness in places usually full of cosmos, both front and back. The poppies had a price. Now it's late, but there are petunias in with *Portulacas*, a funny old plant I love, which fell out of fashion. There are a lot of white salvia seedlings in too, so now I wait to see if it is all too late.

David called today. We walked around the back garden and I showed him the fig with its fruit and silver foil flags to keep the birds off. He felt the smooth grey trunk of the big olive and I explained it is now as tall as the house.

Terry heard us in the garden and passed over cucumbers and tomatoes for us both. We had another of our cryptic botanical talks where Terry gives his country wisdom on growing vegetables, gained from being born on a farm in Queensland. For example, the blood orange I moved yesterday, overcome as it was by the great pink hibiscus, has wilted in shock and looks hopeless. Terry looked down at it below the fence and said, 'If you cut it back hard' — words I hate to hear — 'it will be alright. You know, the leaves that droop never grow back.' Privately, I thought I would still not cut it, in case he was wrong. It has taken a long time for those leaves to grow and the two bits of blossom to come.

David and I walked over to the station with the jacarandas in buckets where they have sat since Ghilly brought them down to me before Christmas. We also took seven or eight small *Ailanthus* seedlings that had sprung up from the big tree.

Once we got through the gate and he felt the high weeds among the plumbago, daisies, geraniums and roses, David bent and pulled them out. I was exhilarated. We walked along beside the platform and decided that six long strides should be the distance between the trees. This is close, but they won't all survive, and if they are too close they can be moved later (did I really say that!). I left the digging to David and ran round to the platform tap with buckets. Handing the buckets over the railing, down to David below, I watched him water the first trees we had put in. Although not all went on the trees (great dips were in the dry mud where a truck had come to do electrical work, and the water slapped over the edges as he walked), much did. It was slow work, because the heavy wide hose won't reach.

After we had planted about fifteen trees, some wilting, some sticks, some healthy, nonetheless all given a chance, we crossed over the train line. Here the bauhinia trees grow and the earliest part of the garden, which is full of daisies, geraniums and the white rose blooming. Among the agapanthus that were there before, we put in eight thorn bushes. Denis had sent these in a heavy sack, along with petunias and tomatoes that he did not want to sell. The thorn bushes went in around the edge and a few in farther where vandals tear up the plants. I had been surprised when I saw the bag of thorns, but I remembered Denis shaking his head one day at the nursery, talking about thieves who climbed the fence and took his pots, saying, 'What we really need is thorny plants.' Now they are in. I had gloves, but David had none and he didn't seem to mind the thorns. Tom, coming down the steps to empty a bin, stood looking worried and I said, 'Tom, you know nothing about this. You haven't seen it.' Meaning thorns may be illegal, like barbed wire. So he walked off. Two boys, who were playing at the station and talking to Tom, got the hose when I asked them and watered the plants. Those who care for things won't destroy them, I hope.

It was three o'clock when we finished. David came back to collect his tomato plants and walked home alone. A furniture truck had arrived in the street leading to the station and had blocked it entirely. I told David it was there, and how he squeezed around it I do not know.

Without sight, everything has a different perspective. But the deeper things remain the same. I keep trying to imagine David's view of the world. North and south, left and right, day and night, all are altered. But a tree is still a tree and a conversation still a conversation. Even though it may be punctuated with, 'Oh, above us now are six pelicans flying behind each other about a metre apart, as if they have measured it.' And no reply is possible or needed.

Tuesday, 5th February

Over at the valiant little railway station, where trees and shrubs are kicked, David and I plug on, replanting. For some curious reason, neither of us has become downhearted yet. Perhaps over time we've become inured to the death of trees because we've learnt that when one is torn up or broken, we can replant two.

Inexorable as the sea, we never give up. I think because it's a vaguely wild thing to be doing, planting a paddock beside a railway line, we are willing to risk loss. The exhilaration of the faintly forbidden cheers us on, as if we were wagging school or hatching some forbidden secret plot like building a hot-air balloon. The fact that David can't see the trees and can only feel their new growth when I put his hands on the leaves, or when I pull a branch over to his face, doesn't affect his ardour at all.

We sit in the shade of a gum we planted ages ago by the platform, David being careful not to hit his head on the platform when he stands up, and drink tea poured from the thermos and eat buns and cake, talking over the news he gleans from Alan Jones on radio.

Sometimes when I decide to alter the shape of the garden, for instance to widen the section by the station steps and to get rid of an unused path, David, who is immensely strong, simply picks up the old wooden railway sleepers that form the shape of the garden and lugs them around as if they were matchsticks, while I try to tell him where it needs to go, nimbly dodging around to avoid the lurching sleeper.

There is now a station rule that we must dress in orange jackets, so recently I helped David put his on while I did up my own. Both soon fell down around our waists as they went on back to front. As David trundled barrow after barrow of old lawn clippings across the line to mulch the trees and roses, I called to him to keep going, not to stop and not to veer off the path. I am at my happiest shouting, mulching, loading and feeling that we are winning the battle to get the trees to grow.

Sometimes I wonder what will happen when we can't garden any longer or one of us moves away. I think then that it is on the trees I must concentrate, as they will outlast us, and whatever happens down below them, what weeds, what Paddy's lucerne or kikuyu grass overtakes the land, the trees will stand. The rest can be mowed and the frogs can croak in the creek among the rushes and the lilies.

After about three hours David and I wheel our barrows across the road with me shouting at the traffic to let us by. We part at the corner, going home to bath and, in my case, to rest.

Among the stones and grass on the western side of the line, a peach tree we planted blooms all pink, and the Claire rose and Souvenir de la Malmaison bloom, also pink, wildly throwing their branches and their petals in the wind. Wild and free as their ancestors once were.

Friday, 15th March

A bird is singing sweetly. A bulbul. In *Silas Marner*, the index calls a bulbul a nightingale, which is a puzzle as the nightingale sings a longer song than this bird. They dart around with their black topknots, like a pen nib.

Yesterday Tabitha at the nursery walked around helping to choose a range of plants to try for a perennial border. It was her last day at work, as she is going to study landscaping full time. I will miss her.

The old rough lavender bushes against the side of the house by the path will go and this trial lot will be planted in their place. The theme is a dusky reddish-pink and while I got enough to cover only about two metres, if that, it cost over fifty dollars, so I see it will be expensive to do the whole side, if this works. I started reading the instructions on some plants, which say to put the tallest plants at the back. This makes me laugh, as it seems obvious.

I have been out tearing at the lavender. The smell is everywhere and the plant is hard to budge. I brought in the labels from the new plants to write them here. At the back Siskyou Pink (*Gaura*) will shelter pink *Echinacea purpurea*, called Kim's Knee High, which is a dwarf variant of the medicinal herb. 'Very alluring to butterflies,' the label says. Then Egyptian Star Flower (*Pentas lanceolata*), in pale pink, will have beside and around it, perhaps (I have to see how they go, away from the placement Tabitha made on the shop counter), the red-tipped grass called *Imperata cylindrica rubra*. And beside these will be a dark brownish-red sedum. In the front, a band of white flowering dark leaf miniature begonias.

This is the look that professionals, and those in the know, get, and now I am on my way towards it. All this because in Mornington I saw Paula's *Sedum*, Autumn Glory, and bought one. That, I forgot to say, will be among these plants, towards the back, because it is a dusky mushroom-pink and should meld with them.

A Barefoot Good Samaritan

WHAT I HAVE LOST

Great-grandfather's stamp collection
A gold sovereign
My mother's silver bracelet (in a sand dune)
Friends
Watches galore
Some hearing
Opportunities
A brace of lovers
Several stone
Parents
A dinner set (at Central Station)
A husband
Luggage
Recipes
My father's moth-eaten maroon woollen bathers
Teeth
Desire for revenge.

Tuesday, 30th July

Bless Ali Gripper. She put the fear of God into me. A journalist on the *Sydney Morning Herald,* she has rung every six months or so for the last two years to see if she could write about this garden. I did not want her to see it because it was still shabby and not at all what I hoped for. I always put her off and gave her the name and address of somebody who had a good garden. So Ghilly and John got a visit among others.

The last time Ali rang and I put her off, I said I would not do it again, and that if she rang in spring, we'd make a date. This has stirred me mightily.

When Gem Flood came in the front gate one day and said, 'Oh, I've been upset about my front garden, but yours makes me feel better,' that stirred me too. There's nothing like seeing something of your own through a friend's eyes. Be it hair, clothes or garden, it can be a shock. And it was merely a passing remark, more of personal relief than malice.

I rang concreters and got quotes for a path to the verandah. Fred came and mixed a colour, with two-thirds white and one birch green, which seemed suitable. He poured a valley, a gully, a river of concrete, while Jack and I stood on the verandah and watched.

When it was dry, I rang Murobond and got a colour card for their cement-covering paints. I painted the side path and the verandah with their Ficus, which looked like pale-green felt when it was done, and matched the new path. Ali, see the effect you have had. I painted the iron railing on the verandah with Murobond Aubergine.

Today Margaret O'Hara took me to Fairy Meadow Nursery. There was a sale of gardenias on. Some were a metre high and I bought eight for five dollars each. It seemed like a dream. I ran around loading up a trolley in a sort of trance, a frenzy of pleasure.

It reminded me of the feeling when, as children, my brothers and I found a paddock of mushrooms, and everywhere we looked, there they were. Such abundance. Such luck and pleasure.

Beautiful plants. I planted them at once with eight bags of organic potting mix. Then I rang my friend Kathy Lake (these watery names are real), because I see I need more gardenias and she will kindly drive me to the nursery. Let's have monoculture at this price.

Stunned with scent, I plan to swagger round like a drunken bee all summer.

Wednesday, 31st July

Kathy took me to Fairy Meadow. I bought sixteen gardenias and eight more bags of that black compost. Few things have made me happier than lugging that trolley up to the counter. I rang Patricia Harry this morning (who has the best eye I know for colour) and asked her what colours I ought to use with these gardenias. Should I have white alyssum for the borders and blue pansies and white petunias? She paused a moment and said, 'Blue pansies? Nah . . . get black ones.' So I did and it is all planted. Now there are forty gardenias in the garden, with glossy green leaves. All planted by 4 p.m. I'm a wreck.

Friday, 9th August

All week there has been a box of bulbs at the back door, but other matters took me away, so the delphiniums have grown shoots in their packets and the Oriental liliums have pink tips bursting out, everything longing to find its place in the sacred dirt.

I have tipped the box out, so that each time I open the door they lie there in blunt appeal.

Once I saw a friend come home from a trip we'd made to the desert and, walking into her bedroom, she took her underwear drawer and tipped it out onto the floor. I have always found this a useful method since, and I copied her. It doesn't exactly work with cutlery but with most other things it's invaluable.

Six white gypsophila are in the box, a plant I've never grown before, and brown bulbs of French shallots, rhubarb and something called the Cut Flower Selection, which must have been a box I ticked back in autumn when I lay on the couch with the Windy Hill's summer bulb catalogue.

Henry Mitchell, who once had a gardening column in *The Washington Post*, says in a book called *The Essential Earthman* that catalogues are one of the most delightful and addictive things in gardening. One reviewer said of Mitchell that he wrote about gardening the way that Herman Melville wrote about whales.

Last year Oriental and Asiatic liliums were a tremendous success all over the garden. I hadn't tried a big order before and they bloomed for weeks. (You might think that there is no difference between these liliums but I assure you there is. The Oriental ones are bigger and more lavishly beautiful; very opulent, like a potentate.)

So what works, I plan to repeat — an old gardener's trick. It has taken me years to learn this or to admit it. I keep saying it but I don't do it.

For instance, rhododendrons are no good by the sea. I have lost half a dozen and should never have tried them here. Camellias I thought were cold climate plants but they thrive here and even the meanest garden with cement, a scrap of well-tended lawn and a few glaring azaleas often has a wonderful camellia tree, pruned within an inch of its life but thriving and abundant.

Dorothy, Diana and I walk to Sandon Point on Saturday afternoons and take afternoon tea with us. We watch the brides (there are always brides here) gavotting in the wind with photographers in black suits running beside them on the cliffs. It is an odd thing that, once dressed for a wedding, people alter marvellously and behave in ways they never would otherwise. Grooms pick up their brides and stand with armsful of silk and tulle on the edge of the cliffs, laughing in the wind. The brides pick up their hems and run, waving their bouquets as if fleeing from a horde. Sometimes I wonder what the fathers think, watching their daughters explode into action.

We have so far never seen a whale even though we search the sea and we know they pass regularly, going north to breed or south to feed. But last week Diana remarked that maybe one day we'd see a bride out at sea and whales marrying.

Recently we went to a camellia show in a Boy Scouts' Hall in Wollongong. The men who compete were there and William and Brad Walker were among them. William, who grew the Laska Beauty I first saw, took us round and we all bought a plant from the stall. Dorothy and I chose Elgans Splendour, a great pale-pink ruffled flower which I put inside my front gate.

Belinda and Clive Jeffery have come to lunch. I wrote her a fan letter, because when I got down to cooking for one, just boiled chicken and noodles or tuna and rice, I thought if I didn't try something new I would break out in sores. I opened Belinda's *100 Favourite Recipes* book and life got a lot better.

What do you make for a food writer? I decided to try something complicated. No reason not to make a difficult situation more so.

Charmaine Solomon's recipe for fried, stuffed cheese balls seemed just the thing. It involves curdling two litres of boiling milk with lemon; rolling it when cool between your palms until your hands become sticky; stuffing small balls of this with almonds, chilli, coriander and sultanas; frying these balls in oil; and then putting them into a sauce made from fried onions and garlic then mixed with half a cup of tomato paste and some of the whey and a cup of cream. The tricky bit is draining the cheese. This involves hanging it in muslin, which is not easy to buy around here, from the ceiling for a few hours over a pan to catch the whey. Don't try this at home, as they say on television about the gymnastics.

When Belinda left, I offered her a litre or so of whey, but she sensibly declined. I thought it strange that you write a letter and end up offering the recipient whey.

Because I told Belinda I'd made Upside-down Tomato, Cheese and Basil Pie a lot, she gave permission for me to quote the recipe. It is a very good dish for lunch or a picnic and will reheat quite well in the oven, but not in the microwave. So here it is:

Upside-down Tomato, Cheese and Basil Pie

1 x 800 gram can of tomatoes

225 grams of self-raising flour

1 teaspoon of salt

1 dessertspoon of mustard powder or mustard paste

100 grams of parmesan cheese, finely grated

125 grams of unsalted butter, cut into chunks

50 grams of cheddar cheese, finely grated

2 eggs

½ cup of milk

6 medium-sized ripe tomatoes, preferably Roma, thinly sliced

a handful of basil, shredded

Method:

Preheat oven to 180°C. Butter a shallow, 26-centimetre round ovenproof dish and line the base with buttered baking paper. Pour the can of tomatoes into a sieve over a bowl and leave to drain. Whiz the flour, butter, salt, mustard and cheeses together in a food processor or rub in your fingers until it is like breadcrumbs. Tip into a bowl. Beat in a separate bowl, the milk and eggs. Make a well in the cheese mixture and pour in the liquid mixture. Mix until it is a fairly stiff batter.

Lie the sliced tomatoes in overlapping circles in the base of the buttered dish until the base is covered. Spread the drained tomatoes over the top and sprinkle them with torn-up basil. Dollop spoonsful of the batter over the tomatoes. With lightly floured hands spread this out evenly, but if there are a few small gaps don't worry as they will fill as the pie cooks.

Bake for 30–35 minutes. The time will vary depending on how thick your dish is. Test by putting a blade in to see if it comes out clean. When, and only when, it does the pie is ready. Remove and let it sit for 5 minutes before inverting onto a platter. Scatter with extra basil leaves.

(If you wish, you can slice one or two red onions into rings and place onto the base of the dish before the tomatoes, which makes the dish richer and more succulent.)

Sunday, 1st September

Peri has come to stay for the weekend. Her station wagon is packed with trees. She has given me three pink-flowering silkwood trees, the pride and joy of Sydney Botanical Gardens. Silkwood *Chorisia speciosa* is written by hand on a white label. The Gardens are now raising and selling them.

There are also a lot of cuttings of begonias wrapped in newspaper, for the dark spots in my garden. I tried these at the station, but the vandals knocked them over too easily. We need stalwart things there. Yet, again, as the garden increases, I feel it will have less damage as it will seem normal to have flowers, trees and shrubs there.

The important thing in public gardening, I've discovered, is to be prepared to lose at least three-quarters of the plants (not necessarily while the planting is actually going on, as that would be too daunting).

I told Peri how one Saturday, after lunch, I was waiting for a train to Sydney and I saw a group of boys wearing back-to-front baseball caps jumping up and down on the benches on skateboards. I realised what had happened to the tall red geraniums beside the steps leading up to the ticket office. There is a steep ramp here and the boys tried to skate down it. But it is so steep, none could do it and they fell off into the geraniums. I saw that it was not malicious, merely that the plants cushioned the falling. This cheered me up, because these children have nowhere to skate: the streets and paths aren't safe, there is no purpose-built rink for them and the station is perfect. They wait till Tom has gone.

I walked around my back garden with Peri, looking for a place to plant a silkwood, as they are superb trees. When we joined the Friends of the Botanical Gardens earlier this year, we were taken for a walk by volunteers and they showed us the silkwood trees in flower. The volunteers we saw later, in their pinafores and hats, were digging up the silkwood seedlings under the trees and potting them.

I thought that if you had an apartment, it would be a good way to go on gardening, if you could be a volunteer, and you would learn a lot too. Some of these women are very knowledgeable about gardens. One of the women we had morning tea with, Margaret Stead, had her own radio talk-back gardening program.

We have decided there isn't any room here for one of the trees. It would only be squashed. So I will put all three in at the station, and may heaven keep them safe.

Monday, 2nd September

Weeded the lawn. Is this madness? Winter-grass is everywhere. It is obsessive and feels like doing a jigsaw.

This weeding, at night I can't stop thinking about it. In bed, I see the weeds and keep prising them out. Am I wasting my time? I've got a sore muscle on my elbow and this wrist feels broken.

Remembering the idea that with one hour of work a day, an acre of bush can be weeded in a month (or is it a year?), I weed the lawn from about three to four, when the children are walking home from the school a few doors away. Their voices rise like waves at recess and lunchtime. The cries of children.

Saturday, 7th September

A day of lilies. Last week, on the way to Diana's on my bike, I saw a creek with arum lilies in bloom. Today I decided to take the barrow and a spade and go and liberate a few. (The road over the creek is to be widened and the lilies will be covered when that happens.) Squelching down into the mud, where the lilies grow in wild abundance, I dug and lugged them one clump after another up the creek bank into the barrow. The mud came up over my knees, and as I tugged the root ball upwards it had to be held against my chest like a child to stop the leaves and flowers falling from the base. As I worked that Michael Flanders and Donald Swann Hippopotamus song about glorious mud cooling the blood, went over and over in my head. Then I thought, this is happiness. We came from the mud and we return to it.

With the laden barrow wobbling from the weight I went slowly home. From time to time I sat on the edge of the gutter to rest. Passing a house with many cars outside and people standing in the street drinking beer, I sat down. An elderly man, with neither teeth nor shoes, came over and said, 'Where are you taking that?' I told him. He said, 'You'd do better if your tyre wasn't flat.' He took the barrow and said he had his pump out because he'd been working on the cars in the street. I stood outside his drive, which had been hosed down, as I was dripping mud. With a few spurts of air the tyre swelled up. Then, calling over his shoulder, the man said, 'Joanne, come down in five minutes and pick me up from the Parade.' I said that he couldn't take the barrow as he offered because he had no shoes.

'Don't like shoes. Never wear them,' he answered, giving me a toothless grin. He set off at a great pace, pushing the barrow with me running beside him. He asked, 'How old are you?' I told him, thinking I was about to get a compliment.

'You are old enough to know better. I saw you come down the road but I thought you were a neighbour who doesn't speak to me so I thought bugger her. But when you passed her house and sat down and came past our house I saw it wasn't her.' By this time his daughter

Joanne had arrived in the car and she drove beside us laughing. We came to my gate and I thanked the man, John.

'I'll take it round the back for you. Who'd you buy this house from?' I told him.

'Jimmy Simpson! I used to work for Jimmy in the railways.' I asked what he did.

'I'm a driver.' And with that John put down the barrow and walked out the gate to the waiting Joanne.

I dug holes and put in all the lilies before night fell. And I leave you to judge with what triumph I stepped into the bath.

Monday, 9th September

Walking around David's garden we were talking about his geraniums, which are in bloom and came from cuttings from my garden (I almost said 'looking at'), when I began to tell him about the glorious day of the lilies. 'That sounds like the sort of thing I like doing,' he said. So I asked if he would like to come with his barrow that afternoon and dig a few lilies.

We walked through the park with me shouting, 'Go left, David. No, right!' as his barrow veered towards new trees that had been planted there. Careening round, we made it to the creek through many a vicissitude. I realised again how often we use the words 'see' and 'look'. They're often used metaphorically too and litter everything we say. Soon after we became friends I gave up trying to avoid words such as these because it made conversation too hard, and in the end I felt it was unnatural and patronising. I think these words don't exclude the blind, they are merely normal speech. 'Watch out!' 'You see.' 'Take a look at that.' 'See how your geraniums are blooming.' And so on a thousand times a day. Now I relax and let the language roll.

I led David down the bank as he held his white cane and a shovel. Coming to a clump of black-leafed lilies and ginger plants, I showed him that he could dig whatever he chose. There was an old bucket lying among the litter and, putting the cane in that beside him, I left him to it and plunged in farther to groups of arum lilies. As I staggered out holding a great dripping root ball to my chest, *squelch squelch*, I lost a shoe. Then we lost the cane and one of the spades. I plunged around, feeling with my other shoe, and after a while found everything and so we went back to work. David's white hat had mud on the back of it, as if he'd been tossing mud like hay over his shoulder, which puzzled us. There was mud on his nose and mud dripping down the front of me, which was for some possibly atavistic reason, amazingly delightful. Perhaps it is a return to childhood. A time of innocence where filth is glorious and free, a most liberating feeling. In the rest of life I am in thrall to filth and spend hours working to be rid of it. Exultant and reckless, I sang the Hippopotamus song to David, and what he made of it I do not know because he stayed silently digging, keeping his thoughts to himself.

After our success, getting home was another matter. With the barrows teetering with plants, we made our way up a slight hill to the edge of the highway. 'Stop. Stop,' I cried as David headed down a sharp bend to the bank of another creek. Worried about us on the edge of the highway, crossing a bridge, I took David's barrow and wheeled it over the bridge, leaving him standing in a field like a statue (or a shepherd listening for a lost sheep with a mud-covered crook). A young man came up and offered to help. With the traffic whizzing by, I think our predicament had become clear. He wheeled the heaviest barrow over rough ground to a smoother safe place and left us, watching over his shoulder as I led David to the barrow.

We were going down a quiet street when an old woman appeared and asked what we were doing. I told her. She began with dire predictions, looking and sounding, in her blue cardigan and shift, like a Sibyl or a member of a Greek Chorus. 'If you plant those lilies they might get into the creek at the railway station.' (We'd be so lucky.) 'You'll be arrested if you plant willows. They are a noxious weed.' I said that the willows I had planted had died, and it is true they have been poisoned by accident for the fourth time by the Railway grass-poisoners. She began to tell me a tale about the RSPCA. I looked behind and saw that David had turned around and was going the other way. I left the old woman and her warnings and ran back and turned him around. 'I think we've had a narrow squeak there,' I said. 'I think we might be careful in future, as that woman knows a lot about the flooding of the creeks and everything that goes on here. She could report me for trying to grow willows.'

Finally we wheeled the barrows in my gate. David offered to dig holes for the lilies so I showed him where to dig. After all I needed had gone in, he agreed to accept some ginger plants and black lilies for his own garden and, as the chill of night fell, he took the barrow from me at the gate and wheeled it home. Night being the same as day, David doesn't need to hurry home at dusk. I asked if I could wash his hat and windcheater and he took the hat from his head. If I'd had my way I'd have whipped off the T-shirt too and he would have walked home bare, covered only in the shelter of the mud.

Now I have a field of lilies and am thankful.

Saturday, 28th September

The silkwood trees are planted at the station. Sinna walked out from the office saying, 'I wondered what was happening. I could see trees waving from the window, and they were moving.' I had been wheeling them over to the northern side of the crossing, where I have not planted before. I thought the trees would be safer there and, with no wires overhead to interrupt them, they could flower in full pink magnificence and frame the crossing. I put two in. Sinna came over with a square bucket, used for mopping floors, and watered them. The third went in on the side near the shops, because that has cyclone fencing and is safer.

Tuesday, 15th October

The lawn is still being weeded and my elbow is so sore I now use my left hand and the dib tool. I put fifteen kilograms of superphosphate on the lawn and watered it in two days ago. And today I threw around a couple of kilos of urea and watered that in. I read this recipe in a garden magazine.

Tom called out as I walked over the railway crossing this morning, 'Kate. Can you come over here? Where did you plant them trees?' Sinna had left the message of how vital it was for the new trees to be watered, but Tom couldn't find them, because she hadn't made it clear that they were in the new northern part of the garden. So I showed him the sticks waving with green mops on top and he said, 'Oh, yeah. I can see them now alright.' I love this concern and co-operation from people who are not gardeners themselves, but who are willing to help. I think back to the months and months I spent asking at the ticket office if we could have some trees planted, and the only reply I got was a puzzled look. Now look at the co-operation of watering the people give.

Wednesday, 23rd October

Today we planted trees in Park Road. I have just come home. Philip Zweers, the botanist from Wollongong Council, chose water gums and tuckeroos. Jack and I letterboxed the residents of Park Road during the school holidays. He'd bring his surfboard and we'd drop the letters in on the way to the sea.

The idea was that every resident should be asked if they would like a tree outside their fence. Philip said it had been found that unless the person wanted the tree, it would not thrive. Wollongong Council were providing the men and the trees so I did as he said. This came hard to me, as I am keen on setting out and hoping others will join in. I always thought it best that way, because then you aren't stopped and at least something gets done. Goethe said: 'Whatever you think you can do, or believe you can do, begin it. Action has magic, grace and power in it.'

I believe this. At the station, I thought that if I asked if I might make a garden, the answer would probably be 'no', because of insurance or other problems. So I began, and it was six months until somebody spoke to me, and by that time the garden had begun to grow. Permission was never asked and has never been given.

This defiance must be in the blood. When my brother Tucker and his son, Ben, got in a canoe and rowed down a salt creek in southeast South Australia twenty years ago, seeing the dead trees and wet deserts and the problem salt was making, Tucker decided to start draining and opening up the wetlands.

Salinity in Australia is estimated to be a sixty-billion-dollar problem. With the stripping of trees to make pasture, the salt in the underground water table rose because the trees were not there to keep the water level down by bringing it up through their roots and dispersing it into the air. The salt now kills the remaining trees and lies in dry salt lakes — patches of poison so large some are visible from space.

After several years of waiting for the government to begin work on a drain they had proposed for a decade, Tucker rang up the Komatsu Company, bought a bulldozer and began. Much of the work was done without permission and the faxes the government sent weren't answered.

Recently I gingerly asked Tucker how much of the drain is done, because he doesn't like answering questions. Never has, never will. 'Eh?' I repeated myself. 'About 250 kilometres is done and in the end it will be about 600 kilometres all up, I reckon. Approximately, that is.'

When Philip and I drove up to the Illawarra Retirement Village in Park Road, heads rose over the fence from a shelter shed where residents had been waiting for us. 'Where are the trees?'

I said they were on the truck down in the park by the station. David and the council workers were also planting in the park — replacement trees for those lost to vandals three years ago. The retired people streamed out while Philip asked where they would like their trees placed. He sprayed the ground with white paint in the spots they chose.

The truck came up, trees waving above the roof. The men got out of the truck and dug. Philip, seeing the soil was just builders' rubble, ordered compost. The truck was driven off and returned with a tonne or so of glorious black soil. While all this was going on, one resident collapsed. An ambulance came, and so in the photographs Philip and I took of the residents, the trees and the workers, the sombre outline of part of the ambulance is in the background. David helped back-fill the holes with trees in them with the compost. The ambulance drove off and, the job finished, David and I walked off down Park Road.

Eucalyptus robusta, or swamp mahogany, went into the park near the drain and the station. They grow fast, and to forty metres. I think that the other trees we established there will protect the tiny ones from vandals by having a psychological effect. The small seen against the large might prompt that impulse of protection we all have for the young. They say that's why animals seldom kill their young, and why, on the whole, we don't either.

The first trees that we put in the empty park seemed to be an affront to people, a temptation or an insult. But now the survivors wave and gleam in the sun. They rustle. I go over and count them like cattle. Each one increases me.

In a fit of energy, David and I went in and dug holes at the station for many geranium and white daisy cuttings. Tom dragged out the hose for us and I watered as we went. Then we locked the paddock gate and left.

Oh glorious, glorious day. While it is true that only about one-quarter of Park Road's residents responded to my letter, the trees are in and where trees go, more may follow.

Friday, 25th October

A phone call yesterday, after months of waiting, from the firm that installed underground electricity wires at the station and, in doing so, dug up geraniums, a frangipani tree which had grown from a cutting and Caro's olive tree. The firm has a policy and a fund to replace gardens they have disturbed. And hallelujah I say to that. Sinna, who is ardent about the garden — my first true convert on staff — told me of the firm's policy and that she had begun to ring and ask for plants.

Two months ago Sinna was called and told that a man would come, and funds were available for him to plant and to spread mulch. I jumped on that, because I knew we could get more plants if we had no labour given. Sinna and I agreed we would ask for the whole amount in old-fashioned roses. We sealed the deal with a slap on each other's arm.

The woman on the phone yesterday said it had been agreed by the firm that we could use a supplier of our choice and buy plants of our choosing. I said carefully, 'And what can we spend?'

'Four hundred dollars,' she replied. I ran over and told Sinna, and took her a bunch of David Austin roses to show her what we will one day have blooming over the white railings.

Coming back from the shops later, I saw Sinna in her neon-orange safety jacket and navy trousers, walking around with the bunch of roses in her hand. I called to her, 'The bride of Woonona!' She answered, 'Well, Kate, I'm scared to leave the roses in the office as

I don't want them stolen, so I thought I'd hold onto them.' I got out *Botanica's Roses* and looked up every name of my favourite old roses and David Austin roses and every gorgeous photograph of a rose that I liked. I made a list and this morning I rang Denis at the nursery. I think, because they have given us plants in the past, they ought to get the business. And, with joy, I read out that sumptuous list: Mermaid, Madame Grégoire Staechelin, the Claire rose, Black Boy, Glamis Castle, Constance Spry, Souvenir de Mme Léonie Viennot, Gertrude Jekyll, Mme Pierre Oger, Mme Isaac Pereire, Loving Memory (also called Red Cedar in Australia), Belle Story (because she was the first nurse in the nineteenth century to join the Royal Navy and I killed it at Leura). I ordered Heritage too, because it has grown so high in my back garden; it is as tall as the lemon tree and Graham Austin, because it has wound its way through the lemon tree and, being a yellow rose, mingles with the lemons (some of which weigh half a kilo).

Yes, I have had my successes. You, reader, have heard much of failure, perhaps because failure has a quality to it that brings out long detail. The fascination with the doomed, the wondering, the puzzle of it. Maybe it is simply a melancholy streak, or it may be false modesty. Hard to know.

Saturday, 23rd November

The roses have arrived for the station garden. Denis pulled up in a van and handed the pots to David, who had to climb the fence as the gate was locked. It was thirty degrees, but we planted all the roses because they may have been stolen if left out of the ground. David dug and I planted in furious haste, because at noon my friend Antonia was arriving to stay from Melbourne.

Among the kikuyu grass and weeds the glorious roses went in, with me chanting their names so that one of us might remember which was which. I buried their names beside them so they would not call attention to themselves and back-filled the holes with rose compost. Sometimes I led David over rocky ground among geraniums, trees and daisies to where a hole was needed. At others, I laid beer bottles, which people had tossed in from the platform, to show him where to dig.

Outside on a fence in the car park we put Mermaid, a beautiful single cream rose, very thorny and a great climber, and may heaven keep her safe. This rose climbs many metres, very wild and tangly.

Nancy Hayward, a red single rose, bred by Alistair Clark, grows in my friend Clare's garden in Rose Park, Adelaide. When Mrs Hayward saw the rose she was not pleased; she said it had too few petals. This makes me laugh: it is a brilliant rose, almost magenta red. Clare grew it from a cutting, just a stick she stuck in the ground. She grew ten Iceberg roses in the same way. 'You only need to dig a hole with a knife and put the cutting in and, for the first year, keep the water up to it,' she told me.

When I stayed with Clare earlier this month, while walking the dog we saw rose clippings jutting out of a rubbish bin with a pink bud on one. We took them home and Clare put one in beside her back verandah post. That's how easy it is. And if it doesn't work, not a lot has been lost. But most will grow. You can't do it with new roses, they say, but I haven't yet tested that. And, after all, Nancy Hayward isn't really new, just mid-twentieth century, so it must be possible with some.

Now at the station, there's a paddock of David Austin and old roses, and that, I reminded myself as I worried over them and the roughness of it all, is how roses first grew. They may feel they've simply come home.

Nobody was at the station office to give us a key, or to unlock the hose shed for us, so we had to abandon the plants without watering them in.

My friend Antonia arrived on a train and sat on a log talking (we haven't met for twenty years) while David and I planted the last three roses. We walked home with red faces and a barrow full of empty black plastic rose containers and beer bottles. If I had been told a year ago that I would have twenty old roses to plant, I would have thought it a miracle, and in some ways perhaps it is.

Sunday, 24th November

So hot that I woke thinking of the unwatered roses and thirty-degrees forecast. At nine Antonia (who is an artist gardener and has made big installations at Mildura where her ancestors, the Chaffey brothers, began orchards) and I walked over to the station with buckets. From a tap on the platform, which, luckily, had the handle left on it, Antonia handed down the buckets of water to me standing in the paddock below. Everything got half a bucket of water and then we walked down to the beach with the buckets still in our hands.

There had been a storm and seaweed lay in heaps on the sand. After washing the seaweed in the sea we filled the buckets and brought it home. Then Antonia told me how to make liquid seaweed fertiliser.

Saturday, 30th November

I wrote a poem to send with Christmas cards today. I began it a month ago, after a walk in the small park next to the station, around the trees that the council, local schoolchildren and I planted. The children, in their green uniforms and hats, ran like a flood of water over the grass as they saw the men and me standing among the seedlings beside the truck. One or two trees didn't make it into the holes that Dave, the council worker who helped me with my garden by building the side path, had dug.

All the advanced box trees we planted around the East Woonona Circle car park were torn up within three weeks. But those close together on the edge of the drain near the fence, planted there on Philip Zweers' advice, survived. 'They seem to make a microclimate and to safeguard each other,' he had said. And so it proved to be. We did lose about a third, but those that lasted are tall now.

CHRISTMAS POEM

>'What is in the East?'
>   Elizabeth Bishop.

What is in the East?
Hope, that's what.
Dawn too
and camels —
they always strode
from East to West
embroidered across
my brothers' shirts.

The washing line
lies in the eastern portion

of the garden
right behind the shed.
Sheets flap there like tents
and in the farthest paddock
to the East are all the sheep
that the drought has left.

The dried-out creek
lies in the East
an arid metaphor
for a time drained
of so much hope and yet
the East exists
and cannot be erased.
Stars emerge as if on strings
pulled up and down on whim
by kings.
The fact is there's always
something hopeful in the East
but only some can see it
and first they need to look.

Counting the Trees

COUNTING THE TREES

Five willows two olives
ten gums four figs
two melaleucas six jacarandas
three silkwoods.

Trees
little dogs
barking and yapping
at the sky.
I count as I walk
by the creek.

The trees meet me
the mother
the lover who dug the hole
and watered them in
who desires them to grow.

One gum was my sick stick
wrapped in a rug
of barbed wire
safe from the vandals.

Now it is taller than I
and circles the sky
silver and rustling.

It nestles its roots
deeper and deeper
stitching the earth to the sky.

I bury my face
in its leaves
and say Oh my love
Oh my great tree.

The willows green swans
grown from sticks
drink in the creek
and sprout leaves
and soon branches.

Willows, I wait for you
to lift the great fans
of your wings.
You are family to me
harmonious children.
I can feel my hair
turning green
rustling and glistening
my feet growing down
arms high
laden with air and mirth.

Monday, 20th January

*Y*esterday Jack and I walked around the Botanical Gardens in Sydney. I looked at the silkwood trees, the offspring of which Peri bought and gave me for the railway station. These are native to South America and are thriving in the Gardens. They had immense pink blossoms when we first saw them, and the seedlings, which sprang up around them, are what we now have.

Here at home, honeyeaters are in the creamy Moonlight grevillea on the edge of the drive. It has grown very fast: in three years it has reached roof height and is full of flowers the colour of clotted cream.

David and I have had weeks of talk about a tulip tree he bought, on my advice, for his front garden. When I read out the description of it growing twelve metres across and extremely tall, he hesitated, because it could touch his roof's gutters. For weeks the tree sat in its bag on the back lawn, until I took Peri round to give an opinion. She said that it was far too big and it would be best to plant something smaller. A *Gordonia* perhaps. We had tried a *Gordonia* before, but it had suddenly died, because, we think, the clay soil gathered too much water, being in a small dip on the edge of the lawn.

David went to Canberra for a few days, and in that time the tulip tree, leaning in the shade of the shed, collapsed. I found it dried out, a mere set of tall sticks. David watered it for weeks, but nothing happened. One day he said he was going to plant it in the back garden: 'I am going to dig a very big hole. As big as a rubbish bin.' Suddenly I felt sick of this tree and knew it was hopeless — digging a hole a waste of time. I tried to disguise my irritability and said that at least the hole would be useful for another tree when the tulip tree didn't grow. It was as dead as a dodo.

I'm eating humble pie. The tulip tree is sprouting. David fingers the buds and small leaves and says, 'These are leaves, aren't they?' Certainly they are. I told Peri and she said, 'Oh, God. Never mind, it will take years to grow.' (Meaning it will shade the whole backyard in its fullness.)

I took some self-sown tomato seedlings around to David a few months ago. He has a small square-fenced vegetable plot where he dumps all weeds and lawn clippings, along with a blown-down wattle tree that he cut up. Now the tomatoes are covered in fruit. We staked them, tying them up with stockings. The fences, covered in vines, keep this area very hot and it is also that which makes everything grow fast. We found two ripe cauliflowers among the weeds, which we picked; one a bit too yellow to eat, but the smaller one was perfect. These had been from a punnet of seedlings given by Denis as too advanced to sell. We had forgotten about them and, with no attention at all, they flourished, hidden by the weeds. This is the best soil I have ever seen. Soft, full of worms, warm and lush. I could get into a bed of it myself. And, of course, will one day, like it or not.

Wednesday, 22nd January

There is something about summer that makes me crave my mother's rice salad. Here is the recipe. She wrote it in her book, calling it 'Shop Rice Salad', because she made it by the gallon for my brother's chicken shop, years ago in Gawler.

Shop Rice Salad

1 kilo of white rice, plus one cup. Cover rice with water to a thumb-knuckle length over the rice. Boil

for ten minutes. Allow to stand, covered, ten more minutes. Pour cold water over it through a colander and leave to drain and to cool. Then mix one grated onion, two tablespoons finely chopped parsley, half a bunch of celery (cut finely), three large carrots (grated and covered with the juice of one lemon and one orange). Add one cup of sultanas and each chopped green and red capsicum.

Dressing:

1 dessertspoon curry powder

1 dessertspoon dry mustard

1 cup sugar

¼ cup olive oil

1 cup vinegar

Mix these things and pour over the rice, which has been put in a serving bowl. Add the vegetables last, stirring gently. At the end of the recipe my mother has written . . . 'Good'.

Diana has gone to Cyprus to write a book about the archaeological dig of the fourth-century theatre. It's been minus eight degrees in Cyprus. She fled the bushfires and only just caught her flight by taking a long trip around the fire. Whenever I see a white *Gaura* flowering I think of Diana, because she told me about it growing on archaeological sites.

Today a card arrived from Nicosia, where Diana writes about buying buds of narcissus 'which have opened with their sweet clean scent filling my room'. She says:

> We walked to the main square at midnight on New Year's Eve, a band playing Theodorakis' old songs, a few rather patchy fireworks — the people dancing, and suddenly I realised they were migrant workers from Sri Lanka and India. Sikhs in turbans, whirling to Greek music, and beautiful blonde Russian prostitutes in lace tights; Cyprus a melting pot as ever.
>
> I went to the markets in the old city on the first day here; the smell is so familiar, a mixture of incense, souvlaki and petrol fumes.

Thursday, 23rd January

A great day in the garden. I rode to Corrimal and bought pink and white and blue *Lisianthus* for the front gate bed. A bargain of white gladioli, *Ismene festalis* Inca lily (I am trying it again after no luck with the first) and white *Nerine* lilies. I moved a small sick rose which has never thrived from outside the front gate.

On the matter of that dream of mine, to have a hedge of cream and white roses like the one I'd seen on television, it was not successful. Inside the picket fence they got only morning sun. Roses are very obliging plants and will endure a lot, but they cannot cope without six to eight hours of sun a day. At Leura, I tried every kind that were supposed to be able to manage with less sun. The only people I ever saw at Leura who had really great roses were Nan Evatt, the nuns in the mall and Cheryl Maddocks. One rose has driven me mad, and every time I return I see it beside a pergola in the mall; it is Altissimo, a great red rose, and it has bloomed once, as far as I know, since it went in a decade ago. It is in the shade. I want to leave a note in the letterbox, but do not dare. The rose deserves a note. The house is dark terracotta pink with mullioned windows. Who will move the rose?

Jane in Adelaide, where everybody, from the best to the worst gardeners, has radiant roses, had a climbing Maria Callas over her front verandah and that's a sight to see. It's twenty metres long at least. Highly scented too.

I moved the hedge of pale roses by the front fence and spread them about in sunny spots and this saved them. The lesson is hard to learn. Over and over, I see that even people who know a lot plant things where they are going to have a hard time.

I didn't know that violets could be weeds. Pulling them from the trunk of the other pink robinia at the front bed, I saw that it has collar rot. I have poured water and fertiliser on that tree. Nothing made any difference. Nan, who gave it to me, said to have a look at the place where the trunk meets the earth. There it was, all spongy and sick. Denis told me to use white oil. He delivered a bottle of it. I couldn't see that there were instructions, such as a booklet taped or stuck on the back, so poured it holus-bolus onto the neck of the tree. Kill or cure. Nan says she will give me another robinia, but I am keen to save this one, so I wait.

Friday, 24th January

Barbara and Ruth rang from Peel to say they have taken the honey from their bees and that they were badly stung, more than any other of the three years they have kept bees. It is a bit too late in the season, Barbara says. They got eleven litres. With no poisons in the house, not even fly spray, and none on the trees, they can sell the honey as certified organic, if they decide to. So far, they have always given it away or bartered it. They were properly dressed for the job, Barbara says, but sweat made their clothes stick to them, and the bees stung through the cloth.

I have been putting out seed for birds on a piece of wood nailed to a corner of the deck railing. A white cockatoo, unlike any I have ever seen, comes. It looks as though it has been rolling in ashes. I can't tell if it is old or young. They live to be about a hundred, I think. My grandmother had one in a cage on her back verandah and it was almost as old as she was, she said. Diana taught me this trick of nailing a board to the railing. She has lorikeets by the dozen, many white cockatoos, which eat the railing, and after they have gone pigeons come. Now green parrots come here, a few minutes after the white cocky. They all come within half an hour of the seed being put out. I do it silently, so I can only say what I have said before: it must be that they smell it.

A huge black fat crow was strutting around the lawn this afternoon and I wondered if I had upset the balance by putting out kitchen scraps. I don't want the nightmare plague of crows that Peri has on her farm.

Christopher Lloyd's book, *Colour for Adventurous Gardeners,* has come in the post. I read him on white. A great burden of unsullied purity of white. Cold, staring and assertive, it draws your eye but makes you wish it hadn't. It is the colour of ice and snow and once was the colour of funeral flowers. Professional landscape gardeners of the worst kind are wild about white. They have a formula of some dark green *Murraya* with glossy leaves, white flowers and scent, white agapanthus, usually the small variety, and a line of black mondo grass and that's a garden. I think you might be able to do better yourself even if you don't know much. At least a garden done by a person without a formula would look interesting. Don't worry, I have had my flirtations with white. I still like it, but it needs blue and some other colours. Blue is a wonderful colour for furniture or buildings in a garden. It's what Henry Mitchell recommends.

Because I am going to leave self-sown white cosmos all through the back bed, I have decided to sprinkle Peri's wild zinnia seeds through. She got several ounces of this seed from a gardener at Nimbin, when we went to see a collective community a year ago. I was afraid that it might become a weed and spread into the native bush near the sea. But it has been a mild, though blazing bright plant, and gives the most wonderful zinging orange splatter to a bed.

I once gave a book by Gertrude Jekyll to Peri for a birthday present and she was so upset she said she went to bed for two days. Her Mosman garden and her farm garden are full of brazen colour. The diagrams Gertrude drew of coloured plants, arranged as a painter would, made Peri feel her garden was a failure. But Peri was a bit before her time. Colour: purple, orange, scarlet, dark blue, yellow; it all goes together now.

The Jekyll book was another gift that didn't hit the spot. I have never given Peri anything that she has truly liked or found useful. She doesn't say that, of course, it is just that later on I work it out.

As I stood on the deck this morning, staring at the garden, I saw that the coastal banksia, one of the first trees planted here at the same time as the olives, is taller than the house. It towers behind the shed, next to the olive, which has no fruit this year. It must have put all its energy into growth. Out the front, beside the road, both olives have plenty of fruit. I am waiting for some to grow black and then I will harvest the green and black as I did last year.

I couldn't find a recipe for pickling, but half-remembered reading about buckets of brine soaking the fruit over weeks. I had read Patrice Newell's book, *The Olive Grove*, where she said something about cutting the olive before soaking. I did that and it was a terrific success.

For about two months the olives lay in a bucket of strong brine which I changed every three or four days, more often at first. Then they were drained and put into jars with garlic, rosemary and olive oil. After about a month, they were ready. People couldn't tell that they were homemade. It was not a big job to put a slit in each olive and it was this that leached out the bitterness.

Once, in Victoria Park, Adelaide, near where I used to live when married, I was flying a kite with Caro and I took a fresh olive from one of the trees. I spat for half an hour. The taste wouldn't leave and there was no tap nearby.

Wednesday, 29th January

The height of summer. A still morning. Only birds calling seem to move the air.

I have decided that two summer crops of flowers in the big back bed may be the best way to manage it. The early big pink poppies fell in the rain and wind, as they always do, and the tall white cosmos fell down after seeding the bed. Now that the barrowloads of cuttings of climbing roses have been taken away, all is bare. I told Peri, on the phone at the farm in Queensland, of my plans for the back bed and that I thought two summer crops, relying on a late summer or early autumn flush, will be the way to do it. As she didn't tell me not to, I think it might be alright. She has saved me from a lot of mistakes with her advice over the years.

I rode to the nursery and Pamela, who has taken Tabitha's place, suggested some dilandrenias, which I bought. I got a white *Gaura* too, called Dancing Butterflies, and a dozen pots of white petunias with some pink and blue. The soil is rich and it's bare of the rose branches that tore shreds from my clothes. Now, eyeball to eyeball, the garden and I stare at each other. I hose myself down head to toe as I work in the sun.

David came over late this afternoon. He offered to water the garden while I am at Peel for six days visiting Ruth and Barbara. I thought of the prickles on the robinia tree at the back tap, the pots of geraniums all around, but said, 'Thank you. Let's have a trial run.' He went to the tap and traced the hose up and turned it on and I handed him the end. Together we traced the brick edging Jack and I had built with cement months ago, showing the edge and length of the bed. I went on planting while David watered. As we stood talking afterwards, he gave me a hosing, but as it was very hot, it was pleasant, though unexpected.

It showed again that David's hearing lets him down, in that he does not know where a sound or a voice is coming from. I try to imagine this and can't. Last month, when I was away for Christmas, David brought in my mail and put out my rubbish bins. He said when I asked him if he'd collect the mail, 'Just one problem, Kate. Where's your letterbox?' I told him that if he traces his hand along the fence from the gate, he will meet a passionfruit vine, a climbing rose and the box. Nothing's easy.

Thursday, 30th January

It is a continual truth about gardening that, whatever successes are waving in your face, it is the weeds, the sick plants, the bare spots, that call out. I keep reminding myself that if I had seen this green and blue alley four years ago, I would have felt triumphant. But that's not the way it works. So today I took a walk around, remembering what was here before.

The side path is the most successful part of the garden. Plumbago on both sides bends over the path and dark blue spikes of bog sage wave around. The whole thing is crammed with plants in bloom, and the look is what I was probably aiming for, although I could never envisage it. A wild, waving, frondy, spiky look, which Philippa first taught me in her garden, is what has grown and I rejoice.

Down the back, under the *Ailanthus* tree, the hydrangeas are in bloom and the arum lilies I got from the creek are thriving. Farther down, Peri's white and pink tall begonias are flowering among bird's-nest ferns and metres of self-sown blue Michelmas daisies. Margaret O'Hara's clivias, which have travelled with her from three houses, are now in six gardens on the coast, including mine, where she has given them to friends.

Along the back fence the jacaranda, which the previous owner planted from a cutting, once used to lever a log during a train mishap, is twenty-metres tall. The pinkish-white oleander I brought here in a pot from Leura nursery has covered the iron fence, and next to it a pink hibiscus is ten metres tall and in full bloom.

Outside my bedroom window the frangipani is in full bloom. I have taken many cuttings from this tree and some have grown beside the train platform. Two which had taken on the eastern side (the place dug up eleven times) were lost in the last disturbance, but then they cost nothing. I was sorry to lose them, because you get fond of a plant over the years.

Outside the bathroom window, in full shade, nothing has ever grown and I have wasted a lot of plants and time there. It has taken years to learn a lesson I thought I already knew. That is, to grow plants in places that give what they need. There is something perverse in me that keeps ignoring this. I can't understand why I keep doing it. Had a camellia been put there, it would now screen the window even though they need some sun to bloom. Instead, I planted grevilleas and these, by coincidence, are in today's green rubbish bin collection — mere dead stumps.

Friday, 31st January
'Girra Girra', Peel

I have been out picking strawberries. Ruth has three strawberry beds, miraculously without snails. It may be too hot here for many snails in the summer, or it could be that and the combination of frost in the winter.

Today I read Martin Luther's biography about him sheltering at the castle of the Wartburg, where he had picked strawberries as a child. It shows how long people have been gathering strawberries. They may have been wild strawberries, it doesn't say, but it seems likely that they were grown domestically, and this would have been in the late fifteenth century.

The native trees we planted when Ruth and Barbara bought this farm are mostly flourishing. The wattles have just finished blooming and some are five metres tall. The eucalypts vary between half a metre and three metres tall. About a quarter of the trees died in spite of a watering system being installed. But all around, dozens of self-sown gums are sprouting. Walking around with Ruth this morning, I asked her about them and she said, 'It's because there are no sheep here any more.' I never saw a clearer sign of the damage sheep do to land. This is why there is so much erosion here, the deep runnels where the water runs, draining out the soil like a haemorrhage. The bales of straw and rock put in the erosion ditches have helped in many places. Over and over I see how the land wants to mend itself. The self-sown trees and the way the land makes the women want to fill the eroded places and help it heal, as if bandaging it. The women themselves are part of the land's healing, as they live on the land and, in empathy with it, they respond as if to a cry.

Each day for five hours Ruth goes out onto the verandah and writes her thesis on sati, the Indian practice of widow-burning. Barbara walks up to the shed and writes her PhD, comprising a novel among other things, and I lie on the couch in the house and read.

Len and Helen came to lunch today. Helen is writing her PhD too, on ecology and feminism. She told me about her trip to India, to a community that grows almost all its own vegetables, and another one of women only, which began in the seventeenth century in Europe.

Last night, at dusk, as we were setting the table, three kangaroos, probably a family as they were different sizes, came to the wire fence which Ruth has put around the garden and ate grass. The female probably had a joey in her pouch as well as the small one that hopped around eating. The two dogs inside the fence seemed to know the kangaroos and simply lay on the verandah on their couches, watching, unsurprised.

Wednesday, 5th February

Hot, with steady rain all day. I took the Peel rose cuttings out of the glass of water and, as Clare told me, dug a hole with a knife's plunge, dipped the cuttings in hormone powder (although this wasn't in her method) and stuck them in. Watered well for a year, some should grow. It feels like saving a cave painting.

It says in an old *Your Garden* magazine (May 2000) that Pat Toolan has a heritage rose register where you can send details of a rose that may be worth saving. Her local council inspired her because, for almost a hundred years, roses had bloomed at a cemetery fence in a thirty-metre bank, which they sprayed and killed the lot. She began a formal register of old roses growing in cemeteries, ruins and gardens. She propagates any that appear to be under threat. Genetic material is saved this way, but heritage and cultural value are better saved if the roses are preserved in their own situation. That's not always possible. Local councils need to be made aware, Pat says, so that they will value what they have, and save it. The number to contact her on is (08) 8564 8286, or write to her at PO Box 61, Keyneton, South Australia 5353.

I had the Peel rose growing for a year, out on the nature strip by the front gate, but it was hit and cut off twice at the butt with the lawnmower. It re-grew; then it was kicked and this time it died. I see now that a rose can take two calamities, but not a third. It ought to have been planted in a safe, sheltered sunny spot. I have learnt these things on the back of many losses. Old people are important for gardening, because they know a lot of forgotten things and tricks that can save plants. They are a bit like heritage roses themselves, some of them.

The heavy cupped mauve-pink blooms of the Peel rose, highly scented, may be known to others by name, but to Ruth, Barbara and me it is a mystery which makes us desperate to save it. Diana, due home soon from the dig in Nicosia, probably feels the same about one of those fourth-century mosaic floors she is always drawing, photographing and weaving patterns from.

I have been over at the station, with an umbrella, planting daisy clippings near the Mermaid rose and the sprouting passionfruit vines. I can't tell you of the zeal and pleasure. I am rabid to have this garden grow.

Thursday, 6th February

The frog is back! As I walked out in the heavy rain to take a bucket (of rainwater caught while I was away) to the pond, I heard the frog calling. After three months away, it's back. Cleansing rain. We have had a quarter of a year's rain in two or three days. The back garden squelches and shines with water.

In the night the frog called like a clock.

As I rode on the bike path south to Corrimal today, frogs were calling in a small creek by the caravan park. It means that within four days of heavy rain, frogs emerge and some reach calling stage. Perhaps it means that the adult frogs have been hibernating, buried in mud. I don't know why the frog left the pond made from the old bath, but I know why it came back. Yet we have had heavy rain while the frog's been gone, not as heavy and fast as this, but regular rain, and the frog did not return all through that time.

I am taking some frangipani cuttings to the station in a minute, and I expect the drain, which is now a creek with trees and vegetation, will be full of frogs' noise.

Peri is coming for the weekend. Her living-room ceiling fell on Monday night, when the big rain began. Some tiles on the roof were broken, the ceiling filled with water and collapsed. It is a Queen Anne Federation house, so now she's looking for a plasterer who can mend it in the same style, and living with intriguing calmness among buckets and plastic.

Later. Only one frog croaked in the creek while I stuck daisy and frangipani cuttings into the bank. I never manage to see a frog there, no matter how quietly I creep.

I see now that the fervour with which I began the station garden has waned a bit, but whenever I go there and start to dig I become engrossed, and as I look down the line to Bellambi I long to see trees receding into the distance. I looked hard for the palm seeds Jack and I planted months ago, but so far no sign of life.

When we were planting Park Road last spring, I told Philip Zweers, the botanist, that we had sown palm trees down the railway line and he groaned. I asked why and he said, 'They aren't natives.'

'Beggars can't be choosers, Philip. I plant whatever I can come by or am given.' But I saw his point. That day, David and I saw a fallen hakea tree in a front garden. The young couple who had just moved in there ran out when they saw the truck with the trees. The man explained that they had lost my letter asking if they would like a tree, and so had not been in touch. They wanted a tree and they got one. David and I tore off the wooden seedpods from their hakea, which Philip, seeing us doing it, said only lasts about twelve years before falling as this one had.

I burnt those seeds and sowed them in a seed tray with smoke chemicals from the Botanical Gardens' shop sprinkled on top. But from the dozens of seeds of all kinds, including flannel flowers, that I sowed in that tray, almost nothing came up. What did come up were some seedlings I had thought were the Guinness black and cream poppies that Patricia Harry had given me. After months of watching these strange fronds, so unlike any poppy, I remembered that there had also been some dill planted at that time. I went out to the bed where it grew and tasted it. Dill indeed. So I lost those poppies too.

Today I took a bag of native seeds I had gathered at Tucker and Patricia's at Watervalley in November and, without any burning, or anything at all, I threw them along beside the train line, past the platform to Bellambi.

The *Eucalyptus robusta* which I bought for seven dollars three years ago is twenty metres high, I saw today. Well, if not twenty, fifteen. Once a tiny thing in a pot, it seems incredible it could be so robust. It is inside the station's cyclone fence, so I think it is safe — well, as safe as any tree can be and that is only a mite safer than a person. (Trees don't walk across train lines.)

When I began to garden here, my ardour was only matched by my ignorance. I was thinking, as I walked home from the planting of the cuttings today, that it takes at least two years, in a new garden with its new geography, to learn the most basic things. I used to watch Philippa when she began a garden: the way she simply dug and slipped things in. She was like an inexorable, benign bit of weather. She just kept coming on and on. The garden was never dug for plots, as some do. Just a knife, a hole and a cutting. Within a year, in both the gardens I saw her make from scratch, she had things waving and looking natural. I learnt from her to begin, to start anywhere.

What I see now is that knowing so little about the climate and the soil meant that while this method has given me trees quickly, most things have to be moved thrice at least.

I watch the vegetable growers, Terry and also Peter Cundall on TV, and the way they prepare their plots as if making beds for people. I watch Daphne, Terry's wife, who, when I first came here, told me that onion weed is such a problem that she plants almost nothing in the ground. She has got around this problem through a series of about a hundred black plastic pots in which her entire spring and summer crop of *Nemesias*, petunias and phlox grow.

You can put a person down anywhere and, if you knew their previous garden, you will be able to recognise the new one within six months. Their hand print will be clear. We think we go around in the world somewhat invisibly, but few things show us as what and who we are as the gardens we make. Recognisable almost, as our faces.

Friday, 7th February

When I plant trees I remember Roger McDonald, who is another frenzied planter. He says in his book *The Tree in Changing Light*, that when his friend's truck came loaded with trees it was like a float in an agricultural show. I remember when Philip Zweers, David and I planted trees in the park and the street, the truckload of trees arrived looking like something biblical. A mass of waving fronds. How long people have been using branches as signs of joy. Think of Palm Sunday. On the matter of tree planting, I saw on 'The Inventors' television finals that a plough has been invented that doesn't tip the soil up on top of itself but rather spins it in a rotary fashion, letting the moisture stay within, and pulls down the weeds to make humus and mulch, all the while letting the microbes from the deeper soil stay where they are healthiest and those near the top stay where they also thrive. I am mad to have one of these ploughs. I could get to Perth along the railway line. The

Nullarbor wouldn't be the Nullarbor any longer. It would have an avenue of trees.

We've had an episode of snakes at the station. Tom greeted me shaking his head recently, saying, 'You're going to have to pull up all of your garden, you know. One of them young fellas saw a snake down there. I've rung Wollongong and they're sending a snake expert.'

I heard this with as much calm as I could muster. Next day the station was swathed in blue-and-white bunting like a murder scene. The whole garden was roped off. They were waiting for the snake man to come. A day or two passed. I asked Terry about snakes at this time of the year. (Tom had said that the snake had been about a third of a metre long and very thin, showing me with his hands separated as if telling a fishing story.) 'They're only little grass snakes, Kate. You're lucky if you get them in your garden. They eat the insects.' I walked over to tell Tom, who said the snake man had been. The bunting was taken down and the event faded away, as these things do, with nobody being very sure of what actually was seen or heard or said or by whom. But it was another lesson to me to keep my head when I hear of orders to tear up the garden.

Saturday, 8th February

Three pink and grey galahs. They were sitting on the deck railing when I walked out this morning. One put its head to one side, blinking, as if pondering a question, almost thoughtful. After a night with Peri interrogating our lives, it seems a perfect illustration of our talk. Giving no answer except its pink and grey beauty, it flew away.

Later. A bonanza. Today Peri and I drove to Wollongong Art Gallery and on the way saw a sign to Bunnings Hardware. Turning in, we stopped and went into a vast store. Peri bought me a watering-can. I got two Majestic palms, self-cleaning; meaning they drop their leaves themselves. A native of Madagascar, they enjoy humidity, so will fill spaces down near the frog pond in the mottled shade. I felt uplifted and radical buying these palms because I've never thought of putting palms in what's really an old-fashioned cottage garden.

As we walked around, I saw a fishtail palm, pot-bound and leafless. I asked if I might have it cheaper for the station garden and the manager, Rhonda, said I could have it free, as it had been left, waterless, behind other plants. Peri went to get the car and I walked out with the green-tipped tall palm and saw a pallet of trees outside the door, reduced to two dollars each. 'Look what you've missed,' I said to Peri as the car pulled up.

'No, I haven't. I saw them on the way out, and I'm going back to get the lot for the station.'

As we loaded some of the trees into the station wagon, Peri said she had asked if there was a man she could hire there who would come and help me plant the trees. There was nobody and that's how I like it. It is a volunteers' garden and I don't want people paid to help. David and I can do it. The trees were in my hair as we drove home. We put them on the verandah and went back for the second lot.

Organic lucerne pellets were on sale at four dollars for twenty kilos, which had been reduced from over twenty dollars. I bought some and asked why it was cheap. I was told it was beginning to break down and they wanted to get rid of it quickly. We loaded everything in, along with six terracotta pots, also a big bargain, and saw a sign to a fair. We went in and bought Indian food and some spices, asafoetida and other mixes. Peri walked around eating a packet of onion fritters while I slumped in the car with the trees.

Beside me on this table are two packets of rare flower seeds: one is of blue butterfly nasturtiums. Nan Evatt and I shared a packet once before, but I didn't manage to get those seeds to grow. I am keen to try again. This has blue flowers with a white throat.

The second packet is a feathered poppy called White Knight. Originally introduced to England before World War I, and then seemingly lost. It has huge blooms, the packet says, twelve centimetres across, resembling balls of finely cut white feathers. To be sown from mid-summer to early winter. I will sow them before I go to

Adelaide for Writers' Week so that they should be ready to plant out when I get back in mid-March.

These seeds all come from Erica Vale Australia Pty Ltd, 1747 Anzac Avenue, Mango Hill, Queensland, or from PO Box 297, Kallangur 4503. A blue perfumed nasturtium and white tasselled poppies. There's nothing like it to lift the heart.

If you are depressed, try digging. Swimming's good, but digging is better. Digging to plant something, I mean, preferably a tree or two.

Sometimes when I feel forlorn, whatever from, I get into bed with Treloar and Ross Roses catalogues and the *Botanica Rose Encyclopaedia* and just concentrate.

Sunday, 9th February

We have been back to Bunnings and got another load of trees and pots. Diana came to lunch, arriving just as Peri and I drew up with the trees. She began to talk to Peri about Nicosia. I was in the kitchen, cooking prawn risotto, and I overheard Diana saying, 'I saw a mandrake in Paphos. It was on the debris of the old city, beside the sea, in rough grassy country. I was walking with Neoptolemos and Eustachios from the Museum. I gave a little shriek when we came to the mandrake. I had the book on Cypriot plants and it had a description by Pliny of the mandrake.'

'Get with child a mandrake root,' I said, having run in and picked up a page of paper to write on.

'Yes,' she said, 'it's an aphrodisiac.'

Peri said, picking up something else Diana had been saying about Greek painted churches, 'Well, the best painted Byzantine church I ever saw was in Budapest. It was like walking into a field of paisley pattern.'

'Don't get off botany, Peri, I want to write this down,' I said. 'Yes, Lotha,' Peri said, referring to me, (her nickname for me, as I call her Mandrake, the magician from our childhood comic books) and I jolted when I saw that Mandrake had appeared in two guises in our talk.

'I'm going to see those painted churches in Nicosia, with the Reckitt's blue ceilings, Diana,' Peri went on.

Diana, seeing I had the pen waiting, plugged on: 'It was spectacular. It's a big rosette on the ground, twenty-five centimetres wide, not more than five centimetres, or two inches high, with bell-like flowers and a rosette of leaves, the size of hydrangeas, all around the flowers, which are violet coloured. I just looked at it and went back later to draw it.'

Wednesday, 19th February

Such a day. For the first time I saw that the station garden is beginning to look like a park, with trees dotted about above old roses and, below, the grass. There comes a time in every new garden when there is a turning point, as if the garden heaved a sigh and emerged.

I planted the last trees that Peri gave: a golden rain tree (*Koelreuteria paniculata*), which grows to fifteen metres and comes from Korea and China, a tropical peach, the shrub Snow in Summer, and nameless others. Down the track, where David and I had moved the ficus, I took a barrow of water and two buckets, along with some clay-breaking mixture in a bottle. I read the instructions and, taking the best and thus the easiest way, poured some capfuls of the mixture into the buckets, filled them with water and poured it among the roots. I dragged the barrow back through the ditches and got more water. Then I gave three jacarandas the clay-breaking treatment.

As I walked back the three hundred or so metres to the station, I counted the frangipani cuttings that have taken root alongside the platform. Eighteen. Ten more went in there too, the idea being that what flourishes should be repeated. One day, in a summer far away, the whole platform will have frangipani trees and jacarandas in bloom.

Three unknown native trees Diana gave me have taken too, but her guava was mowed and sits torn and valiant like a ripped flag. I stuck a three-metre long green-painted bamboo stake beside it which I had bought at

Bunnings. I had been meaning to tie up something in my own garden with that stake, but I could no longer remember what. Now the guava has a tall green-painted flagpole next to it, and this may keep it safe.

Tony, who is an occasional worker at the station while Tom is on holidays, said that Tom had been back to check on things, and it may be that he will agree to changing the mowing people, because they have mowed the daisies by the cyclone fence for the third time. I saw this when I got off the train on Tuesday and, suddenly, found myself engulfed in fury. I walked home, trying not to think about the lost bushes that had once again started to grow, along with two passionfruit vines that have stalwartly withstood two previous mowings. Until then I had not been upset when things were dug up or when the children fell off their skateboards into the red geraniums. But now I was gripped by an unholy rage.

Sinna had sweetly put a notice on the board inside the station, saying that staff looked at this daily and therefore the mowing men would be told again that the daisies beside the fence needed to be avoided. I again felt that wave of impotence which comes when you have tried every way you can think to tell somebody not to harm a plant. When the person doesn't know the plant is there, you can be sorry, shrug a bit and feel that it is nobody's fault. I took a bath and calmed down.

Having plenty of geranium and white daisy cuttings, because Peri had pointed out that the pots in my garden needed pruning badly, I stuck these in among the frangipanis down the side of the platform where some geraniums from other plantings have begun to bloom.

I am now wondering why I am gardening in a long line towards the south. Why not spread out and widen the plot towards the back fences of houses that face away from the line? It makes an eccentric garden, this long line of trees and now flowers. I think the answer is that more people will enjoy the longer line of garden than if it sped by their eyes in a flash as their train passed. And as they walk down the platform, coming north from Wollongong, they will see the trees growing up through the railings.

Over and over in my mind I can hear Philip Zweers saying, 'Why not natives?' And I say again, 'Beggars can't be choosers, Philip, I plant what I am given.' But his voice is there, like a moral.

Glorious Days

GHAZAL 3

Here, in nights of light,
you can't hear anything except the sea.
At dawn the clouds
can't sear anything except the sea.
Forget-me-nots, indigo plants, old roses,
this is autumn.

Days of ease and langour mean lately you
can't fear anything except the sea.
Lucid hope, floral ginger scents,
sky blue plumbago, the comforts of old
age.
Fighting siblings drift apart
Christmas means they
can't steer to anything except the sea.
A monument, a book, a psalm. Thomas
á Kempis gives more comfort as a
seer than anything except the sea.
Running on the beach, does it matter
if the sand is soft?

With flesh
that's had a tear
don't try anything except the sea.
'Weeping may endure for a night
but joy cometh in the morning.'
Persecuted, think of this. Even
if inconsolable, you can't
be near anything except the sea.
Kate, accept your daughter's gifts and
trials
remember her in childhood when she
called
a frog a flog. So dear, she can't be
compared
to anything except the sea.

Friday, 21st February

Today I read in the free local paper that fifteen thousand people commute to Sydney daily from the south coast and that doesn't include the rest of us who go up and down intermittently. That is enough reason, I think, to keep planting in a line rather than veer out and widen the garden.

I have only reached the far end of the platform, with one palm a few metres further on. It will be a long trek with the barrow if I try to reach Bellambi, which, as you know, is a foolish dream I sometimes have.

I have found an enormous pink frangipani tree and took ten cuttings on the way back from the sea pool at Bulli today.

There is four hundred kilos of lucerne pellet fertiliser in bags on the front verandah. Half for my garden, half for the station. As I planted at the latter yesterday, I spread some around the trees and piled up the lawn compost among it. Then I laid grey rocks over all as extra mulch, to keep the moisture in. That saying of my brother's, 'The best fertiliser for land is the owner's feet', came to mind when I saw that the fig tree David and I moved had fallen over in the clay. Too far away to be seen, when I was spreading fertiliser and watering in trees, it was lucky I had walked down to check. Propped up now with rocks, it looks healthy enough.

I did a matron's round of the garden and thought I should tell you of an angel.

On a cold morning (concerning the exact date there's no possibility of being precise), a train loading mainly elderly people, with a busy male conductor wearing a necklace, let me board carrying a rare plant at Spencer Street, which is in Melbourne, going to Central, which is in Sydney, as a spring day was dawning.

The plant was *Acacia cognata* and I had got it from Plantmark at the Landscape Garden Conference in Camberwell Town Hall. For three days I had sat looking at this plant, more like a green cat than a shrub, as it stood decorating the edge of the stage. It was said that the plants were not for sale. But I had to have one.

Andrew, a young man from Plantmark, was supervising the loading of a truck with the stage decorations and I persuaded him to sell me this weird and beautiful green shrub. Antonia, with whom I was staying, drove me home to her house and put the plant into a box ready for the train trip the next day.

When the conductor saw the plant he took my ticket, turned it over, pointed to the fine print and said that there was a rule against taking plants on interstate trains. I told him I would nurse it but he said, 'Don't be ridiculous!' Then suddenly he had a change of heart and agreed to let the plant come on board with me, as I told him it was rare and that I was alone and there was nobody who could take it away. It would have to be called a surfboard and I would need to pay the price a surfboard costs to travel. I did this with alacrity and relief.

At Central I saw that it wasn't possible to carry the plant in its metre-square box at the same time as wheeling my suitcase. I took the box, leaving the case beside the train, and put it onto the Wollongong train. Then ran back for the case, which was still there.

Because it was nine at night when the train reached Woonona, I had been wondering how I would get home from the station, because Tom would not be there to mind my case and there was no waiting-room in which to leave it. As I stepped off, thinking I would leave my case on the platform and carry the plant home first, because I could risk the loss of the case more than the plant, a young man stepped up and offered to carry the plant home for me. It was out of his way but he strode along holding the box to his chest, chatting. I told him about the plant and the station garden we were passing. He said, when I explained that the garden was made by somebody who was blind and me, that his mother was also blind.

I have never seen him since but if the archangel Gabriel had stepped up and lifted the box I could not have been more surprised and grateful.

The green acacia has flourished. I took it out of the pot and put it into the ground. Now, brushing against it on the side path, it feels like a cat stroking your leg. It forms a soft mound, the size of a labrador dog, and is still growing bigger.

Monday, 7th April

A glorious day. David and I gardened at the station to good effect. Kikuyu grass, being easy to feel, and Paddy's lucerne, the weed with the deep root and yellow buttercup flowers easily traced down to the soil and pulled, were tossed over the fence onto the ramp by David. I put in another tropical peach left over from the load Peri gave me weeks ago, along with a barrowload of cuttings.

David and I ate ham sandwiches and drank a thermos of tea under the old wattle tree, surrounded by the roses, which are thriving. We seemed invisible to all that went on on the platform above, and were glad of it. We began our work again, David hurling weeds over the fence up onto the platform with vigour and me using a spade to weed (a new rough effective way I've found). The prickly bushes of holly Denis gave me ages ago have mainly thrived and help to thicken the garden there and, perhaps, to keep it safer. I know nothing's really safe, but it's a pleasure, sometimes, to think it is.

At the university one of my students, hearing about the garden in an aside I'd made, said, 'Oh, we could never have a garden where I live. There's too much vandalism.' I didn't say anything because I couldn't think of a reply that wouldn't take a lot of energy. But I treasure that remark.

Having taken two barrows, one by one, to the station, I asked David if he would like to help me take them home. Eager and willing as ever to do any work, he agreed. Together we crossed the road with the barrows and empty buckets, my heart beating faster as I showed David where the road was. He can't use his cane while driving a barrow but we came home safely and I have been exhilarated ever since. Unique and game for anything, David took the best barrow down the side path and left it at the shed.

We came inside and had afternoon tea, laughing. My wreck of a second barrow, which I'd used to cart over the lucerne pellets, is useful nonetheless, and I see now a person can always do with two barrows, and that's not a widely known fact.

Tuesday, 8th April

I have asked people what they think comprises happiness for them. Independence, freedom, health, they say. Yet you can have all these and be unhappy. You can be suicidal and have them. I've been there. There is never time to tease the whole matter out because I ask at lunch and the food and other talk gets in the way. The American Declaration of Independence ends with something about the right to the pursuit of happiness. I keep going over this matter and only see that it is when I am engrossed that I am happy. The joy of abandonment, of forgetting oneself. So when I am under the camellia, tearing at the weeds, things fall away and then later, standing, the world appears and is astonishing. During those minutes of lostness, happiness grasped me. In his book, *The Wreck of Western Culture*, John Carroll says that Shakespeare, although leaving no lucid readily clear code of behaviour, seems to be saying that to live well and wisely a person should be honourable, and that it is important to be honest and loyal to friends while also being gentle, even given the turbulence of life and good and bad fortune. These things can be clues to how to live well. Nonetheless, you can do all these things but happiness may not necessarily be yours. But you will possibly be happier, and so will those around you, if that is the way you choose to live. Walking indoors to replenish the teacup I feel I am a person who is always grasping after something that is just out of reach. Something sometimes glimpsed that fades away. Clues, there are always clues.

Happiness comes unexpectedly. For instance, a woman bringing in the washing that has dried in the afternoon sun hears pigeons cooing on the lawn and sees shadows growing; she walks inside with her arms full of warm linen, puts it on a chair and locks the door against the night.

Saturday, 17th May

A silver day. Very still and full of conundrums. For instance, should the *Magnolia soulangiana* at the front gate be removed? Shocking thought. But nothing beats taking a long hard look at a plant over a year to see if it really is successful. The mere word 'magnolia' sets me off into a romantic denial and a deeply ingrained unwillingness to actually look. The tree, planted with such belief and ardour, is often a shabby tattered grey crocheted sort of doily. The west winds tear at it and shred the leaves. I have stood by it in the last fortnight shaking the branches to make the leaves drop, to let the buds show forth.

Looking round at other magnolias I see the same problem, and it is not just here by the sea that they are grey and tattered. The *Magnolia stellata* in the back lawn doesn't give much pleasure either, and I wouldn't plant one again. I still think David has the best tree in Woonona, a *grandiflora*, a tree for all seasons and all people. Cream flowers, the size of dinner plates, that scent his whole garden and which I pick and keep on my dressing-table, watching them turn pale brown, as if in an invisible oven, a lightly browning custard. The scent is with me all night. I know I am sleeping with magnolias, even while I dream. It reminds me of the time Barbara Pak Poy stayed and said that she knew she was in white damask sheets, even while she slept.

Peri came to visit and, after parking her car in the drive, stepped out beside the pink robinia tree Nan Evatt gave me. It was weak from collar rot that no amount of pest oil could cure, and she said briskly, 'Get rid of it and plant something decent. It will never be any good.'

I had told Nan how sick the tree was and how superstitious I was about taking out a tree that had been planted to remember somebody (what if they got sick?). Nan said, 'Take it out, darling, I don't mind at all.'

On Mothers' Day, Hugh dug it out for me. I saw when it had gone how ugly the shape, so sickly and weakly waving, had been; few leaves and flowers, more like a dying giraffe than a tree. I was glad we'd put it out of its misery. Now, of course, there is the pleasure of deciding what tree to plant in its place. This pleasure gets rarer as a garden goes on, simply because there is no space left and the decisions, right or wrong, stand there letting you know for all time whether you were wise or foolish. (Unless you can face their removal if they're wrong, that is.) I'd take out the magnolia in the front, but it is healthy and was planted for Sophia, and I don't want to tempt fate.

Jane rang from Adelaide last night and told me she has catalogues of tree peonies. Would one of these thrive here? I think if a *Magnolia soulangiana* is in trouble, so too would be a tree peony. I need to enquire widely. There was an avenue of yellow tree peonies a century old at Sorenson's Nursery at Leura which were removed when it was sold for housing. Some of us will never get over it.

The smaller peonies of the bulb type are beautiful and not widely grown. They are thought to be difficult, but Don Burke says that the most common problem is that people plant them too deeply. They need to be planted with the tip almost uncovered. Delicate, delicate, that's what you need to be. Bulb peonies are the cream sponges of the garden. Yet, I want one of those trees.

When Jane read out the list last night, I said, 'I bet they cost about five hundred dollars each.' But I was wrong. The price ranges between a hundred and fifty to three hundred dollars. Here is a sample of what's available: Qing Xiang Bal (delicately fragrant white), flowers early.

Growth, vigorous. Tolerance, average. Flowers, many. Size, tall erect. And: Gui Fel Cha Cul (Superior Imperial Concubine), proliferate form, pinkish-red. Flowers, mid-season. Growth, vigorous. Tolerance, average. Flowers, many. Size, stalks long, stiff and upright, tall erect. And, finally, one that can stand tougher conditions: Wu Jin Yao Hui (glossy black). Rose form, dark purplish-red/lustrous. Flowers, mid-season. Growth, medium. Tolerance, tolerant of adverse conditions. Flowers, many. Size, medium height. The address of the supplier is Hilltop, Cherokee Road, Kerrie, Victoria, 3434. Phone (03) 5427 0260. Fax (03) 5427 0594.

Veering away from the peony for a moment, there is the possibility of the most perfect of all tree shapes, and that is the persimmon. Planting something you can eat has always seemed to me to have a moral value to it. The world has only got enough food in stock for two years or so, maybe a bit more, but what if the weather failed in both hemispheres? Wouldn't you wish you had put in some citrus, nuts, figs or potatoes? If a war came, wouldn't it be good to be able to dig up a few potatoes and give them to a beggar if you, by some miracle, had enough for your own family? I am thinking this way, about the beggar, that is, because I heard a woman on radio talking of her war years, when she starved and begged food from farmers who gave 'a few potatoes'. I have never understood why we don't have streets lined with orange trees, or apples or quinces or figs, or anything at all that we could eat on the way to school. In the Barossa Valley children used to pick quinces, smash them on posts, leave them to sweeten in the air, and would then eat them raw on the way home. I have not tried this but read about it in *The Barossa Valley Cookbook* by Angela Hoezenroeder.

Friday, 30th May

Peri and I have been to the Botanical Gardens in Sydney for her to photograph some tropical trees for her friend Margaret Barwick to use in her book, *Tropical & Subtropical Trees: A Worldwide Encyclopaedic Guide*. We wandered in soft misty rain under our blue umbrellas, discussing plants and talking about what we wanted next for our own gardens.

Great swathes of clivia and begonias were in bloom and above us the bats swung chirping in the great trees. Peri has a sweet habit of linking arms as she walks beside me, so arm in arm we strode along until she saw the sort of tree Margaret had asked her to photograph. She would bring out her list from her bag and scan it, then, having taken the photograph, we walked on looking for the next. We found about six on the list of ten and so went and had lunch in the bistro above the creek.

Margaret has been writing this book for about a decade and there will be a photograph of Bend of the River's homestead at the place where star fruit is described, Peri says.

Saturday, 21st June

As I tipped barrowloads of woodchip mulch from the platform down onto the station garden, I wondered again if this was a fool's job and if the resulting mess would make me sorry. But I kept on, with David loading one barrow while I took another over, ran up the platform and tipped. When no more mulch was needed in that place, David came and lifted the barrowloads up over the wooden sleepers that make the edge of the garden. I had spread thick layers of newspapers from the newsagent over the weeds and around the plants. The rhythm of loading the barrows in this way exhilarated us both as we were faster than ever before. We had a thermos of tea and some cake while sitting on the railing and talking. Sometimes David runs his hands over the plants behind us as we sit and deciphers what they are: geranium, daisy, bauhinia tree, Caro and Peter's wedding olive tree.

By one o'clock we had covered quite a lot of the garden and had to lock the gate where the pile of mulch stood because Tom was going home for the weekend.

We crossed the road with our barrows and said goodbye. How a man, completely unable to see the path, a car, a barrow or a tree, can cross a road alone, pushing a barrow, as David now often does, is as mysterious as flight.

Sunday, 22nd June

Walking out to go for a run, I noticed smoke coming from the station garden. I ran over and saw that a fire had been lit from the papers we'd laid under the mulch, and in about six other places the paper was burnt but the fire had died out. My worst worry is I've made a fire hazard. I kicked the fire out with my shoe and picked up the burnt papers blowing around. A group of boys about twelve years old were standing near the takeaway food shop so I went over and casually asked if they knew anything about the fires. I don't know that I expected a confession, but it seemed possible they might agree not to do it anymore.

I have never felt so beaten. One boy pulled two lighters from his pocket and I said, jokingly, 'Oh, so you must be the guilty one.' I didn't want to antagonise them but wanted them to see that somebody loved that garden and it was ours. I wanted them to realise they don't need to destroy it, no matter how terrible their lives. Oh, this is deep water, but I wanted them to see that it was not an anonymous thing, but something valuable. I pointed to the dark-green cast-iron table and benches in the park among the newly planted trees and told them I'd got the council to put that there for them to sit and eat at. 'For you,' I said. Did it touch them? I don't know. But if they want to, they can go back and relight fires if they were the ones who did it.

The sea was calm, the sky blue and people were out on the bike path, walking with dogs and children. Once, those children at the food shop were also in pushers, innocently going along beside the sea. As soon as I began to run thinking was not necessary. The wind was in my hair, the sun on my face and the sea stretching away with its infinite peace.

Monday, 23rd June

The new method of watering at the station, which I invented from need a few months ago, is wonderfully useful. Because it's now dry, and the new trees given to me by Richard Bird, who grew them from seed, are shrivelling, I needed to get water to them. It was too far for the hose to reach, so I asked David if, once I'd turned on the hose from the tap up on the platform, he'd water whatever he could while I ran back and forth with the barrow filled with four buckets of water and the bowl of the barrow itself full of water. Each time I came back,

David filled everything and I rushed off again. It took only a short time and saved a lot of carrying.

After the watering, we finished off by covering the newspapers with mulch. We put on so deep a layer, which we then hosed, that it would be a hard job to ever set it on fire again. Well, that's what I tell myself.

I have a theory that, facing old age, it's a good thing to work or exercise until you have only just enough strength, with your hand trembling as it puts the key in the lock to shove open the front door. Working within your strength will only keep you at your present physical level, or even imperceptibly slightly less, whereas really knocking yourself out might just extend strength.

David, who is about ten years younger than I am, works out on an exercise machine and is strong. He picks up the loaded barrow as if it's a balloon. A week ago, on a bleak day, I walked around to see him and, finding the shed door down, his cane not at the back door, and no answer to the wind chimes being pulled, I was walking away when he pulled up the shed door from the inside. He'd been exercising there on the machine in the dark with the door down, for privacy from passers-by.

Tuesday, 1st July

In Balmain for a week to visit Philip Martin in hospital, I didn't go back to the mulching of the station. The day

I left, I went over to tell Tom about the fire. He said before I even began, 'I've been putting out a fire down there in the garden.' I asked, as I had to catch a train and didn't have time to do it myself, if he'd hose down everything so the mulch would be too wet to burn, and he said he would. If you want frisson in your life, start a public garden.

Friday, 4th July

A windy week. Chairs and branches are tossed onto the lawn. The wind howls while its silver rag polishes the trees. I crouch indoors, muttering, afraid and yet enjoying it.

Margaret O'Hara's two King Charles spaniels were lifted off their feet by the wind and moved sideways, which surprised them mightily. Marg was laughing about it at lunch at the Balgownie pub's restaurant yesterday. We looked out onto the wild bush of Mt Keira and a pink flowering gum at a side window. I haven't had grilled sausages, gravy and mashed potatoes for years, and left the restaurant feeling less anxious about the howling wind.

We drove to Bunnings and I bought a Laurie Bray creamy-pink camellia for the back deck. I have cleared off the deck, given it two coats of oil and decided to have only three citrus in pots and one camellia. All the dross has gone. It is easy to have a pile of pots slowly accumulating, littering, taking the space. Since this new revelation I want to be austere. The deck looks twice as big. It's odd the way we put things in our way to trip ourselves and slow us down. In the end, I could be left standing with only a place for my feet, surrounded by a cluster of messy pots, all the while thinking I was gardening with purpose. And odd, too, the way people hold their tongues and do not tell you what a mess you are making. Or maybe they don't notice. But once you do so yourself, everything, as in your personal life, gets swept away and you wonder how you stood it for so long.

The howling, the beautiful voice of the wild. Wind calls to wind as whales call to whales. Howl on, screaming wind, I try to remember my place in this beautiful dangerous world.

Wednesday, 9th July

Nowadays, change is the most constant companion. Once, dragging a bucket through the bathwater meant pain in the night. Now it no longer does.

The changes in the garden have been so gradual that I hardly notice them. Yet, once in a while, walking down the side path I get a shock at the thickness, the way the plants sway and loll and how the bright blue forget-me-nots, which came years ago from a packet of Blue

Cottage Garden seeds, has lavished itself in the natural way plants do, and which is so hard to imitate. It is always thrilling to see.

For all that's been lost (for instance, the jacarandas and frangipani at the station, which held such promise), two ginkgo trees, a beautiful slow-growing pair, male and female, have green shoots in spite of the fact that they were never watered by hand, not even on the day they went in.

The roses in the back garden are a bounty beyond words, and Jude the Obscure has proved itself a triumph. Like a great horse, it has all one ever wants: perfect conformation, vigour, performance at the highest level, every attribute worthy of its kind. There are many favourite roses but when the last rose contest is held, Jude the Obscure will be among the finalists.

David's sasanqua hedge, which I nagged for years to have him plant, is a triumph and he knows it. His fig, peach and apricot trees, which he planted somewhat reluctantly, have given fruit and he has put a wooded edging round the plot to save the trees from his mowing. When I call in I say, 'The sasanquas are a triumph, David. Those fruit trees love it there. You've even got a few more figs. Look!' And I take his hand and run it up the branches to the fruit, which he picks and takes inside.

Roses at the station wave above the rocky ground, even though it's almost a year since they had even a bucket of water, let alone a hose on them. I'd always thought they might be hardy and so they proved to be. Perhaps it was the lawn clippings and the newspapers we mulched them with that saved them. Or maybe they are like some wild child, strong, muscular and vital, who seems stronger for a sort of benign neglect which, combined with good air, wind and sun, has made them thrive.

Recently Nan Evatt gave me *Yates Garden Guide* to look up trees to plant. She took me outside, into her most green garden, to show me a tall lacy green-and-white-leafed *Acer negrano*, only eight years old, which scrapes the sky. 'It would be even more beautiful if it didn't have those other trees so close by,' she said, standing there in her blue dressing-gown, looking up with all her pleasure in the beauty of the tree.

Year after year Nan has taught me about plants and gardens. It's the knowledge in people who have been gardening for over fifty years that I worry will be lost when they die. It feels precious when I listen to her, like a rare archaeology of the mind that I long to save in some museum, a sort of intellectual invisible catalogue in space. Yet it flows away like water through our hands unless it's written down. And there is so much of it that it can never be entirely caught.

Last night the wind dropped. The silence was broken only by a magpie singing and the great trees stood above the birdbaths in massed abundance. The gardenias were blooming white in the dusk, abandoned stars with their distinctive scent; and around them the white hydrangeas had water gleaming from their leaves. The olive tree flowed downwards, shedding a white fountain of blossom, its silver leaves slithering above the tap.

Monday, 14th July

Yesterday Diana and I walked to Sandon Point. On the way we leant on the bridge railing above a creek and watched a fat brown duck paddle below. A few metres away, the surf ran onto the sand. A girl on a white horse rode past on the bike path, clopping along. We both need a bit of luck at the moment, so I made a wish. Two simple things, but vast as the sea to achieve. Miracles are what we need and they, I have found, are often about.

We walked around the clifftop where a house has been demolished. The garden remains and tomatoes are growing on the edge of the sand. We walked on past the protest tents, where the new development now has bulldozers working during the week. An Aboriginal flag is woven from streamers into the fence around the site. Every weekend the fence is pushed down, which doesn't have any effect except, I suppose, to relieve the feelings of the protesters.

We passed the place where, on a different day, we had seen a woman in the paddock who I thought was washing up. Diana said, 'She's not washing up, Kate, that's archaeology she's doing.'

We had walked over and had a talk. It turned out the Land and Environment Court had decreed that a search be made for proof of Aboriginal occupation. The woman, wearing a linen hat and rubber gloves, was sifting the soil into a basin. It was a hard job that found nothing of interest because, as she said, 'The site is so disturbed — there was a train line here taking coal down to the jetty.'

The sea turned pink and the sand was opalescent. Waves broke backwards in high curves of white spray. We kept saying, 'How beautiful!' Diana went home white-faced from the exertion, as her asthma is troublesome. Sometimes you get a glimpse of the shortness of life and I think, who knows how many times we will do this together again, at peace with each other, laughing with chagrin and happiness. And then she drives off to her studio on the hill.

A card came today from Peri in the south of France. The all-white card has a pile of folded all-white linen on it.

> Such beautiful old linen one finds in many village markets around this area. Almost every day there is a market in a neighbouring village. I've tasted the very best prunes ever. Margaret never passes a plant nursery

so I've plenty of chances to suss out the local produce. Picking raspberries every day and the cherry trees are laden. Rabbits are in their hutches waiting to be slaughtered. The vegetable garden next door is a work of art. Such a lovely place this is.

I have been trying to think about what my garden means to me. A green walk in silence. A sleepy lizard beside the flowering plumbago, my companion. The *Ailanthus* tree sheltering the lilies, the frog pond and the clivias. The loyal lemon tree, triumphant, laden and undemanding. Purple bougainvillea still climbing through the jacaranda beside the Turkish fig which leans towards the sun. The peace of walking round with a cup of tea soon after dawn in my dressing-gown.

Trailing the damp hem along the gardenias beside the zigzag path. No eyes can see me here alone, triumphant in my sweet hermitage, the vine the shed wears as a hat. All these things I planted desperately hoping for some shelter and grace, something away from harshness, noise and criticism.

This small green place of peace that the birds, the frog and the fat lizard share. The wind, the moon and stars, the reflections in the birdbaths when I walk out to simply be another animal alone, peaceful and grateful.

Saturday, 19th July

I've gone deaf. Three weeks ago I caught the flu and one day I woke up to silence. The wind blows and I do not hear it. People's lips move and what they say is a mystery. It is quiet and essential in here in this new world. Strangely, I am more myself than ever before and yet less so too, as I can't talk except in the most simple way, as if in a foreign language. Honed down to the fine detail of the perfection of silent things, I feel free. Not yet lonely — that would come if this were to last, but it is not expected to. Crossing the road I see cars pass and am surprised, so must remember to be careful. The pure white world of silence. Suddenly I see that the litter of sound somehow sullies the world. Essential things are sharper and more pure. The mandarin tree, shining in the sun, moving gently with three bright fruit, does not hear either. The clear blue sky arches over, indifferent to anything noisy. But then Mozart could fill the house and I would not know, except by seeing the label of the record and the switch turned on. Would the door hear? Or the tap, whose water now flushes out silently? But if my daughter laughed, I would not know the fabulous sound, pearls and roses, except from memory.

I walked around to David's and, not feeling well enough to mow my lawn, asked him if he would. He nodded and went to the shed and pulled out his mower. Taking an old black bag, he put a can of petrol in it with a couple of rags and a funnel and together we set off.

Remembering that when David mows his own lawn he uses white poles laid on the ground to flash in the sun against the dark grass, and having no poles, I decided to use white pillowcases to mark the edges of the lawn. Laying out half a dozen pillowcases in a deep rectangle on the lawn, I sat on the back step and watched David rev up the mower and begin. Suddenly I realised the differences between the sighted and the unsighted. Standing at my back door, I look out over the deck towards the end of the garden. The sides run parallel and it was there that the pillowcases were lying, each under a stone to hold them down. But that is not how somebody who can't see approaches the space. David began to mow as if the garden were a hologram. He went backwards three steps, and fanned out from there, backwards and forwards. Not once did he run in a long line as I had expected. He never noticed the white flash of pillowcases because he never faced them; being involved with another logic of seeing altogether, he simply ran over them backwards. From time to time he spoke to me, but I reminded him that I couldn't hear. It was enough that he could hear and I could see, and so, with me running to pick up the pillowcases behind him, and him going on from green space to green space like a butterfly, the lawn was mowed. It took hours of this elegant dance, more like a ballet than anything else. I thought of what a beautiful silent film it would make, the man and the woman moving around the lawn according to their own gifts and deprivations, not at all unhappy, quite the opposite. A smile doesn't have to be seen to be given, nor does a voice need to be heard for friendship to be there stalwartly. It was the man's gift of his work and the woman's pleasure in watching that remained. Also, her astonishment and enchantment.

From time to time David stopped the mower and I ran with the catcher full of grass to the compost heap. Then, occasionally, he wiped the funnel, which he took from the bag on the back step, and filled the mower with petrol, dipping his finger every few moments into the tank to feel how full it was.

There remained the problem of the swatches of grass missed by the mower going slowly in its fan-like dance. David took out a handkerchief and, crawling over the lawn, laid it down where he found a tall thin pattern of grass remaining. Then he had to find the mower, having moved away from it, so he circled around with his hands out until he hit it. Seeing this, I put the pillowcases down on every patch of the mohawk haircut patches of lawn. Then David caught the flash against the dark and mowed towards it as I snatched back the cloth. In this way, slowly, the long grass was cut. All this took so long the moon came out.

Let us leave them there, the man and the woman, engrossed in the garden.

Bibliography

David Austin, *Old Roses and English Roses*, Peribo, 2002

Margaret Barwick and others, *Tropical and Subtropical Trees*, Thames and Hudson Ltd., 2004

Len Beadell, *A Lifetime in the Bush*, New Holland, Australia, 2004

Maggie Beer, *Maggie's Orchard*, Viking, Penguin, Australia, 1997

Elizabeth Bishop, Robert Giroux (ed), *One Art: Letters*, Noonday Press (Farrar, Strauss and Giroux), New York, 1994

Botanica, The Illustrated A-Z of Over 10,000 Plants and How to Grow Them, Random House, Australia, 1997

Botanica's Roses, Random House Australia, 1999

John Carroll, *The Wreck of Western Culture*, Scribe Publications, 2004

William Dalrymple, *From the Holy Mountain*, Flamingo, HarperCollins, 1998

Don DeLillo, *Underworld*, Picador, 1999

Henry Doubleday Research Association of Australia, 3 Paget Street, Richmond NSW 2753

Philip Dowell and Adrian Bailey, *The Book of Ingredients*, Michael Joseph, 1980

George Eliot, *Silas Marner*, Collins Classic, London, 1959

E.M. Forster, *Howard's End*, Penguin, 2000

Janet Frame, *You are Now Entering the Human Heart*, The Women's Press, 1984

Antonia Fraser, *The Gunpowder Plot*, Phoenix (Orion),

Masanobu Fukuoka, *One Straw Revolution: An Introduction to Natural Farming*, Other India Bookstore, 1992

Rose Gray & Ruth Rogers, *River Café Cookbook Two*, Random House, UK, 1997

Germaine Greer, *The Female Eunuch*, Flamingo, HarperCollins Publishers, 1999

Jane Grigson, *English Food*, Ebury Press, 2000

Emile Guillaumin, *The Life of a Simple Man*, University Press of New England, 1982

John and Rosemary Hemphill, *What Herb is That?*, New Holland, Australia, 1997

Ted Hughes, *Birthday Letter*, Faber & Faber, 1998

Belinda Jeffery, *Belinda Jeffery's 100 Favourite Recipes*, Viking (Penguin), Australia, 2001

Gertrude Jekyll, Richard Bisgrove (Preface) *Gertrude Jekyll's Colour Schemes for the Flower Garden* — Frances Lincoln Ltd, 2001

Thomas à Kempis, *The Imitation of Christ*, Fount, Great Britain, 1980

Raymond Kersh, *The Edna's Table Cookbook*, Hodder Headline, Sydney, 1998

Peter Levi and Georgis Pavlopoulos, *A Bottle in the Shade: a Journey in the Western Peloponnese*, Sinclair-Stephenson (Reed International), London, 1996

Christopher Lloyd, *Colour for Adventurous Gardens*, BBC Books, London, 2004

David Mabey and David Collison, *The Perfect Pickle Book* (third ed.), BBC Publications, 1995

Richard Mabey, *Home Country,* Ebury Press, 1990

Roger McDonald, *The Tree in Changing Light*, Random House, Australia, 2002

Henry Mitchell, *The Essential Earthman*, Houghton Mifflin, 1994

Prosper Montagne, *Larousse Gastronomique,* Hamlyn, 2001

Andrew Motion, *Keats,* University of Chicago Press, Chicago, 1999

Patrice Newell, *The Olive Grove*, Penguin, Australia, 2000

Mary Oliver, *Winter Hours: Prose, Prose Poems, and Poems*, Houghton Mifflin Company, New York, 2000

Eleanor Perenyi, *Green Thoughts: A Writer in the Garden*, Modern Library

Mary Pickford, *Sunshine and Shadow*, William Heinemann Ltd, 1956

Jerry & Skye Rogers, *Bend of the River: A Family Pastoral*, Lansdowne, Sydney, 1998

Sheridan Rogers, *The Cook's Garden*, HarperCollins, 1992

George Schenk, *Moss Gardening: Including Lichens, Liverworts and other Miniatures*, Timber Press
Simon Sebag-Montefiore, *Prince of Princes*, Phoenix (Orion), 2004
Charmain Solomon, *Vegetarian Food*, Reed Books, Australia, 1993
Sophocles, *Antigone*, Oxford University Press, Oxford, 1998
Wallace Stegner and Page Stegner, *Wolf Willow: A History, a Story, and a Memory of the Last Plains Frontier*, Penguin, 2000
Virgil, *The Eclogues, Georgics and Aeneid of Virgil*, translated by C Day Lewis, Oxford University Press, 1974
Gilbert White, *A Natural History of Selborne*, Everyman, London, 1993
Diana Wood Conroy, *Fabric of the Ancient Theatre: Excavation Journal from Cyprus*, Moufflon Publishing, Cyprus, 2004
Virginia Woolf, *To the Lighthouse*, Vintage, 1992
Yates Garden Guide, HarperCollins Publishers, 1998

Acknowledgments

Some of the poems in *Playing with Water* have first appeared in the following publications:

Pages 2–3: 'The Day', *The Canberra Times*
Page 43: 'Summer', *The Oxford Book of Modern Australian Verse*, edited by Peter Pierce, 1996
Pages 45–46: 'Autumn', *Quadrant*
Pages 158–159: 'The Lodger', *The Australian*
Page 274: 'Lips', *The Canberra Times*
Page 304: 'Dirt', *The Canberra Times*
Pages 318–319: 'Ghazal 1', *Eureka Street* magazine
Page 336: 'What I Have Lost', *Eureka Street* magazine